EXPOSURE

EXPOSURE

A Novel

KURT WENZEL

LITTLE, BROWN AND COMPANY
New York   Boston   London

Little, Brown and Company
Hachette Book Group USA
237 Park Avenue, New York, NY 10017
Visit our Web site at www.HachetteBookGroupUSA.com

First Edition: July 2007

The characters and events in this book are fictitious. Any similarity to real persons, living or dead, is coincidental and not intended by the author.

Library of Congress Cataloging-in-Publication Data
Wenzel, Kurt.
Exposure : a novel / Kurt Wenzel. — 1st ed.
    p. cm.
ISBN 978-0-316-09397-2
1.   Motion picture industry—Fiction. 2.   Actors—Fiction. 3.   Digital media—Fiction. 4.   Technology and civilization—Fiction. 5.   Twenty-first century—Fiction. 6.   Los Angeles (Calif.)—Fiction. 7.   Satire. I. Title.
PS3573.E573E97 2007
813'.6—dc22   2006038193

10   9   8   7   6   5   4   3   2   1

Q-FF

Printed in the United States of America

FOR DAD

EXPOSURE

The widespread addiction to Bliss seems the only appropriate response to the culture. In fact, in this new benumbed epoch of overexposure, media fatigue, image anxiety, and advertising-induced depression, an attraction to Bliss may actually be the last proof of one's humanity. Your senses are alive to the catastrophe, at the very least. You're not too deadened to need a little help. And it's a damned sight better than being a noise junky.

— *from the* Black Book,
author unknown

S*he was waiting there at dawn, as instructed, where the pines get thinner and the earth was worn sandy from parked cars — teenagers who came to screw. It was the farthest point inland where you could still see the ocean, bruise blue and white veined, scrunched between the cliff's edge and the horizon like a long loin of beef. Field jacket, jeans, hiking boots — might be some rough terrain, she'd been warned. No one had mentioned the cold.*

From the small pack she took the black pillowcase and fitted it over her head.

She knew what he sounded like from their phone conversation. Initially this had given her some scant sense of security, until someone had reminded her that he had likely modulated his voice. Breathing a little less comfortably now, she realized just how risky this all was, how dangerous. Sure, drop me blindfolded in the boondocks while I wait to be picked up by some guy for whom there isn't even a photograph, never mind a name. See if I care.

Tired of standing, she crouched, leaning her weight against a small, jagged boulder. Pungent scents seeped their way through the hood: pine sap and cedar, rabbit piss (a guess), the crisp wafts of Pacific brine. Like a seaside pet shop, she decided. And cold. *Goddamned cold. Her nipples chafed against the khaki.*

Finally, in the distance, she heard the whir of a motor, then gravel skipping like bingo balls through the wheel wells. Instead of relief, she felt a mild panic. What if it wasn't him? *she thought suddenly.* What if instead she was stumbled upon by a carload of drunken louts? Or what if it was him and he was deranged, a rapist or a serial killer? Wasn't he after people in media anyway? *As the vehicle came closer, the urge to take off her hood was nearly irrepressible—though the moment she did, of course, the interview was over. In fact, if she saw him at all, even by accident, he would kill her. "Terminated," he had said, adopting the jargon of espionage fantasy.*

"Good morning," someone announced, the vehicle having pulled up dangerously close to her, pebbles and shell flakes ricocheting off her field boots. It was not the voice from the phone, she noted, though by now she wasn't expecting it to be. Now he sounded flat and ominous, the voice of a farmer in winter, a midwesterner. Was this his true voice, or had it been the one on the phone that was real? Probably neither of them, she thought. Maybe both.

"Congratulations," he continued. "I don't believe anybody's ever been this close."

She heard the sand gnash under his feet as he approached. He tugged at the edges of the pillowcase, then sifted the material in his fingers, testing the opaqueness.

"*You're shaking,*" *he said, putting a hand on her shoulder.*
"*Just cold.*" Screw you, *she thought.* Let's drop a hood on *your*
head out in the freezing nowhere, see how you do.
"*Give me your pack,*" *he said.* "*I'll help you in.*"
She stepped into the passenger's side of some sort of Jeep—a pre-
hybrid, she guessed, from the gasoline smell—as he guided her to a
spot behind the front seats. He wanted her to lie down. Once there, she
felt him securing the hood with a piece of twine.
"*Will we make it to East Berlin by midnight?*" *she asked, showing a twinge of annoyance. She had meant to strike a blow at his self-
importance, maybe even make him laugh. But there was nothing.*
"*Stay low,*" *said the man known as Mr. Black. He climbed behind
the wheel and started the engine.*
Writers, *she thought, struggling to breathe through the petrol
fumes from the Jeep's floor.* Such drama queens.

ONE

From his tomb at the Ming Blue, Marshall Reed watched the curtains part along the bearings with a cool silence.

A Ming thing, he murmured to himself, setting down the remote. Men like him — whose lifestyles were predicated, to a large degree, on privacy, and whose behavior the trades characterized as "unpredictable" — usually found themselves a few blocks down at the Marmont. But Marshall preferred the stark precision and monastery silence of the Ming. The Marmont, he'd decided, had grown self-conscious. Television stars on tasseled Harleys, party in the Belushi bungalow. *I'm past that now,* he'd thought, *or maybe behind it.* Either way was fine with him. He was thirty-nine and had done his share, without the self-congratulations. Real self-destruction, he knew, went on secretly. And alone.

Plus, he could work at the Ming. In this new cacophonous age, the Ming Blue offered the most elusive of contemporary luxuries: silence. A hotel on *mute.* No squawking plasmas blaring at you in the lobby, no thumping P-hop at the bar. Of course you weren't allowed to open the windows, but in L.A., who cared? All this had made the hotel a popular destination for two primary groups: the faddish weekend media fasters—those who couldn't get to the mountains for the full cure—and high-priced screenwriters who could afford to work away from the lot. Marshall Reed was one of the latter. Though he had but a single screen credit to his name, the murder mystery *Chula Vista* ('09), the script was generally considered one of the greatest ever written and had guaranteed him gainful employment in Hollywood for the rest of his life. Why he had failed to deliver on this promise, even now, almost ten years later, and why he contented himself with what in a different era might have been called hackwork, were riddles still pondered by cineastes the world over.

Deciding to take his breakfast by the pool, Marshall shook out his shaggy brown hair and dragged his slight frame into faded jeans and a denim shirt, which he wore untucked, in defiance of local fashion. He rode the elevator to the roof and found a table under a cool niche of palm planters. There he sipped coffee while discreetly lifting his sunglasses as a young Nubian performed the breaststroke, legs lissome as the tail of a spermatozoon. Not until she had tucked herself away in a towel did he begin to scan the newspapers on his Pod. Mr. Black was all the rage, of course. *National Insider* was announcing it had indeed secured an interview, and precoverage had made the front page of the *L.A. Times*. Marshall had just started to read the article when he noticed his waiter, a young Asian male in a blue Nehru jacket, hovering behind one of the palms.

"Hello there," the screenwriter announced, somewhat annoyed.

Though his own celebrity quotient was blessedly low, there was a certain young Hollywood type, usually male, for whom the name Marshall Reed inspired a sort of cultish awe and, at times, an intrusive curiosity. He realized now that the waiter had been peeking over his shoulder at his Pod screen.

Knowing he'd been had, the young man stepped out from behind the palm. "Sorry," he said, trying to keep his voice down. He pointed at the screen with his tray. "I was just wondering what you make of this guy."

"Ah yes, the infamous Mr. Black," Marshall replied with a chilly sarcasm. The waiter had the look of a budding screenwriter, he was sure, and so would now have to be dispatched with benevolent firmness, the usual modus. "Nice publicity stunt. The book has its moments, though." Marshall lifted his coffee cup to signal both a refill and dismissal.

The waiter overlooked the gesture. "I'm about halfway done with it. I think it's great."

"Well, good for you," Marshall replied, surprised at the rapture. "Most people haven't bothered to read it, though everyone seems to have an opinion, don't they?"

Mr. Black, as he was known, had been named by default. It was nearly two years ago now that a conspicuous volume had appeared on the nonfiction tables in bookstores. It had a completely black cover—no title, no jacket copy, no author photo. No *author,* far as anyone could tell. And the publishing house wasn't saying a thing. As for the book itself, it turned out to be an augury, a digressive warning on the dangers of media saturation. There was actually a glut of such books these days (such were the ironies of the media age), and the whole thing would have been dismissed as the rant of another killjoy except that the author's anonymity lent the whole thing an air of mystery, if not legitimacy. If for five hundred pages you were going to harangue the age of the moving image billboards (or MIBs, as they were known, the new giant digital plasma screens that had replaced static billboard advertisements, and smaller versions of which seemed to be popping up just about everywhere—on the sides of buildings, on the hoods of cars, on changing-room mirrors and the interior of bathroom stalls), at least this "Mr. Black" had the good taste to do it anonymously.

However improbably, the book had become a cult sensation. The author had defined some universal malaise in the mass subconscious: an unease with the new visual technologies, a disgust with the insidious psychology of advertising. Owing to a particularly virulent strain of Hollywood self-loathing, Mr. Black's message had even been embraced by the entertainment industry. The author's suggestion of "media fasts," for example—extended dry-outs from the image world—had become Los Angeles's most fashionable new diet, and there was not a person of stature in Hollywood who did not have a copy of the *Black Book* proudly displayed on the office desk.

"You're Marshall Reed, aren't you?"

Marshall nodded with a pained grimace.

"Daniel Lee," said the young man, putting out a hand to shake. "I'm a screenwriter too."

Marshall shook the waiter's hand, lowering his sunglasses for a quick look. Daniel was new, he'd surmised, and not particularly well polished by Ming standards. Hovering near guests was forbidden, and engaging them in conversation was near blasphemy. Marshall thought to warn the waiter he was probably being watched on the Eye this very moment but decided it was too late. Daniel Lee would be gone before lunch.

"Hey, I gotta ask you—"

"Sorry, buddy," Marshall said, his hand shooting up reflexively. "I don't read other people's scripts." He always felt like a heel saying this, but he remembered those times he had tried to be nice and had regretted it. Hollywood was enjoying its most profitable decade in history, which of course only thickened the city's sheen of desperation. Marshall had had his Pod address hacked countless times and on other occasions had found screenplays taped under his hybrid, planted there like car bombs. One poor soul had even sent a girl up to his room at the Ming. Under her *Umbrellas of Cherbourg* raincoat she wore nothing but thigh-highs and a copy of her employer's spec script, strapped in between her legs like a fig leaf.

"Here's the deal," she'd announced, unhooking the script and spreading her legs with a flourish. "I sit here and watch you read it. When you finish — and I hear it shouldn't take you more than an hour — you get *this* . . ."

"Nothing personal, Daniel," he said. "Just my rule."

"No, no, that's not what I meant." The young man laughed softly, shaking his head at the misunderstanding. "I wouldn't do that to you, man, don't worry. I was just going to ask you about . . . you know, your *career.*"

Marshall straightened a bit in his chair. "What about it?"

"Come on, you know." Daniel chewed his lip, courage waning. "What happened?"

Sunglasses hid Marshall's eyes, though his mouth betrayed his irritation. Of course it was common knowledge he hadn't written a feature since *Chula Vista.* He performed "polishes" now, arguably the most sought-after practitioner of his kind. He also understood that young film geeks, having accomplished absolutely nothing — and therefore still able to harbor pie-in-the-sky notions about "art" and the sanctity of "career" — took a dim view of this. To them the life of Marshall Reed had become a cautionary tale.

Again he gestured for more coffee and was ignored, the waiter continuing on with the digging of his grave.

"Like, we have this group of screenwriters that gets together, for support, you know, and we argue about this sometimes. 'What ever happened to Marshall Reed?' I mean, we realize it's the system. These idiots at the studios, right? Even though you wrote a masterpiece, your stuff's just too smart for mass consumption. It's not financially viable. The system strips—"

"*Wrong,*" declared Marshall with a quiet malevolence. He pushed himself back in his chair, the better to examine the young man in all his clueless glory. "Where do you guys get this stuff from anyway?"

Daniel didn't reply.

"I mean, here you are, a bunch of ambitious young screenwriters, and this is the best you can come up with? Some dreck about a writer and the system?"

Marshall took off his sunglasses, setting them on the table.

"Okay, look, Daniel, let me clear up some things for you before you become all bitter before you even get started. First of all, the people at the studios are *not* idiots. All right? Don't ever think that. That's boring and a waste of time. The studios are a *business,* Daniel. Big news flash, I know, but you brought it up. Don't blame them because you and your coffee klatch buddies can't get your mediocre scripts produced. What do you think, a great project crosses a studio exec's desk and he says, *No, this is too good, we can't possibly produce this. We're too stupid and evil!* It's about money, Daniel. Movies are expensive; they want a good return on their dollar. If you look at the profits, I'd say they're doing a pretty damned good job. Hollywood made more money this year than anytime in its history. That, I'm afraid, is precisely its function. Nothing more, nothing less."

Marshall glanced to see the young Nubian standing to adjust her chaise.

"Now here's a suggestion, Daniel: *Go out and make your own film.* Seriously. There's no excuses anymore. You can shoot a movie on a cell phone now, for chrissakes. Your script's that good? Go make your own movie and stick it up their ass and stop whining."

Still steaming, Marshall leaned forward and sipped at the dregs of what was apparently going to be the last of his coffee, infuriating him even more. He had gone to bed just past dawn and now believed he was willing to kill for caffeine.

"Now, about my career," he concluded. "I wrote a pretty good movie some years ago, and I've parlayed that success into a steady gig punching up dialogue that affords me a nice living. I eat well, Daniel. I drink the good stuff and only do the best drugs — when I'm feeling so inclined. I live here at the Ming. That's what's *happened* to my career, since you asked. How you doin'?"

Daniel stood fingering his tray, face absolutely stricken.

The screenwriter stood, flipping closed his Pod. He threw some money on the table and made his way around the pool, passing the elegant breaststroker stretched out on her chaise. Her sorrel skin shone like a mirror in the sunlight, her knees supporting a large glossy magazine.

"You were lovely out there," Marshall whispered to her, slowing as he went by. "You made my morning." He did not look back to see her smile.

Waiting for the elevator, he snuck a last glance toward the café and noticed two men in suits talking to Daniel. One had already taken the tray from him and the other had a hand firmly on his shoulder, ushering him from the premises.

TWO

They're going to put advertisements on the moon. This is true; it's already in negotiations. A satellite is going to throw images off the surface, six days a month, while the moon is at its fullest. Why? you ask. Because they can. Because they know you're too numb and worn down. Because you can't live without your noise and busy simulacrums.

Outside the confines of the Ming, the image world unfurled itself before him.

Marshall called for his hybrid and pulled out onto Sunset, the MIBs immediately looming above him and stretching down the boulevard as far as he could see. It was more spectacular at night, of course, but the day still found them formidable: sixty, eighty, a hundred feet tall, some of them, and just as wide across. One after the other, like a mass grave for drive-in movies, except that these were digital, and *alive,* relentlessly alive—the DPIs on these things were incredible. Slowed by thick traffic, he watched the images flash around him with a stunning unctuousness. Creamy thigh here, strong jawline there, the side swell of a melon-sized tit. All of it in highly saturated digital color.

Then, at a stoplight on Doheny, a digitized Humphrey Bogart relaying the urgent message: *Pepsi Now!*

Marshall grumbled, trying to think of some pithy expletive to mutter in the name of decency. It was hopeless, he decided, a lame stab at self-respect. He had, in his own way, he knew, contributed to this malignant bile. There were plenty of movie advertisements among the MIBs, and every so often some bit of purple dialogue he'd written would rise up before him in letters twenty feet tall.

Sometimes the feel of a trigger is the only thing that makes sense.

The light changed and he drove on, Lon Chaney Jr. passing a Norelco shaver across his lupine face. Among the few remaining living icons, it was his friend Colt Reston who most dominated the billboards. To say Colt was a famous movie star was like saying the universe was full of wide-open spaces. With the help of the new technologies, he was arguably the most recognized, most photographed, most exposed human being who had ever lived.

The irony of all this had never escaped the two friends, their trajectory to Hollywood being anything but typical. They had met fifteen years ago as minor league baseball players for the Palm Springs Angels, a single-A affiliate of the major league Anaheim team. It was Marshall who was the star in those days, a bonus-baby pitcher out of Stanford with a major league fastball and an irascible demeanor he used to his advantage.

"Hey, you!" Marshall would call from the mound to the on-deck hitter, having just whistled a ninety-four-mile-an-hour fastball under the batter's chin. "You're next."

Colt, on the other hand, was a light-hitting outfielder with good speed and occasional power, basically going nowhere. By their second year together, while Colt continued to struggle at the plate (the dreaded slider, bane of the mediocre hitter), Marshall had a meeting with the general manager. He explained that he had heard some rumors about Colt and just wanted to let it be known he would be very unhappy if his friend were released, could very well be thrown off his game. It was a threat on which he was probably not prepared to follow through, though fortunately he never needed to: Colt was saved. And as soon as he was promoted to triple A — which was imminent, Marshall had been told — he would take Colt with him there, too. And so on, forever.

Their fortunes reversed shortly after this, however, catapulting them into a completely new destiny. It happened in an instant, on a scorching desert night in July of their second year. Marshall had cinematized the event, like most of the salient moments in his life, his memory breaking it down into the spare dialogue and clipped visual sequences of the movie mind:

```
EXT. MINOR LEAGUE BASEBALL STADIUM, PALM
SPRINGS — TWILIGHT

CLOSE-UP of a rugged, determined face
framed by a baseball cap. This is the
pitcher, MARSHALL REED. He wipes sweat
from his brow, awaiting the sign from the
catcher. In the background a desert dusk
throws blush on the palm trees and, behind
them, the looming San Jacinto Mountains.


WIDER ANGLE

Marshall winds and throws. The ball ex-
plodes from his hand, making a crackling
sound in the catcher's mitt. The batter
swings too late. He's struck out.
```

NEW ANGLE—THE STANDS

Two major league SCOUTS sit among the fans.
One holds a radar gun. They look at the
speed reading, then nod and scribble in
their notebooks.

ANGLE ON—PITCHER'S MOUND

Marshall winds and throws, though this time
there are gasps from the stands. The BALL
dribbles up to home plate. The batter looks
up, incredulous. Marshall has collapsed on
the mound.

CLOSE-UP—COLT RESTON—CENTER FIELD

Colt's face—showing a piercing,
otherworldly handsomeness—collapses in
disbelief. He sprints toward the pitcher's
mound, pushing past the circle of players
and coaches. Finally he sees Marshall,
who is holding his shoulder and writhing
in pain. Colt cradles his friend's head in
his arms.

> COLT
>
> Get back. Give him some room!
> (*Pushing aside players and coaches.*)
> What's going on, Marsh? What's
> happening?

> MARSHALL
>
> (*Writhing.*)
> My ... *ahhhhh* ... shoulder!

It was the rarest of pitching injuries: Marshall had broken
his arm throwing a ball. The MRI showed a large benign tumor

around the shoulder (most likely from years of pitching stress), which had precipitated the break. The injury was so severe that the doctor worried the arm might have to be amputated but then found enough good tissue during surgery to save it.

Naturally, his career was over. After the operation, when the doctor told him the news, Marshall wept for the first time since he'd been a boy.

Ironically, that same night, Colt went on to have his best game as a professional. He played with a furious abandon, as if in retaliation for Marshall's injury, smacking two home runs and making a diving catch on the warning track to seal the win. After the game there came a dramatic serendipity, one that was now part of cinematic lore, as familiar a tale as Lana Turner at Schraft's drugstore — except that this one was actually true. Vacationing in his Palm Springs hotel room was the then up-and-coming talent agent Dre McDonald — NetTalent's first prominent African American agent ever, and soon-to-be most dominating presence in Hollywood. He was half reading a script and idly flipping channels on the plasma when he stumbled across a postgame interview on a local access channel. The banter was not particularly interesting: some hillbilly ballplayer waxing banal about "doing my best" and saying "a prayer for my friend." But what he saw there nearly knocked him from his chair.

A face contoured as if by the gods.

Dre's girlfriend, too, found herself enraptured. Peeking over a mass-market paperback, she offered, with reluctant delicacy, "Dre, honey, don't take this the wrong way . . ."

The agent continued to stare at the screen, transfixed. "I know," he said.

"You *do?*"

"Yes, but go ahead, say it anyway. So I know I'm not crazy."

"Well," she said, clearing her throat, "that is the most beautiful-looking man I've ever seen in my life. Baby, that's a *movie star*. Who is he?"

"No idea," replied Dre, already reaching for his cell, "but fuck me if I'm not going to find out."

When the Angels released Colt the following week, the agent was waiting, offers extended. The depressed, heartbroken ballplayer showed up in L.A. with a used pickup truck and zero knowledge of the craft of acting. Dre urged Colt not to worry, hiring a good car for him and getting him a suite at the Beverly Wilshire. They wanted him to come by the next day, to run him on the monitor for some people.

"You mean like a screen test?" Colt had asked, hick accent still intact. "I didn't think they did that anymore."

"They don't, actually. Just for you."

Seeing Colt in person, Dre felt a searing disappointment: he was shorter than expected (though weren't they all?), with some mismatched skin tones and a gentle swath of pockmarks the agent hadn't noticed on the plasma. Dre couldn't help wondering if he had a dud on his hands. But what he and his colleagues saw on the monitor that next morning—the thing that happened to Colt Reston's face when assimilated by the grains, pixels, and effusions of digital film—changed the world of movies forever.

Traffic was thick, and Marshall got to the studio late as usual. Having misplaced his studio pass more than a week ago, he pulled up to Panoramic's arched entrance and tried to get past the gatehouse with just a wave.

Tuten, however, flagged him down. The screenwriter rolled his eyes and lowered the window.

"Carrying any weapons or explosives today?" began the portly guard. Ordinarily Marshall would be spared the morning gatehouse questionnaire, but since he had lost his pass, Tuten was obligated to put him through the tedious security check reserved for guests. "That includes small firearms, knives, blunt objects—anything at all that can be used as weapons. This is strictly prohibited by the studio and should be turned over immediately. Are you carrying any illegal substances? Drugs of any kind? Drugs are strictly—"

"*That,* I may be able to help you with," Marshall said. He leaned out of the window, asking conspiratorially, "Whatcha looking for, T.?"

Tuten pinched his lips sourly. "C'mon, Marsh. Every day I tell you we're on the Eye here, and every day you give me a hard time. Just bring your damn pass already."

"T., there's a scan up a hundred feet that's going to read me down to the fillings in my teeth. What's the point?"

"Doing my job, man. Don't like it, go home."

"Don't have one," replied Marshall, who then seemed to brighten at an idea. "Hey, maybe I could stay at your place. Move in with you and the little lady."

"Sure," said the guard, who finally broke a smile. "That's gonna happen." He opened the gate, allowing Marshall to make his way up through the garage-shaped detector and onto the Panoramic lot. The vehicle moved slowly, passing the rows of lush palms, the hacienda-style offices, the large warehouselike studios and airplane-hangar soundstages. Driving farther, he ran into a large detour—they were filming a movie about filming a movie—and finally found Colt Reston's absurdly elongated Airstream on the farthest reaches of the lot.

Marshall parked just behind the trailer and some plasma-sized MIBs sprang instantly to life as he strode by: Gucci, United Technologies, Skittles. Reaching the entrance, the screenwriter was recognized by two solemn-looking PAs with mikes around their necks, and who bookended the front door like guards at the palace gates.

"Guys, lighten up," he told them, tugging their Panoramic caps as he passed. "It's just the movies."

Inside he found Colt on the couch, playing a hologram video game, enemy planes swirling above him like bees. On the floor a few feet away from them, a husband-and-wife team from wardrobe sat tailoring the uniform of a futuristic, quasi-fascist policeman.

"Hey, everybody," Marshall announced, making a beeline for the bar. Giving up on the idea of coffee, he opened the small Sub-Zero and dropped some cubes in a glass, the ice popping as he splashed them with vodka. Seeing he was ignored, he decided to continue: "You know, I finally realized what this ridiculous excuse for a trailer reminds me of."

Colt seemed to smirk as machine-gun fire burst from the handset.

"A huge dildo," the writer said, turning toward the wardrobe couple, who were only brave enough to mirror Colt's smirk. "Somebody's got *size* issues, people, know what I'm saying?"

"Mr. Vancouver," Colt said, abandoning his game and rising to his feet. He and Marshall embraced passionately, with rugged slaps on the back, while the wardrobe couple moved out of sight. "How'd things go up there?"

Marshall shrugged, flopping down onto the couch behind them. "Weird set," he offered ambiguously. "Cool city, though." He sipped his drink.

They hadn't seen each other in nearly a month, and despite the embrace, it was clear that the awkwardness between them had not subsided. All was not well with their friendship. The days when they had been inseparable, when barely anyone in Hollywood would mention one name without the other, had begun to wane. Marshall could not say he was completely surprised. In fact, what seemed more surprising was how long they had managed to stay close. Of the fourteen years they had been friends, Colt Reston had been the number one movie star in the world for the last eight, while Marshall's career had been in permanent retrograde for almost as long. There was still a strong bond between them, mostly based on nostalgia, Marshall had concluded, but in practical terms (that niche where Hollywood alliances tended to subsist) their alliance no longer made sense.

In fact, Marshall took Colt's allusions to Vancouver as a subtle dig. He had been called there for some last-minute rewrites on a spy thriller that had spun out of control and, on arriving, had found disorder and rampant self-indulgence—his choice environs. There were stories in the trades about a druggy set, and though the name Marshall Reed was never specifically cited, it was assumed that he was in the thick of it.

"Orlavio," Colt said, referring to the director. "Running a loose ship these days, eh?"

"He's old now," Marshall answered with calculated vagueness, virtually assuring himself an impending interrogation.

He patted the couch, hoping Colt would join him. By now Marshall had mostly accepted that it would never again be like the

old days, when they would share a joint and play hologram baseball, hiding from the demands of the set like spoiled teenagers. But
now Colt had begun pacing in front of him, and Marshall caught
him sneaking nervous peeks at him out of the corner of his eye.

"All right, Colt, you want to sit down, please? You're making
me crazy."

But the actor kept pacing, and now Marshall realized that
Colt was not sneaking peeks at *him* but just above, looking repeatedly in the mirror hanging over the couch.

"Marsh, I gotta talk to you about something. Something that's
been on my mind for a while now."

On the couch, Marshall arched ever so slightly. Despite some
freelance work, he was essentially Colt Reston's private rewrite man,
though *writing* was probably far too generous a term. Working for
Colt mostly meant *eliminating* dialogue from a script, stripping away
the chatter to get at the images, the brutish physicality. But now a bitter smile pursed Marshall's lips. He was sure of what was coming.

*My God, I am about to be fired by the only friend I have left in
Hollywood.*

He understood that Colt had been under pressure to get rid of
him. Executives at Panoramic (the studio for which Colt worked
almost exclusively) were sick to death of watching their biggest
star spend half his morning making calls for a troubled screenwriter, trading in favors, throwing his weight around to cover up
Marshall's various mishaps. They must have gotten to Colt while
he was away, the screenwriter decided — the rumors from Vancouver having sealed the deal — and now, inconceivable as it had
once seemed, their friendship was about to be thrown onto the
great Hollywood ash heap.

"I can barely think about anything else," Colt said.

Marshall waited sullenly. *Get on with it already.*

But instead the actor reached out a hand, urging Marshall off the couch.

"Come look at this," Colt said. "I want to show you in the good light."

Confounded now, Marshall let himself be pulled to his feet and herded into the trailer's tiny bathroom. There the actor turned on the lights and stood in front of the brightly lit stage mirror, leaning his face closer to the glass.

"Now, don't bullshit me," Colt demanded, turning his head side to side to show every angle of his face. "I want the truth."

Marshall didn't know what to make of this. Had Colt's vanity hit some new plateau while he'd been away? He found himself pulling away from the reflection until Colt slipped an arm around his back and kept him still.

"Well?" the actor said expectantly.

"Well what?"

"Come on, I know you see it."

Marshall laughed a little. "What am I seeing?"

"There's something different, right?"

Pressed closer now, Marshall had no choice but to consider the face of Colt Reston. It was, by anyone's measure, an extraordinary countenance: the broad, jutting jaw, the sharp nose, the impossible green eyes framed by sandy hair. But then he also understood that Colt was very much a product of the digital age. Just as some actors had thrived with the advent of sound — others finding themselves displaced — so did Colt Reston owe much of his iconic status to binary pixelation. Only in the digital monitor did his somewhat rough-hewn features seem to gain otherworldly focus and definition; only then did they reach the warm, ethereal perfection they did not otherwise possess.

"Can you give me some idea of what I'm looking for here?" Marshall asked.

Colt looked annoyed. "It's right *there,* man! Come on."

Marshall tried to stifle a laugh. He'd watched Colt grow increasingly narcissistic in recent years but had chosen not to condescend to it, giving his friend the benefit of the doubt. Who but Colt Reston could say what it was like to carry the fate of an entire studio on your back (probably an agency, too) or to endure the gaze of tens of millions? Nobody before had ever experienced Colt's level of popularity and exposure, so there was really no telling which of his eccentricities were universal and which were truly neurotic.

But clearly something had happened to him; here now was a psychosis not even Marshall could excuse.

"Like what?" he asked, trying to play along.

"There's something *wrong,*" Colt said, poking at his face with his fingers, as if trying to heighten some flaw. "It's right goddamned there if you'd just *look.*"

Marshall gave his friend another cursory examination and then, mostly out of boredom, became distracted by his own reflection. He did not particularly like what he saw. Underneath the carefree appearance—the bed-head hair and the light beard and aviator glasses, which it was assumed he wore to hide his eyes—Marshall could see that his features were beginning to deteriorate. There was, most obviously, the sallow skin tone, and then the deeply etched lines that were coming too quick for someone not quite forty. He was running down, getting that rummy look.

I could do with some serious pixelation myself, Marshall thought.

"All right," he told Colt finally, "maybe you look a little tired." Desperately wanting to move past this episode, he was willing to concede some darker hues under his eyes.

"So you see it, then."

"I said you looked *tired,*" the screenwriter repeated. "Whatever else you think is there, I don't see it. Have you been to a doctor?"

"Yes."

"And?"

Colt looked loath to admit it. "Exhaustion, they said."

"You see? It's what I've been telling you. You're over-worked."

"Overworked, overexposed — over*everything,*" Colt added glumly. "Just ask Mr. Black."

Ah, the Black Book, thought Marshall, almost relieved to have found some source for the neurosis. Colt had been singled out for ridicule in the work, and he was surprised to see how much the actor had been stung by it. With Marshall away in Vancouver, the words had obviously begun to nag at Colt again.

Advertising is the new fascism, via the MIBs, and Colt Reston is our Mao, our Big Brother. Shameless, banal, and overexposed, we are force-fed his amorphous, characterless image like ducks fattened for foie gras . . . He is nothing less than a scourge, an affliction . . .

"I told you a hundred times, fuck that guy," Marshall said, Colt finally settling in next to him on the couch. "A year from now no one's going to remember Mr. Black, his book, or *any* of this crap. It's a publicity stunt to sell copies. It will pass."

"Can't help it," Colt replied, smiling sadly. "The bastard put a bug in my ear, Marsh. And let's face it, he's right, in a way. People are sick of me. My career has gotten away from me lately. Six movies a year, all the publicity, the MIBs . . . You've heard about the vandalism?"

The screenwriter nodded. "The Blackheads," he said.

No matter what you thought about the new landscape of Los Angeles, pro or con, Marshall figured you had to be intrigued by the Blackheads. These were the hard-core fans of the *Black Book*, believed to be mostly college-age kids, and though there was no telling how many they numbered, they were proving a formidable nuisance nonetheless. Almost every morning the city woke to find another few MIBs slashed and spray-painted. Damage estimates were into the millions and not a single vandal had been caught, the rumor being that many in the city were secretly rooting for the Blackheads and had turned a blind eye.

There was a knock at the door now as one of the PAs stuck her head in and let Colt know he was due back on the set in fifteen minutes.

"Thanks, sweetheart," the actor replied, flashing a smile that would probably make her month. Marshall couldn't help but feel a surge of pride; fame had done many terrible things to his friend over the years, but Colt had always remained inordinately decent to the people around him. There were times this took nothing less than a Herculean effort, Marshall knew—a man in Colt's position—and he admired his friend for it.

"Oh, and some bad news," the young woman added. Her eyes flickered as she played with the mike around her neck, obviously dreading this part of her mission.

"Yes?"

She hesitated. "Your . . . Web site."

Colt lifted his billion-dollar chin. "What about it?"

"Well, we got a call. I guess somebody must have hacked in."

"Hacked!" Colt exclaimed.

"There's a new intro. It's doctored or something . . . I don't know, Colt, it's just really gross. I wouldn't even look at it if I were you. The webmaster said it should be under control by the end of the day."

Marshall, however, was already there, typing in "ColtReston. com" on the plasma. Immediately the pop-up advert that paid for the site appeared: Clark Gable's hair tousled by Veronica Lake, each extolling the wonders of the latest dandruff pill. Then Marshall scrolled down until he came to the offending image: Colt's face altered to a hideous death mask, eyes bugging out of a gaunt and ravaged visage, and underneath this, in a font simulating a handwritten scrawl, the legend:

Leave us alone!

THREE

She woke as she always did, an hour before the alarm, skittish and tinged with an anxiety leaning toward aggression. Not a bad state to be in, Lindsay figured. After all, there were deadlines to meet, ambitious upstarts, daily-changing technology, ratings pressure, Bliss-addled copywriters, and in-house crushes. Not to mention people who resented your color, your gender, your still-tight ass and law degree.

Nope, better to wake up mad, she thought. *Better to go to work bleary eyed and coiled, ready to strike.*

Lindsay and her morning ritual: quick call-out to the coffee maker, followed by a three-minute hand job, barely satisfying. Sipping her brew, she would part the curtains to let in some gauzy L.A. sunlight, gazing down at the apartment complex pool to see how cold it looked for laps, trying to psych herself up. The Beverly Court was a "luxury" building, inhumanely expensive, but somehow they'd forgotten to heat the damn pool.

This time as she looked down, however, she flinched, dotting her curtains with coffee: perched at the end of the low-slung diving board was a large mountain lion. It balanced tentatively, the board vibrating ever so slightly under its weight as it leaned over to lap at the chlorinated water, the pool turquoise and blushed with henna highlights from the morning sun. The lion's shoulders and haunches were duly rippled with muscle mass, but the cat itself was a bit flabby, if she was not mistaken, somewhat adipose around the neck and chest. It was then that she remembered . . .

Junk Food Big Cats!

It was a great story. The *L.A. Times* had recently had a small item about it, but none of the television newsmagazines would touch it. *Might not be too late,* Lindsay had told herself. It certainly wasn't going to get better anytime soon. Urban sprawl had reached the foothills of the San Gabriels, luring wildlife down from the mountains and slowly reshaping the food chain and delicate ecotone systems. Along the outer sprawls of Northridge, Burbank, and Pasadena, deer by the thousands now feasted on the verdant lawns of gated communities, while the raven population had exploded due to the sheer tonnage of new roadkill. Then there were the catamounts themselves, who came down at night to binge on the poorly secured Dumpsters of fast-food restaurants and waste-management facilities and were now hooked, even more susceptible than humans to the addictions of MSG and a high-glycemic-index diet.

Naturally there had been ugly attacks — the dead night watchman, a mangled jogger (still alive), the dozens of missing house pets — and so new systems of garbage lockup and disposal were quickly enforced. But then the lions and their overstimulated opioids simply lumbered west, migrating toward regions where waste management hadn't yet caught on. Lately there had been rumors of fatal maulings in Benedict Canyon and Los Feliz, of a foot taken to the ankle outside a health food store in Malibu. Then one morning's rush hour offered the bizarre spectacle of nothing less than a *family* of lions loping down the middle of Wilshire Boulevard—mom, dad, and little male cub—while distracted commuters slammed their cars into one another and terrified pedestrians huddled in doorways, trying to muffle their shouts of terror. There were estimated to be as many as forty lions in the North Hollywood–Santa Monica–Malibu triangle, and it was said with a touch of hyperbole that there hadn't been such anxiety in Los Angeles since the Manson murders.

Make that thirty-nine, Lindsay thought now, watching a new scene unfold below her. Across the court a woman had appeared on her balcony with a cell phone, and sirens could soon be heard in the distance. Minutes later two police officers were followed into the court by what seemed like a gratuitous band of six SWAT team members (inexplicably wearing their bulletproof vests). An appointed shooter stepped up near the pool's edge, on the animal's left flank. Resting a knee on a reclined chaise, he took aim.

Lindsay shut her eyes until she heard the shot, a surprisingly muted, air-rifle pop, and when she opened them again she thought the marksman had missed. There was no reaction whatsoever from the lion, though the shooter himself had fallen back in apparent satisfaction. The balconies were now filled with Beverly Court residents standing in their robes, calling friends or taking video on their cells. The lion simply sat on its haunches licking its paws, and it was only when it started to let out a few histrionic yawns that Lindsay knew it had been hit.

Soon the diving board began to shake—a rapid quavering, seemingly in opposition to the lion's own gentle movements—and then the big cat tumbled, legs splayed, like the drunken fool at a pool party.

Lindsay stared fixedly as the lion sank, a furry blur, to the bottom. No resistance, she thought, no fight. It was not until the blood had turned the pool the color of a large Negroni that she thought to call the network and ask for a rush on a vid team. *Too late now,* she decided. She'd have to hope for some good cell footage, for which they'd end up paying a fortune. Finally Lindsay wiped away a drop of moisture heading down to her chin—a bead of coffee that had escaped her lips in the excitement—and chided herself for faltering in the face of such good luck.

The restaurant was at a hotel in Bel Air that had been around since the early 1980s, which, by Los Angeles standards, made it a classic, practically Old Hollywood. Marshall entered the lobby and walked straight past the crowd at the maître d' stand. Trying to look casual, he made his way up to a large standing vase and, peering through a thick copse of yellow roses, found Dre McDonald at his usual table. Sitting next to him was Lindsay Williams, the television personality who, one would assume, would now be riding a wave of success with her impending Mr. Black interview, and who had the kind of statuesque good looks that had kept Marshall secretly tuning in for years. She and Dre were kitty-corner, maybe a touch too close for business—a late breakfast meeting turned into a flirt.

Fair enough, Marshall thought, deciding that this afforded him some extra time for his own bit of business.

He walked to the VIP men's room, a special annex lounge that was the new L.A. status symbol and for which, somewhat shamefully, he had a key.

"Marshall, dammit," he heard as he entered, "I was about to give up on your ass."

Dana Wiggins was leaning up against a urinal, smoking a cigarette with the convincing aplomb of a gun moll — perhaps she had once played one, Marshall thought. She was a talented character actress whose career had done a sudden flameout, because of either her smart mouth or her widening hips — both, of course, irrevocable sins. Marshall was upset that she'd taken the risk to smoke in here with the alarms, and he jutted his chin at the two guys in suits behind her at the vanity, bent over what looked like an extravagant amount of Bliss for lunchtime.

"You were late," Dana said with a shrug. "They wanted to party." She took a last drag and threw her cigarette into the urinal, above which flickered a small MIB for children's vitamins. "What, we're all friends here, right?"

"Marsh," a voice said as one of the men straightened up. When the man stopped digging the heel of his hand against his nose, Marshall could see that it was Derek Samuels, a midlevel exec from Panoramic.

"Oh, great," Marshall murmured, and when the other man straightened up he recognized him, too: Lamont Turner, one of NetTalent's new agents. *Degenerate fools, each of them,* Marshall thought immediately, and he was reminded all over again of what he hated most about this drug for which his name had become virtually synonymous: the people it put him in proximity to, the Hollywood monsters he found himself adjoined with in secret rooms.

"I got three more out there that want to join us," Dana said, so excited that a lesser actress would have rubbed her hands together. "You're my good-luck charm, Marsh."

They blamed this on Colt Reston, too, Marshall reflected. It was Colt's success, after all, that had created this latest golden age, pouring hundreds of millions (billions, if you took the large view) into Hollywood coffers. This, in turn, had its usual trickle-down effect: from Colt to the studios; from the studios to the producers and agents; from the producers and agents to the actors, techs, and peons; from the actors, techs, and peons to the car dealers, landlords, waiters, and so on . . . *Everybody* in L.A. had too much cash, and just in time for Bliss to hit the streets. The drug was prohibitively expensive—therefore instantly glamorous and desirable—and reportedly the best high ever invented, possibly excluding mainline heroin. Production was not yet equal to demand, but in the Hollywood subculture of Bliss—of chasing Bliss, of knowing Bliss dealers and how to track them down, of using Bliss indiscriminately at parties, in screening rooms, studio parking lots, and restaurant bathrooms—Marshall Reed was *the man.*

"Join us," said Derek, nostrils aflame, as Lamont held up a small platinum tube designed for snorting.

"With you bums?" Marshall said, turning away from the spread. "I wouldn't piss in your shoes."

The two men grinned, loving it. They were used to this by now—the scorn of Marshall Reed. They found it reassuring. Derek and Lamont were midlevel wonks, their days spent in anesthetized politeness with people too frightened to say *Maybe,* or even *I'll think about it.* So Marshall's freewheeling cynicism had just the masochistic sting they craved. It played to the self-hatred they hid from the world and knew required tending.

"Yeah, why not, Marsh?" added Lamont. "Shit ain't cheap. We're feeling generous today."

Marshall looked again at the vanity. There was about five grand's worth spread out on a small tray — the beach-sand texture of high-quality Bliss. He sighed heavily and then, with the hauteur of teaching them a lesson — nothing for himself, you understand — stepped up and did a line for each nostril, dropping the tube with a disdainful clatter when he had finished.

Now Derek and Lamont smiled, waiting for the speech, the caustic bile they'd come to count on from Marshall, which would be ignited by the rush of the drug.

"Well, guys," he began, stepping back to sniff up the residue that hung upon the edges of his nose, "I guess this is when you know it's really over. When you've officially bottomed out." He either grimaced or smiled bitterly as he handed Dana the roll of bills he had taken from his breast pocket, and she stuffed something there in turn. "When you're tootin' off in the VIP room at lunch, risking a career you've no right to have in the first place. That's when you know —"

And then it hit him, the rush slamming him like a jolt of electricity. He was jackknifed forward at the waist, retching, eyes burning in the furnace of his skull as he reached out for something to hold on to. Finding the contours of a urinal, he remained there, hunched over, gasping to find his breath.

"*Christ, you okay, Marsh? You all right?*" He heard Dana's panicked voice above him, muted as if from underwater, her hand rubbing his back. "*Oh, shit, don't die on me in here. Come on, Marsh, tell me you're all right. Don't die on me, goddammit . . .*"

After a moment he spat into the urinal and nodded.

"Oh, Christ, I'm so sorry," she said with relief as he slowly began to straighten. "I should have told you about this new stuff—it's *nuts*. You have to cut it big-time. These two bozos are trying to kill themselves, what do they care?"

From the corner of his watery eyes he could see Derek snorting another line. "Lookin' a little pale there," said the Panoramic man with a smirk.

"Maybe he needs another," Lamont added. "Something to bring the blood to the head." He went down for a quick hit and came up high-fiving Derek.

Dana gave them both the finger and then turned to Marshall. "How do you feel now?" She held him tight at the shoulders and looked into his eyes, apparently seeing something there that she liked. "Better, right? Go on, tell me how you feel."

Marshall rubbed his fingers against his cheeks to make sure he still had a face. It took him a few seconds before he could speak.

"Fuckin' amazing," he said.

Lindsay dragged her fork through the remnants of a fruit tart, thinking, *Enough already. I'm impressed, brother, I'm impressed.* Dre was laying it on thick. Naturally she was flattered. There were people everywhere—at every seat in this restaurant, in fact—who would gladly have given a limb to be signed by Dre McDonald. Even her father, who drove a livery back in Bellville, Ohio, had heard of NetTalent, though he had no idea what an agency did, dear man, nor could he understand its importance.

"Fifteen percent?" he would tell her on the phone. "For what? You do all the work!"

She knew this was mostly Mr. Black's doing, that this so-called heat she was generating was testimony to the grip he had

on the media's imagination. The interview, which would air
tonight on her show, *National Insider,* was hardly expected to be
a ratings monster. Outside of L.A. and New York, the average
person probably didn't give much of a damn about Mr. Black. But
everyone in the industry knew about him and would be riveted,
and so Lindsay was suddenly now, at thirty-three, a bona fide
commodity: a good-looking African American female journalist
with an intellectual bent.

The irony was that the interview had come to *her,* had basically fallen into her lap. There'd been a series of calls to the station, each fielded by Spencer, her personal assistant and a human
firewall. Lindsay always got a lot of weird attention from men,
hundreds upon hundreds of telecrushes, and Spencer, whom
Lindsay had nicknamed the Diva (owing to his bitchy business
style), dispatched their letters and e-mails quickly enough. But
he'd never run into someone like this.

"Who's calling?" the Diva had asked during their last conversation.

The voice expressed some casual amusement. "I'm the one
they're calling Mr. Black."

The screen on the vidphone was dark, the Diva noted, but
then didn't all the weirdos hide their faces?

"C'mon, creep, give us a break. How'd you get the number?"

"Let me speak to Lindsay."

"I said, *how did you get it?* This is a very private line."

"I told you who I am," the voice said ambiguously.

"Yes, you did, and now I'm telling you to fuck off."

Spencer threw the phone into the nearest trash bin and paid
top dollar for a new ultrasecure number—not once, but three
times over the course of a week, and each time the man had called

back without a hitch. When threats failed to dissuade the man, Spencer finally explained the situation to Lindsay, both of them agreeing it could not possibly be the real Mr. Black but also understanding that at this point it was probably only Lindsay herself who could discourage him.

"Okay, what is it you want, buster?" She'd taken the call in the editing room, picking at a salad with chopsticks and examining the footage of a frat-house hazing incident at the same time. "My boyfriend's in the LAPD and he's just *dying* to meet you. Should we set up a date?"

Laughter on the other end of the line.

"You're *laughing* at me, you pervert? Get a girlfriend already. *Stop calling here!*"

A calm, virile voice said, "I happen to know, Lindsay Williams, that at the moment there is no boyfriend. But pretty as you are, that is not my concern."

She set her salad aside and leaned back from the monitor.

Lucky guess, she decided: television journalist too busy for a relationship. Shot in the dark that had landed.

"I'd like to be interviewed," he continued. "On television, believe it or not, and I'd like you to do it."

"Interview?" Now it was Lindsay's turn to laugh. "Since when?"

"I've had a change of heart recently. This is why I think we should talk. I don't think anonymity is doing any good for my cause."

Lindsay frowned; she was still annoyed, but had to admire the fraud's pluck. She fast-forwarded through more of the increasingly lurid hazing footage, still half listening. "Supposing you *are* Mr. Black — which I don't believe for a minute, by the way. How'd you pick me? We're a midlevel show here at best. If you are who you say you are, any of the big networks would jump at the chance—"

"*No, no, no,*" he'd said, tersely cutting her off. "I don't want a big network. I need a show like yours—quirky, adventurous. There's some freedom there, some leeway with interesting material. I'd at least have a chance to say what I have to say."

Well, Lindsay thought, he certainly was media savvy, whoever the hell he was. *National Insider* prided itself on "risky" material, which too often meant the vulgar, shameless stuff that nobody else would touch. But occasionally it would surprise you. Mr. Black was probably too esoteric for the majors anyway, and *NI* would let him riff in a way the networks would not.

She scooted her chair away from the monitor, signaling to a few techs to keep their voices down. She was intrigued now—skeptical, but intrigued.

"Plus, I've seen your show," he continued. "I like you. There's something genuine there. Not like these other charlatans. Are you familiar with the book?"

"Somewhat," she replied, playing it down. In fact, while most of her colleagues knew the tome only by hearsay, she had actually finished the *Black Book.*

"And?" he asked, somewhat anxiously. "What do you think?"

The Diva stuck his head in, pointing at his watch: Lindsay was due at a producer's meeting in exactly five minutes. "Look," she said into the phone, "I don't have time for book-club discussions. Unless you can prove to me you are who you say you are in the next thirty seconds, I'm going to have to hang up."

After a pause the man said, "Do you happen to have your copy of the book nearby?"

"In my office. Why?"

"Get it."

She sighed, checking her watch. "How do I know you're not going to waste my time?"

"Just get the book, Lindsay."

Keeping him on the line, she went to her office and found her dog-eared copy in a stack on her desk. "Okay," she said with a smile. At the very least, Lindsay told herself, this was sort of fun.

"Open it to the title page," the voice instructed.

She did, and seeing what was there made her chest drum with fear and excitement. Just below the title, written with a blue ballpoint pen, was the inscription

To Lindsay, from Mr. Black

"How the hell did you do that!" Lindsay exclaimed. When he didn't answer, she said, "There's no way you could've gotten in here. This place is a freaking armed fortress! *How did you do it?*"

"You know I can't tell you that."

There was a long pause, during which Lindsay was unable to take her eyes from the inscription on the page. "I'll need to guarantee my safety," she announced finally.

"Of course," he answered. "You'll want corroboration. I'll have my publisher call you from New York. There'll be all the assurances. Though there is one thing about which I won't compromise."

"Yes?"

"When and if we do meet, you cannot see me at all. I don't mean that my face cannot appear on television—that goes without saying. What I mean is that if you get any glimpse of me, even accidentally—a strand of hair, the tip of my shoelace—the interview will be terminated and I will kill you. I will kill you without the slightest hesitation, and I will get away with it because nobody knows who I am. I hope that's understood."

"Anyway, my dear," Dre continued now, "what I'm really saying is you couldn't possibly be in any better position than you are at the moment." Lindsay had not yet signed anything with Dre, but she was already letting him field some of the inquiries that had started to come in for her, a sort of trial run. "*Sixty Minutes* has been in contact, the Google Channel, ESPN—bunch of other majors. But please, listen closely, because I want to tell you something very important." He reached out and took her hand, which she realized only later was probably inappropriate. "You have to understand that no matter what happens in your career, you will most likely *never* be in this position again. You've got exactly one shot to get it right. Just one."

She looked up into Dre's eyes, noticing the tincture of blue there from his contact lenses—then watched them suddenly narrow, apparently spying something unpleasant across the restaurant.

"Oh, Jesus," she heard him murmur, "here he comes."

It was Marshall Reed, trudging heavy legged through the dining room as if it were a muddy riverbed.

He was stopped twice along the way. First to shake hands with a director who longed to work with Colt Reston. Then, a few tables down, he was intercepted by an old actor friend whom he used to run with in the early days, the man sober now since his marriage. After some quick catching-up, he whispered to Marshall that if he had his sunglasses handy he might want to put them on.

"Thanks," Marshall responded, already reaching into his shirt pocket.

Lindsay and Dre stood waiting as he arrived, two black faces against the bright pastel decor and slanting California sunlight. In his slightly woozy state, Marshall saw this juxtaposition as significant, even profound.

"Ms. Williams," he said, taking the woman's hand and noting the unusually long fingers and cool palm. "*NI,* one of my favorite shows. You bet." Relaxing the press of his grip now, Marshall couldn't help noticing how the half-moons cut in the side of her dress highlighted her lovely cinnamon-colored skin.

"You lie," she rejoined with a pleasing smile. "But thank you. *Chula Vista* is one of my all-time favorite movies."

"Ah, so now we're *both* lying," Marshall replied, glancing toward Dre and seeing himself fixed in a choleric gaze. The agent obviously knew he was high, and seemed to regard Marshall's sunglasses as an especially appalling touch.

As for the prince himself, Dre was sporting his habitual sartorial chic. Armani remained de rigueur as ever for agents, but the CEO of NetTalent preferred light Savile Row and bow ties, giving him a look somewhere between a Howard University dean and a Harlem Renaissance bandleader.

"I actually own a copy of the script," Lindsay continued now, somewhat bashfully. "I keep it on my nightstand. It's a real work of art, Marshall. You should be very proud."

"You hear that, Dre?" he asked. He was trying to tweak a smile out of the man, soften him up. "Work of art, she says."

The agent nodded sourly, inviting everyone to sit, though Lindsay begged off, claiming she had to return to work. Marshall was unable to hide his disappointment.

"Come on, I've been dying to ask you about this Mr. Black interview. What happened? Who is he?"

"Sorry," Lindsay replied. "You'll just have to watch tonight along with everybody else." She used his shoulder for support as she came around the banquette. "Since it's your favorite show and all," she added with a wink.

She thanked Dre for lunch and then strode off, each man daring the other to sneak a look back. Somehow both defeated the urge.

"Lean over here," Dre commanded when they had sat. He reached out and lifted up Marshall's sunglasses, frowning at what he saw. "Your eyes," he remarked, "look like two gunshot wounds."

Marshall readjusted his glasses but did not reply.

"You should hear the latest news from Vancouver, Marshall. Oh, it's rich. We got a little call from the minister of culture, explaining how she's considering banning Panoramic from shooting there anymore. Not just in Vancouver, mind you, the *whole country.* You guys had one hell of a party up there." Dre leaned over now, trying to keep his voice down. "What's going on with you, anyway? How could you come here this high after an incident like that? It's goddamned insulting."

Marshall adopted a sulky look, gazing out across the dining room. Ordinarily he would volley with Dre, friction being part of their rapport. But today he knew he was on shaky ground — with Colt, the studio, *everyone.* Whatever leverage he'd once had was gone.

"You're right," he admitted. "What can I say? It was stupid. Won't happen again."

Dre sat back, searching for traces of irony.

"I'm serious." As if to attest to his sincerity, Marshall flagged a waitress and ordered a coffee. "I need to reel it in a bit. I'm actually sick of the whole thing myself, believe it or not."

The agent continued to watch Marshall, then made a dismissive gesture with his hand. "Well, fuck it, it's your career. I don't really care anymore." Dre sipped from his glass of Arctic water, washing away the bad taste. "Anyway, the real reason I asked you here is Colt. I wanted to bounce some ideas off you about what's going on."

"There's something going on?"

"Yes, I believe there is." Dre looked over at the next table and leaned forward again, lowering his voice. "I think Talent United is trying to sabotage Colt, ruin his career."

All set for a juicy rumor, Marshall felt deflated. *Sabotage?* he thought. So what the hell else was new? Were they not all smack in the middle of the so-called talent wars? It was well known that TU ran interference on Colt's career, just as Dre and his boys tore down TU's biggest stars. You paid off reviewers, spun salacious gossip, undermined test screenings, and so on. NetTalent had a whole department dedicated to it, and so, presumably, did TU. What you could not have for your own, you destroyed, as a matter of course. Sabotage was a quaint anachronism.

"You heard about the incident today on Colt's Web site?"

"The Blackheads," Marshall said, nodding. "I was with him this morning when he saw it."

"How'd he take it?"

"Not great," said the screenwriter. "This whole *Black Book* thing's got him very shaken. I think he's lost a lot of confidence lately. He's been acting strange—or at least with me he has."

"Yes," Dre said, nodding, "I agree. He's not the same. This is why I wanted to throw some ideas out at you." He sat up straight,

Dre being the kind of man who regarded good posture as an advantage in business matters. "Like, what if today's incident wasn't the Blackheads?"

Marshall rubbed his temples. As intense as the womb glow of Bliss could be, it usually faded almost as quickly, and so he was surprised that his concentration still hadn't fully returned. "I don't follow."

"Well, have any of them ever been caught? Has anyone actually ever *talked* to a Blackhead? What if the reality is there are no Blackheads and TU has just stepped up their mischief?"

Marshall looked hard at the agent as his coffee arrived, wondering what could have set him on this bizarre train of thought. No doubt Dre was still distraught over the death of Carmela Montoya, the petite actress and NetTalent client who had recently succumbed to an "undisclosed disease," generally thought to be lung cancer. Internationally popular, Carmela had been, in many ways, the female counterpart to Colt Reston, and rumor had it that when her death was announced, Talent United was all high fives in the office.

"Look," Marshall said, "I know it's been a tough month, but this is pretty far out. I mean, why not just say there's no Mr. Black at all, that he's the invention of Dick Vale and his people over at Talent United?"

The agent raised his eyebrows excitedly.

"Oh, come *on,*" Marshall said, looking away.

"Well, why not? Look at what the book's doing to Colt psychologically. It's shattered his confidence, like you said. Already he wants me to cancel two projects for next year. I mean, what better way to neutralize my biggest star, Marshall, than with somebody like Mr. Black?"

"Dre, he's tired, that's all," the screenwriter said, leaning forward to emphasize his point. "The guy's exhausted, he's overworked. You'd have to be *blind* not to see it." The blessed caffeine was finally making Marshall feel more lucid, and he drank heartily from his cup to keep up the momentum. "And get Colt off the MIBs already, would you? I don't know how long I've been telling you this. There's a saturation point for everyone, Dre. The audience has had it with all this—never mind what it's doing to Colt. You can't see yourself everywhere and not go a little insane."

As if for confirmation, Marshall glanced down at the MIB on their table, a small plastic ziggurat that held the salt and pepper, where a *Mr. Smith*–era Jimmy Stewart pleaded the case for a local law firm, the volume mercifully turned off.

During the pause, the maître d', who had been hovering nervously the last minute or so, saw fit to cut in. Dre had an urgent phone call.

"Excuse me," said the agent, rising immediately.

Alone now, Marshall ordered some more coffee. The Bliss buzz was gone and he was suddenly very hungry. After ten minutes of perusing the menu and still no sign of Dre, Marshall made his way to the maître d' stand.

"What's happened to Mr. McDonald?" he asked.

The maître d' looked apologetic but said nothing; apparently he'd been put in a spot. Highly irritated, Marshall turned and noticed a crowd three-deep at the bar, unheard of at lunch, their necks craning toward the row of plasmas above them. Approaching, he saw on one of the screens an aerial view of what looked like the lot at Panoramic, the scene swarming with ambulances and police hybrids.

"There's been an accident," said a shaky voice behind him: it was the maître d', trying to make amends. Marshall did not turn his gaze from the plasmas.

On each screen now was the face of Colt Reston, the photo from the *Chula Vista* era, the man at his most impossibly handsome.

"What accident?" Marshall asked, still looking up, then suddenly reaching for the back of a barstool, trying to steady himself.

Below Colt's face now was a caption, the words displayed in large, definitive letters. Almost involuntarily, Marshall found his eyes skimming from left to right across the bank of plasmas, though all were tuned to the same channel, as if in hope that the next screen's message might herald a different revelation.

Film Star Feared Dead . . . Film Star Feared Dead . . . Film Star Feared Dead . . .

FOUR

The final day of shooting—a sort of celebration, usually. Three or four hours at the most, with everyone taking phone numbers or talking about what they'll be wearing to the wrap party. Hollywood's version of the last day of school.

Today, however? A collapse into petty squabbling, into egos run amok at the end of a long, joyless slog.

The screenplay had been through six writers and nine official drafts, but it was Marshall Reed who had been called in to write the conclusion. Doing what he did best, Marshall had parsed a rambling, three-page monologue on guilt and the tragedy of violence to one tidy, low-production-cost paragraph, the scene set down as follows:

```
Distraught at the carnage he has wrought
in the name of justice, Glen Raymen takes
the 11 millimeter, points it at his temple,
and pulls the trigger. CLICK . . . there are
no bullets. The chamber is empty. He tosses
the gun away and then buries his head in his
```

hands to weep—for those he has killed, for
all humanity.

FADE TO BLACK.

Colt, playing the lead, wanted the gun pointed at the temple,
in allegiance to Marshall's exposition. The director, meanwhile,
the precociously youthful Martin Drago, wanted it placed verti-
cally beneath the jawline, because, as he'd said, it "looked cooler."
Thus the morning had passed in stalemate: Colt holed up in his
trailer playing hologram *Fighter Jet,* and Drago stomping through
the set and lashing out at his crew, half a million dollars (he had
executive producer points) down the crapper. Just before lunch,
one of the studio's numerous vice presidents arrived to negotiate
the standoff. The trick here, the man knew, would be to make
both parties feel like the nexus of importance. Colt's opinions carried huge weight, obviously, but then Drago was on a roll, two
titanic hits in a row, his youth and long-term earning potential
to be weighed against the actor's advancing age, not to mention
the recent backlash against him. He would not be Colt Reston
forever, after all.

Finally, a détente was brokered. Why not shoot the scene
both ways, the VP advised, then see later on which worked better
dramatically? Colt, who had final cut, ipso facto, agreed, as did
Drago, who knew that the actor probably wouldn't be anywhere
near the editing room when the film was put together.

As for what happened next, there would be only marginal
variation from witnesses. Colt finally emerged from his trailer,
agreeing to try the shot Drago's way first—a stab at cordiality
the director instantly distrusted. Three times Colt held the gun
under his chin and three times Drago cut the scene before it could

begin. The angle of the gun was wrong; Colt was too far back on his heels; he looked too fucking *happy*—he was trying to sabotage the take! Infuriated, Drago yanked the gun from the actor's hands, placing the 11 millimeter under his own chin. As Colt retreated to the wings, sharing a bemused smile with the crew, the director beckoned to him, shouting, *"Is this so fucking difficult, Mr. Superstar?"* and, pulling the trigger, proceeded to blow his twenty-seven-year-old brains into a billowing, balloon-shaped cloud above him.

Fade to black.

After the ensuing chaos—the screaming, the trampling, the guns drawn by security—the cast and crew eventually found their way outside to the lot, where they held one another in their blood-stained clothes, trying to make sense of what had happened. Colt, meanwhile, was missing, the actor having quickly been ushered by security to an undisclosed location as police and media flooded the scene. Of the twenty-six witnesses, three stated that it was he, Colt Reston, who was in fact dead. The statements were obviously false (two of the witnesses had been distracted at the climactic moment, a third stoned on Bliss), but then the actor's absence lent enough credibility for the media to run the attention-grabbing headline.

Film Star Feared Dead . . .

Colt's image could not have been a more conspicuous presence as Marshall drove back to the studio, its prominence on the billboards appearing like a staged counterpoint to the afternoon's news. The report seemed to have stupefied the city; traffic was nearly immobile as drivers slowed to confirm the news with other drivers or pulled over to the side altogether, having lost confidence in their ability to continue on safely. Marshall decided to try some neighborhood streets to save time and found that even the tree-lined mausoleum of Bel Air had been disturbed. People were actually out on the sidewalk talking to their neighbors, as if to gain strength in accepting the impossible, while a group of schoolgirls tried to quell their hysteria in a three-way hug. Then, at a busy intersection, Marshall watched in horror as an obese woman repeatedly tried to dash into oncoming traffic, timing each lunge with the change of the traffic light, glossy photograph of Colt Reston held tight at her breast.

Finally arriving at the studio gates, Marshall was met once again by Tuten. This time the big man came out of his booth to greet him at the driver's-side window.

"He's not dead, Marsh. The news got it wrong. He's okay."

"I know, I just got the call," the screenwriter replied, gripping Tuten's forearm in appreciation. "Hey, can you put me through here?" Marshall was trying to shout over the horns. In front of him was an endless queue of police cars, studio security hybrids, satellite media vans, and the like.

"Nothing I can do," Tuten told him. "If you can get past here, I'd try going around to lot Q, then coming up around from behind. I don't know, man, the whole thing's a mess."

Marshall followed the advice and still had to park three lots from the scene. After much faulty information and conflicting stories, he eventually learned Colt was back at the Panoramic offices. He walked the whole way, a quarter mile at least, and when at last he located the room, the large security force barred him from entering. He was about to get nasty when he noticed Dre McDonald down the hall talking on his vidphone.

The writer marched right up. "Thanks for leaving me back there at the restaurant, you prick. We could've come over together."

Dre put away the phone, nodding apologetically. He looked in a state of utter distress, his face wan and his bald pate slick with perspiration. "I'm sorry. I was so upset I just bolted. I wasn't thinking." As if in a stunned afterthought, he added, "Someone tried to *kill* him, Marshall."

"Where is he?"

Dre put his hands on the writer's shoulders, guiding him into the spacious but crowded office.

They found Colt sitting behind the desk of one of Panoramic's VPs. There were people everywhere, all shouting at him from different directions, though the only one who seemed to have his ear was a large man in an ill-fitting suit, quite clearly a detective. The actor was responding to him wearily, as if his questions had already been answered many times.

"Hey, Marsh!" Colt said then, catching sight of his friend. Immediately the actor came around the desk to embrace him.

"What happened?" Marshall whispered in his ear. He was giving Colt a chance to answer discreetly, to say freely whatever he wished. But the actor held him out at arm's length as he explained.

"The gun had a fucking *bullet* in it, Marsh. Some maniac gave me a fucking loaded gun!" Amazingly, Colt's mouth had turned into a little smile, as if it were almost funny. His eyes, however, looked frightened.

"Drago pulled the trigger, the poor bastard," Dre interjected. "It was a miracle Colt wasn't killed."

Marshall turned his head to hide his anger. For the first time this afternoon he was completely sober.

"They've got the prop supervisor in custody, but of course he's denying everything," Dre continued. "And the assistant is missing."

"Missing," Marshall repeated.

A crush started to form again on Colt's right flank, and now some of Panoramic's handlers had to step in to hold off the new herd of media that had crashed the room in the confusion.

Colt was suddenly encircled, the ever-constricting momentum drawing him away, voices pummeling him from all sides. He looked out pleadingly from the maelstrom.

"Take him home," Dre shouted to Marshall over the din. "He's given his statement fifteen times already. He's done here. Get him *out*."

Marshall managed to catch the actor's eye, silently mouthing to him, *"You wanna get out of here?"*

Colt held out his hand while Marshall reached over and pulled, freeing him from the herd. Then the two of them bulled their way out of the room like fullbacks and continued down the hall. Outside they realized they were being chased, and so they ran the entire distance to Marshall's car, bursts of adolescent laughter overtaking them along the way.

Colt's Bel Air compound was out of the question: the media army would be there waiting for him with their troops, entire battalions at the ready. Instead they rode the Pacific Coast Highway north toward Malibu, the larger MIBs mercifully dying out just past the Palisades. Marshall didn't know whether it was the day's frightening events or the post-Bliss blues, but a heavy melancholy began to envelop him as they drove. He couldn't remember the last time he and Colt had been to the Malibu house together, and the idea of heading there now began to fill him with memories of a simpler, more carefree time.

The house had been Colt's first big movie purchase, back in the days when his celebrity was still sane and their friendship indomitable. After his injury, Marshall had retreated to San Francisco, living with his new wife in the big Victorian on Diamond Street. There was still some bonus money left over and so he had become a man of leisure, somewhat aimless, searching for what to do next. He took a graduate cinema class at Berkeley to no definite purpose and came down to L.A. on weekends to replay for Colt the films he'd been studying, as well as to escape from his wife, Marshall's marriage off to a rocky start. The house in Malibu had a small screening room, and on weekends friends came by to watch films by candlelight. These were, by all accounts, memorable evenings, the scent of ocean breezes mixed with Colt's world-class marijuana, throats salved by the wines commandeered from the fully stocked cellar. They'd go all night — *I vitelloni, Out of the Past, Last Tango in Paris* — one after another, and at dawn crawl to their bedrooms to sleep it off until the late afternoon.

It was during this time that Marshall began to fiddle with screenwriting. It was not completely out of the blue: during the winter months at Stanford, Marshall had been a force in the theater department, writing and directing a number of one-acts, and then of course had always been a voracious reader and filmgoer in the margins of his baseball life. Colt was being offered ten movies a week back then, and so there were always stacks of scripts lying around the house. As Marshall read through them he began to think, as many do, *I can do this, I can pull this off* — while in fact he actually could. He was a natural. With screenwriting he was able to exploit his ear for dialogue (the ballplayer's clipped vernacular, overheard in a thousand dugouts), and after a while he began to make notes for an ambitious script that had been growing in his imagination. It was a film noir set in a desert town very much like Palm Springs, a mystery concerning small-town corruption, immigration abuses, the death of a minor league baseball player, and ultimately terrorism. Uncompromisingly pessimistic, it was a landmark in that it revived, for a short time, adult cinema (thought to be long dead), and dozens of writers, directors, and actors had none other than Marshall Reed to thank for the handful of serious dramas green-lighted in its wake.

The name of the script was *Chula Vista*.

The film had been the turning point for Colt Reston's career as well. He was one of five or six leading men in Hollywood at the time, his ascension hindered not so much by his limitations as an actor as by his extraordinary good looks, which made it difficult for audiences to take him seriously. But in *Chula Vista* they had roughed him up a bit, prosthetically adding twenty pounds to his frame and giving him the now famous "fishhook" scar that ran from his ear to the corner of his mouth. And then there was the performance, which had to be one of the biggest surprises in Hollywood history. It seemed to come out of nowhere, Colt finding a frightening verisimilitude in the character of the racist, alcoholic police chief who redeems himself through the love of a local Mexican girl (Carmela Montoya in her first big role). The critics, who'd always been hard on Colt, seemed to echo John Ford's reaction upon seeing John Wayne in *Red River:* "Who knew the son of a bitch could *act?*"

Colt did better than that; he won the Oscar, scolding the Academy during his acceptance speech for failing to nominate

Marshall Reed in the screenplay category. But Colt's trajectory was set. The film was hailed as a contemporary classic, and Colt Reston became the undisputed King of Hollywood. It was a title he'd held for a time and then quickly redefined, a title he ultimately transcended altogether, until there was no longer a name for whatever it was he had now become.

And they had done it *together,* Marshall now reflected, as swatches of Pacific blue flashed in the driver's-side window, the car snaking along the winding highway. He was wondering if Malibu might again become a refuge for the two of them. Certainly their lives had gotten away from them over the years, a penchant for self-indulgence and greed, among other things, having taken its toll. Shrouded in this effusion of nostalgia, however, Marshall began to entertain the hope that they might find their friendship again in the place where it all began. The place where they had been at their best.

Then they passed a final MIB, embedded in a shelf of rock along the highway. As the pixellated Colt smiled at them, his raffish, twenty-foot grin somehow corrosive in the wake of the day's events, Marshall hit the gas, hoping salvation lay just a little farther up the road.

FIVE

What am I doing standing in the tall grass, you ask, in what looks like the middle of nowhere? You won't find any MIBs around here, nor are there any houses, or even paved roads [camera pans], and just a few hundred feet to my left you can see the steep cliffs that lead to the Pacific Ocean. It is a desolate and somehow ominous place. On a map you'd find me somewhere between Carmel and Big Sur, but more important, it is the exact spot where a week ago I met the extraordinary writer they call Mr. Black—though "met" may not be the exact word, since I was required to wear this [holds up the black pillowcase] just before he arrived. This man pulled his Jeep up this dirt path right here [she walks, camera follows] and I entered the vehicle, head still covered, with the only items I was allowed to carry with me: a video camera and tripod.

Colt hadn't used the Malibu house in nearly two years, and it took he and Marshall a few hours to get the place in order. They pulled the bedsheets from the furniture and opened all the windows to get rid of the musty sea smell. There were dishes to dust off, bulbs and fuses to replace. Marshall called a Thai restaurant in Zuma Canyon and brought up a few bottles of gewürztraminer from the cellar, pleased to see the stock not completely bare.

It was time for the Mr. Black interview.

One of Colt's bodyguards had been summoned: Ryan "Rip" Jansen, six foot three, iron stare, muscles like garlic knots. He had, over a long, restless career, protected any number of princes, despots, and drug lords but now seemed to have settled into something permanent with Colt (and had been having a blast lately playing the heavy in a number of Colt's films). Rip had immediately begun to make the rounds upon his arrival, though at eight o'clock even he could not resist peering in through the deck door at the plasma, curious as anyone to see what had peeked its head out from under the rock in northern California.

[CLOSE-UP on Lindsay.]

What you are about to see tonight is a rarity in our world of celebrity obsession and seekers of fleeting fame: the man who does not wish to be photographed, the man who thinks, in fact, that getting your picture taken is literally dangerous to your health . . . But I'll let him explain that one to you. You will not see the man's face but you will hear him speak, and you may find that his words cast a dark shadow over what he calls the "image world" — the place where, for better or for worse, we all now live. You may not agree with Mr. Black — I'm still not sure what I think — but I promise you will find him fascinating.

Seeing Colt looking grim and nervous, Marshall offered him a glass of wine but was refused. So here then was another rift in their relationship: the actor's newfound sobriety.

On the screen Lindsay was sitting in a chair on what seemed to be the deck of a small, isolated cottage, strong ocean breeze blowing her hair ravishingly across her forehead, eyes covered with a thick blindfold. Naturally, Mr. Black was off-camera, offering himself to the viewer as a voice exclusively, disembodied and godlike, though occasionally a bit of shoulder would move momentarily, tantalizingly, into the frame.

Lindsay: What is the basic message of the Black Book?

Mr. Black: That we're drowning in images, Lindsay. The MIBs, for example, have completely changed the landscape of America and, slowly but surely, the rest of the world. The MIBs are pollution, pure and simple — image pollution. There are no vistas anymore.

Lindsay: Is "pollution" really the right term? Don't the images appear and disappear at our whim, with the click of a button?

Mr. Black: Really? Then tell me how I can turn off the MIBs immediately, please! Look, when I say "pollution," I'm referring to the manner in which they have defiled and corrupted our lives. In fact, I do believe that the MIBs defile us spiritually. They crowd out our reality, batter us with constant commerce. We're all worried about the earth's ecology, and with good reason. But I also believe there is such a thing as spiritual ecology, and the MIBs do violence to that spirit.

Consider the ReStars program, for example. Can you think of anything more vulgar or depraved than to resurrect the great old movie stars to shill products? Products that they had never heard of and probably would never have endorsed in the first place? This is not only grave robbing; it's selling the bones. It enrages me just to think about it.

Lindsay: In the Black Book *you suggest that the proliferation of images may have some link to the current epidemic of anxiety and depression. Could you elaborate on that a little bit for us?*

Mr. Black: We have already been told that there is a finite amount of visual stimuli a person can assimilate. Tests show that an overstimulated brain becomes anxious, overwrought, exhausted. And this epidemic of anxiety coincides almost precisely with the appearance of the MIBs.

Of course it's everything else, too — television, Podcasts, vidphones, car plasmas, et cetera. It's been slowly building till now we cannot leave our homes without being optically assaulted, visually mugged, if you will. We're cognitively overwrought on a massive scale.

Lindsay: Is this why you won't show yourself on-camera? Because you don't want to contribute to the assault?

Mr. Black: I refuse to be photographed because I want my ideas to be taken seriously, to avoid being labeled a hypocrite. And then there's a part of me — if you'll allow me to be a bit paranoid here for a minute — that's sincerely frightened of the technology. I mean, we have a generation now basically living in the camera's eye, pointing these ever more powerful machines at one another, without having really explored the dangers of the hardware.

Lindsay: Photography has been with us for nearly a century and a half. What are the "dangers" that you foresee?

Mr. Black: You must admit that in the era of digitalization we've entered a whole new realm of photography and image exposure. And it's clear now, judging from our vast ecological problems, that there's nothing free when it comes to technology; it always exacts its price on nature. And we will pay a price, Lindsay, I assure you. We have not even begun to reconcile this world of ultrafame and photography.

I can't help but think of Marilyn Monroe, for example — those final nude photographs just before she died. There's something so clearly washed-out about her in those photos, something exhausted and malformed. It's as if all her loveliness has been stripped, like she's dissolving before our eyes. Blame it on the drugs if you must, but I am convinced that Marilyn Monroe was photographed to death . . .

"Hey, Marsh?" the actor ventured, as programming bled to a commercial. Colt was clearly stricken by what he'd been hearing, and he turned to find Marshall slumped next to him on the couch, obviously lost in some grave reverie of his own.

"Yeah?" came the equally weak reply.

"I think I'll take that wine now."

"How do I look to you?" Colt was asking the next morning.

He was in the master bedroom, sitting in front of the dresser mirror, Ray Manuel — fifty, ponytailed, heavily paunched — behind him, his wares spread across the bed for easy access. Finding what he needed, Ray came toward Colt with a small plastic bowl filled with a white paste, which he began to smear on the actor's face. This was applied swiftly and with no regard for comfort, Colt's head jostled with each swab.

Colt repeated his question.

"I heard you. Now turn a little to the left," Ray commanded. The actor did as he was told.

There may have been no one employed by Colt more vital to him than Ray Manuel. Ray was his lifeline to the outside world. If Colt wanted to go out to Anaheim to see the Angels with Marshall, for example; if he wanted to dine in a restaurant; if he wanted to stroll down the street, make a simple stop for coffee—he was at the mercy of Ray Manuel. It was makeup or mayhem. And although the new breathing latex-and-elastic prosthetics had been banned ever since the Day of Terror, Colt paid him exorbitantly enough to assume the risk.

"Why aren't you answering me, Ray?"

"Because, I'm trying not to hear you."

"Why? I'm telling you this is important," Colt implored. "You *know* me. You know my face as well as anyone. Why won't you help me?"

"Because, I refuse to let you debase yourself like this."

"De*base* myself?" Colt's eyes flashed up from a mask of white foundation.

"That's right, Ray, ignore him," Marshall said now as he entered the room, while Colt lowered his eyes like a child caught with matches. "He's not thinking straight. We watched the Mr. Black interview last night."

"Yeah, I saw some of that," Ray replied, his hands working vigorously. "That guy's *crazy*."

"Hear that, Colt?" Marshall sat down on the edge of the bed. "There you have it—a disinterested opinion. The guy's crazy. Now forget it."

Ray was applying the latex now, daubing it from the actor's forehead down to his upper chest and back. He cocked his head in hesitation, reaching for Colt and then withdrawing his hand, deciding finally to lean back for perspective—an artist looking for the next stroke to his canvas. Ray never gave Colt the same face twice.

And all this just to go home, Marshall thought sadly. Word from the compound was that the chaos had only increased since yesterday, the extra time allowing the foreign press to arrive, more fans to congregate. Still, Colt had insisted on getting home. He missed his dogs, he'd said, his chef, the double-king-sized bed and Egyptian cottons.

"A man should not be too intimidated to go to his house," Colt lamented.

"Ideally, no," Marshall replied.

"I'm thinking of quitting, Marsh. I don't want to be a movie star anymore. I'm serious about this."

"Fine, but that won't change anything. You'll still be a movie star even if you never acted again."

Ray pulled back as Colt turned brusquely to look up at his friend. "Someone tried to *kill* me yesterday. Do you understand that?"

Seeing his friend straight on now, Marshall was amazed at the change under Ray's artistry, the transfiguration as credible as it was rapid. "Yes," he replied.

"Why? Why would they do that?"

"Colt, I don't know."

The actor fidgeted in the chair. "Christ, I feel like shit," he said, slamming his fist down on one of the armrests. "I'm sick . . . I'm sick and nobody fucking believes me!"

"Go to a doctor," Ray said, trying to steady his subject's head.

Colt muttered something inscrutable, then leaned past the makeup artist to look at himself in the mirror. The results seemed to impress and sadden him at the same time.

"Sometimes I wonder how Carmela died," he mused, calming a bit now. "You ever wonder about that, Marsh?"

"No," came the flat reply. "What's there to wonder about? She died of lung cancer."

"She never *smoked,* Marsh. You know that."

"The two aren't always connected," the screenwriter countered.

"And how come she never contacted me when she was sick? Why wasn't I invited to come see her at the end, Marsh? You either? We were as close to her as anyone."

"Keep your mouth still," Ray said.

"Goddammit, I *have* to be able to talk," Colt snapped. "This is important."

"All right, fine then," the makeup man announced, slowly backing away from Colt. There was an unusual look in Ray Manuel's eyes suddenly, and the ordinarily mild-mannered man tore the rubber gloves violently from his hands and slammed them down on the vanity. "Finish it yourself, you fucking asshole."

"Hey, hey . . . ," Colt said, stunned by this.

"No, fuck off. I don't have time for this prima donna shit today!"

Colt and Marshall stole a glance at each other, obviously concerned.

"What the hell's up with you?" Marshall asked, though gently now, after a pause.

The makeup man breathed deep, leaning with two hands on the vanity as he tried to gather himself. "My studio was broken into the other night," he said finally.

Now the two friends sat up a little straighter.

"What happened?" Colt wanted to know.

"They *stole* things, what do you think?" Ray replied. "Mostly prosthetic and latex stuff. And I think a voice modulator might be missing, too." When he turned around to look at them, his face was lined with worry. "It's not about the money, you guys know that. This could be big trouble for me."

"And us," Colt murmured.

"What's so strange is I have no idea how they got in," Ray

continued. "The alarms were intact. There's no sign of any kind of forced entry."

"What about your assistant?" Marshall asked.

Ray shook him off. "I only use her at Panoramic. I never let anyone near those other materials. Nobody even knows where I keep that stuff. I've never told another living soul."

There was a long, uneasy silence.

"How about just a random break-in?" Colt finally asked.

"I doubt it. What they took was pretty damned specific. I'd say they knew what they were doing." Ray's worried look was back again. "If somebody uses this stuff and they trace it . . ."

Marshall finished the thought. "We all get a long vacation."

"I know I sure will," said Ray. "They used some of this stuff for their disguises on the Day of Terror. They'll come down on me hard."

"It's life in prison," Marshall added. "That's the *minimum* sentence."

There were grave nods all around. Grudgingly, Ray began to put his gloves back on. "Anyway, I'm sorry to dump this on you guys. I moved the rest of my stash again this morning. At least if this guy gets busted, they won't be able to trace it back."

The room was silent as Ray went back to work. Marshall excused himself, explaining that he was going down to the beach to make some phone calls. He reminded them that Rip would be out front if they needed anything.

A few minutes later Colt was gesturing for Ray to lean down toward him.

"Fifty grand," he whispered.

"What?"

"Fifty grand extra to tell me how I look. The truth this time."

Ray looked up, catching Colt's reflection in the mirror. "You're going fuckin' crazy, you know that?"

"Yes," Colt replied.

Later they arrived at the compound, Colt and Rip, with Marshall at the wheel, their incredulous eyes all growing wide in the crepuscular light.

Several thousand people were milling outside the walls of Colt's home, all looking toward the front gates as if waiting for an oracle to emerge.

The property sat a few hundred feet above the Sunset Strip, a 1930s villa converted from a hotel, complete with stone bridges, Japanese gardens, water-nymph fountains, and, most significant, a ten-foot-high stone wall surrounding the eleven-acre compound. Marshall edged the car along slowly until the phalanx of onlookers became too thick for them to move any farther. Colt asked Marshall to pull off to the curb to take in the scene. Dotted among the crowd were dozens of media vans and police hybrids, and there was even an ambulance set off near a makeshift first-aid tent. In the trees, paparazzi were perched like grotesque fruit, their infrared cameras trained at the house; and then, higher still, loomed the helicopters from Channel 6 and CNN and the interminable drone of their propellers.

"What do we do now?" Rip asked, stroking his tough-guy goatee.

"How about the next street over?" Marshall suggested. "We'll call the house, tell them to let us in from the back. You can't risk the front entrance, even in the makeup. Not with this crowd."

All this just to go home . . .

From the backseat Colt simply shook his head, staring out at the scene as if hypnotized. He seemed both appalled and fascinated. "Let me just take this all in for a minute."

As they waited, Marshall found Colt's face in the rearview mirror, the writer still marveling at the skill of Ray's handiwork. Colt had been transformed to a pale-faced man with thinning hair, glasses, and, as a final aesthetic masterstroke, a slightly cauliflower drinker's nose, every inch of it convincing. Marshall was suddenly reminded of that infamous day two summers ago when they had stopped for pizza in the Valley. Sick to death of the inconveniences — the bodyguards and makeup jobs and presidential-style motorcades — Colt had begun working with a "fame-management consultant." His advice? Scale back, forget the entourage, become a "real person" again. Colt was assured that if he acted ordinary, people would treat him as ordinary. Personally, Marshall thought the consultant was insane; the man didn't understand that Colt Reston was something beyond fame, a kind of walking deity, and that his presence, for whatever reason, made people hysterical. But the actor was determined to give it a try, and so this had been the first experiment: pizza on Ventura. They got their slices and took a window seat (Marshall suggesting this might be pushing it a bit, but Colt insisting), and of course within minutes the restaurant was filled with fans, with hundreds more waiting outside. Soon Colt found himself standing on a table, trying to quell the crowd, but as usual the chaos quickly turned violent: soon the restaurant's plate-glass windows were shattered and some cars were overturned, the two friends making a hairsbreadth escape out the service entrance with the help of two starstruck dishwashers.

Turning his eye now to the compound's hungry throngs, Marshall wondered if maybe Colt should have made an appearance today, perhaps issued a statement of some sort, waved to his fans from a window—anything at all to dispel the mystery. His absence might be making things worse, he surmised, turning up the heat of anticipation.

Then Colt's car door suddenly opened.

By the time they'd figured out what had happened, it was too late—Colt was gone in a flash, and Marshall had to hold Rip back from pursuing the actor. They could *not* risk a scene now, he explained. Absurdly enough, both Rip and Marshall were recognizable to Colt Reston aficionados. There was nothing to do but sit back and watch.

With a flamboyant hauteur, Colt wasted no time in mingling with the crowd. Marshall and Rip looked on stupefied as the bulbous-nosed man began chatting up one stranger after another. Fans, policemen, entertainment anchors in between reports—it didn't seem to matter; Colt gabbed away and moved on to the next group. Though Rip remained completely baffled, Marshall felt he understood what was going on: The son of a bitch was amusing himself. Colt was exploiting the freedom of his new face, getting in right under their noses—these crowds that had demanded so much from him, these so-called fans that had enjoyed such power over him for so long.

There was a jauntiness to his step, Marshall noticed. He was animated, grinning profusely. It was the most fun he'd had in months.

"How do you think he looks, by the way?" Rip asked. "I mean, for real, before the makeup."

Marshall's eyes followed Colt under a tree, where the actor

began speaking through cupped hands to one of the lower-slung photographers.

"How he looks?" the writer repeated. He appeared nonplussed, as if the question had snuck up on him. Marshall understood now that ever since returning from Vancouver he *had* seen something in Colt he didn't quite like, though he'd been denying it to himself. "I don't know," he said, putting off any concession. "Tired?"

"Marsh, have you really looked at him? I'm seven years older and work twice the hours. *I* don't look tired like that."

Something unpleasant flowed through Marshall's stomach, suddenly queasy now in the face of a horrible truth. "What do you want me to do?"

"Well, how about when Colt tells you he feels like shit, you believe him. That would be a start."

They watched now as their masked friend leaned himself against the trunk of the tree where he'd been speaking to the journalist. He was hunched over, apparently short of breath from his brief jaunt.

"I'll call Dr. Heilman tomorrow morning," Marshall said.

SIX

Interviewer: At Arizona State you were known for your long, flow-ing locks, but Clippers team policy is the close-cropped haircut. Is this something you think could actually affect your level of play? How much is comfort a factor for the professional athlete?

Player X: It's a factor, sure, but I think if you're a good player you get over stuff like that. Plus, I use Prep conditioner, which makes my hair so full bodied it almost feels like my old hair.

Interviewer: Yes, but your old hair was down to your shoulders, so . . .

Player X: Well, Prep's pretty amazing stuff, man.

I thought that buzz agents and advert cars and product tattoos were the end, that there was nowhere else to go. But apparently there is no bot-tom. Now we've tainted basic human conversation. (How much was the player paid to say "Prep"? How much the interviewer for leading with the hair question?) And this will spread, of course, till soon the day will come when you and I will never again be able to talk with a friend or neighbor and be entirely sure that the dialogue has not been manipulated by a small monthly stipend from an advertising consortium.

A s aptly named as so-called smart buildings were these days, the NetTalent offices in Beverly Hills might have qualified as a mind-blowing genius: thirty floors of opaque ribbed glass, its basement holding one of the largest mainframes of any building in the state of California. The offices had taken Dre five years to build and were his supreme pride and joy, lauded in the *L.A. Times* (by a writer whom Dre later agreed to represent as a screenwriter) as "one of the city's greatest marvels." Nevertheless, the average Los Angeles citizen seemed ambivalent about the imposing black monolith, and ambivalence turned to loathing when the building's unusual sentient qualities became publicized. Here was an entertainment agency with sensory systems attuned to temperature and humidity and that adjusted themselves accordingly; a building with panoptic cameras that ceaselessly photographed everything within a four-block radius and a skyward vector of sixty thousand cubic feet, not to mention a finger-mapping biometric security system and the latest in image-clarification and face-recognition software. It was a touching, seeing, thinking, breathing *entity,* and something about its sleek design made it difficult not to see in the structure an obvious personification. It was ebony, impudent, supremely intelligent, and overtly paranoid. It was Dre McDonald all the way.

Marshall himself claimed to have no opinion at all about the NetTalent offices, though sometimes he did like to do a line or two of Bliss and watch the look on the guard's face as he made his way through the retinal scanner. Today, however, he arrived sober. This was less in deference to Dre than to the fact that Colt was in obvious trouble of some sort, and Marshall wanted to be lucid as he waded through the latest news—the various rumors, disinformation, and self-interested perspectives that passed for anything relating to Colt Reston in Hollywood.

Marshall cleared security and took the elevator to the penthouse, two o'clock as requested. He was admitted without delay, finding the agent at the far end of the room, gazing out the famous angled edge.

"Hey, Marsh," Dre said without turning. "Get a load of this."

The screenwriter ambled across the absurd expanse past Dre's desk and joined him at the peak. Here was another of the building's famous architectural feats—NetTalent's top floor shaped like an arrowhead, its crux pointing at the Talent United offices, which sat almost directly across the boulevard. This structural aggressiveness only heightened the already volatile proximity between the two agencies. Each kept cameras trained on the other's entrances, for example, monitoring foot traffic not only to see what deals were being made and what potential clients were being wooed but also to help discourage poaching (the greatest fear of all). Rival agents might even exchange heated words as they strode the concurrent sidewalks to their offices, the insults actually turning to blows one morning as commuters were treated to the sad spectacle of talent agents standing toe-to-toe in the middle of Wilshire Boulevard, flailing Pod cases and scorching lattes at each other.

"What are we looking at?"

Dre pointed past the TU building to the far intersection, where some electrical trucks were huddled under what appeared to be a dead MIB. "It was vandalized last night," the agent reported unhappily. "They got three of my billboards, the little bastards. Two here on Wilshire and a little baby over on Western."

"Who's 'they'?"

Dre showed a flash of annoyance. "The damned Blackheads," he quipped, "who else? Apparently they were inspired by seeing their great guru on television last night. Meanwhile I'm paying every electrician in this city triple time to have them back on by the end of the day. Hopefully this'll send a message."

"Which is?"

"The futility of their struggle," he announced, looking over at the screenwriter. "Powerlessness in the face of corporations with unlimited resources." The agent smiled, punctuating this with a wink. He was well aware of the huge skepticism surrounding the billboards; in fact it was the *Black Book* which had revealed how Dre's other company, the technology and advertising corporation known as Mannix, had secretly developed the MIBs and that the agent had a huge stake in their content and proliferation. Furious with the leak, Dre was put in the position of having to field the onslaught of criticism about the MIBs — which, by all accounts, he handled deftly. Instead of being defensive, he admitted to having some ambivalent feelings of his own about the billboards, claiming to "love them and hate them, depending on the day of the week." This gave the illusion that Dre McDonald was a thoughtful, ambivalent power broker and tended to mitigate further criticism.

"Anyway," he continued, "the Blackheads want publicity for this and I'm not going to give it to them. I've asked my friends in the media to lay off the story, and I'll offer no comment if I'm asked. The billboards will be back on by the end of the day. Basically it never happened."

Marshall watched the traffic swell along Wilshire as the cars struggled to pass the repair trucks. "I thought yesterday you said there were no Blackheads."

"Well, yes, I still think TU is behind this, one way or the other. I mean, the Blackheads could be anybody, just like Mr. Black could be anybody."

"TU stepping up their mischief," Marshall said without enthusiasm.

"You got it," Dre replied. Then, perhaps conscious of the screenwriter's fatigue on the subject, he added, "But forget about that. Let's talk about something important, like our great friend Colt."

They sat, Marshall trying in vain to get comfortable in Dre's industrial-motif furniture. His own affairs were usually conducted two floors below in the writer's wing, with its puffy couches and loose atmosphere, and he always hated the times he'd had to do business with Dre in the penthouse. Quite frankly, the feng shui sucked. The gleaming, exposed beams and sharp angles were disagreeable, casually hostile, and the space was absurdly cavernous; your body took up so little volume it made you feel inconsequential. When you spoke, your voice seemed to disappear into the void. This was all, of course, strictly by design.

There had been one concession to warmth, Marshall noticed, since the last time he was here. To his left, on one of the previously blank walls, was a large plasma screen. Showing now on the display was a life-sized version of Velázquez's *Las Meninas*. The digital reproduction was exquisite, right down to the work's original frame, and the designers had even taken pains to capture the texture of the paint, the cracked patterns of centuries-old oils. It was so palpable that Marshall had the urge to reach out and touch it but then realized there would be nothing to feel but the silky gel of the plasma.

"I spoke to Colt this morning," Dre said, settling into his chair. He tugged at his bow tie—canary yellow today and insistently Ivy League, though he hadn't quite finished a semester at Antioch before starting in the NetTalent mailroom. "I thought he sounded okay, all things considered."

"All things considered."

"I've also talked to the police. I take it you haven't had the chance."

Marshall shifted in his seat, wondering if there were metal nodes in the cushions made specifically to dig into your ass. "No, I've been dealing with Colt. You want to fill me in?"

"You know the props guy? The assistant who issued Colt the gun?"

"Yes."

Dre paused for effect, swiveling back and forth on his chair. "He's dead."

Marshall stopped fidgeting and crossed his arms in front of his chest.

"They found him over in Will Rogers Park, torn to bits. Apparently a mountain lion got him, maybe more than one—he was pretty far gone by the time they found the body. Clearly the kid was hiding there after the shooting. He'd built this camp, the little shit."

"What about the supervisor?"

"Doesn't seem to be much there," Dre said. "He *supervises* all right, though apparently not much else. He's sort of deadwood, from what they say—been at the studio forever. Says he doesn't know anything about real bullets."

"Of course he doesn't know anything," Marshall said, sitting slightly forward now. *"What's he going to say?"*

The agent nodded, registering the anger.

"I mean, the guy's the supervisor, Dre. He's *responsible* . . ."

"Of course he is. Look, the investigation just started. Nothing is off the table yet. All I'm saying is if you're looking for motivation, I don't think you'll find it with the supervisor. Thirty years at the studio, million-plus pension around the corner. I just don't see the impulse. But hey, like I said, it's early."

"What about the kid who died? What's his story?"

Some colors were flashing on Dre's vidphone; he took discreet notice and kept his attention on Marshall. "There's not much on him yet. He hadn't been at the job all that long. But yes, it will be fascinating once they piece it together, won't it?" He smiled then, righting himself in his chair as if invigorated by the idea. "That's the whole thing right there."

"What whole thing?"

"The *motivation,* Marshall. Why would somebody try and kill Colt? A beloved star like him? I figure there are three basic possibilities. The most obvious is that the kid is a devout Blackhead, a true believer. He's inspired on the eve of Mr. Black's big interview, showing solidarity for the cause . . . I don't know if I buy any of it, but I'll tell you what: if it's true, it carries big consequences for Mr. Black."

"Why?"

"Incitement to violence. This whole antimedia bit has been cute, but I think the writer loses a lot of sympathy if they believe he's inspiring people to kill movie stars. I know the FBI will not be amused."

"Or," Marshall countered, "the kid could just be some John Hinckley type, a deranged loner. Colt averages a death threat a day, Dre, you know that. Killing him is the Holy Grail for lost freaks."

"That's possibility number two," Dre conceded. "And then, of course, there's the idea you simply refuse to entertain."

He watched the screenwriter slump a little in his chair.

"Huge motivation, Marshall. Obvious, overwhelming motivation."

Dick Vale, Marshall thought. *Yes, I know. Dick Vale Dick Vale Dick Vale* . . . The insistent loop in Dre's mind.

The story was now a famous one, of course, the morning junior agent Dre McDonald brought in the ballplayer with the already iconic name of Colt Reston and usurped power from Dick Vale. Dick, who was NetTalent's acting CEO back then — the man responsible for swallowing both CAA and William Morris whole, digesting even the bones — had been the person least impressed with Colt that day. But then he was predisposed, he would later admit, blinded by ill feelings toward the ambitious upstart Dre. "One day this guy's going to have my job," he had explained to a confidante. "You can tell just by the way he walks. Like a *panther.*" There were other clues: the sui generis clothes, the lone-wolf attitude, the persistent challenging of authority. Dick had been advised to get rid of him, but then you try to fire the first black agent in NetTalent's history, he'd argued, not to mention one of its biggest moneymakers.

So on this memorable morning, Dick Vale is summoned at 8 A.M. to the video room in the old NetTalent building. Dre has a can't-miss star on his hands, the CEO is informed. (*Making his move,* Dick decided immediately.) By chance he runs into Dre and his ballplayer as they're entering the lobby, the CEO instantly shocked by what he sees. Standing with the agent is a hayseed-looking character with close-set eyes, iffy skin, and a charisma quotient of *zero,* far as Dick can tell. *Forget the next Tom Cruise,* he thinks, *this guy's not even Chuck fucking Connors!* But then Dick checks himself; his confidence has been shaken lately. NetTalent has slipped to third place among the major agencies—a distant third—and the CEO is taking the hit. Word has it Dick Vale's lost his touch with talent, and things are going so badly as of late he's almost ready to believe it. He decides to hold back, tempering his certainty that the ballplayer is a bust.

They all board the elevator together, gliding upstairs in a taut silence. Waiting for them as they arrive are the CFO, some major stockholders, and a pair of top producers from Panoramic. Dick smiles. This is it: the reckless junior agent has pushed all his chips to the center of the table. Suddenly regaining his confidence, Dick rolls his eyes at the waiting coterie: *Get ready, folks, we have a bomb on our hands.*

They light Colt and mike him. He reads a few lines. The results are mortifying, Dick thinks, avert-your-eyes bad. The man can barely read, never mind act, the words dribbling from his lips like reluctant turds. The whole thing is an embarrassment. Dick is mentally assessing Dre McDonald's severance package (*I'll be stingy,* the CEO thinks, *the black bastard*) when he is asked to join a small huddle at the monitor, the faces fixed with a ghostly awe.

And then there it is, the *face*—or the way light reacts to a face. Who has ever adequately articulated the *how*? How someone can be a star just by the way he stands or holds a cigarette, by the odd pitch of a nose (half a centimeter the difference between a major actress and a waitress), by the magic tonalities of a voice?

There is the story of the director Raoul Walsh spying a young man carrying a chair on the set of one of his films, a young grunt named Marion Morrison. Something about the way he carried that chair, he'd thought, a certain swagger and flair.

"Put that young man in the movie," Walsh had said.

The young grunt later known as John Wayne.

Say this for Dick Vale: he had had the decency to nod. Looking away from the monitor (and he found that his eyes did not *want* to look away, that there was a resistance there), he discovered Dre already locked in on him from across the room, triumphant smirk lavishing his face—and Dick had had the decency to nod. To concede with honor.

It was still a project, he knew. The agency would have to show patience with this one, nurture him. The guy needed a speech coach and a dermatologist right off the bat, just to be allowed back in the building. But if it was done right, they had a star of major proportions on their hands, no doubt about it.

Too bad I won't be around to see it, Dick thought.

"You took the business from him," Marshall said now. "Maybe you feel guilty."

"I didn't take it," Dre countered. "It was *given* to me. Shareholders decided to make a change." Once again the agent tugged at his bow tie. "And anyhow, I didn't exactly ruin Dick Vale's life. What does he do next? Goes out and forms Talent United out of nothing, and in five years it's the number two agency in the world. He's dedicated his professional life to making me miserable. Really, Marshall, he's obsessed with getting his revenge on me, and I'd say he's been at least partially successful. He's poached eleven of my clients in the past three years. There's barely a department in my company that's not compromised."

"*Compromised?*"

"Spies. Little rats feeding him information. There's no telling how far up it goes."

Marshall was grinning as he shook his head. "And you believe this?"

"I'd better; I've got six corporate detectives on payroll. Dick's got *spies* here, Marshall. We've flushed three of them already this past year. I told you, the man is obsessed. I know for a fact that Dick makes decisions detrimental to his own agency as long as he thinks it will hurt NetTalent."

Both men looked over at the wall suddenly, the painting now in dissolve. *Las Meninas* was breaking down into small digital blocks and then, remarkably, re-forming as Gauguin's *Spring of Delight*.

"Hey, how about that?" Dre said, very pleased. "It's working."

"What just happened?"

"The plasma is sensitive to the heat in the room, Marshall, the growing tension. It's trying to soften the atmosphere." Dre could see that the screenwriter wasn't following him. "It's sentient. Here you have the bright colors, the pastoral scene. You should see when I start to scream and the lily pads come out."

Marshall squirmed again on the chair's hard nodes, not knowing whether he was stirred or repelled.

"Anyway," Dre continued, "I see you're still skeptical about my Dick Vale–Mr. Black connection. Fair enough. But let me leave you with one last little tidbit to chew on, if that's okay." He folded his hands, smirking confidently. "Are you ready?"

"Can't wait," Marshall said, deciding now to simply be amused by Dre's paranoia.

"Mr. Black works in Hollywood."

There was a long pause. The agent sat back and swiveled again, as if to admire an expertly landed punch. Meanwhile, Marshall's eyes flickered away for a moment and then narrowed to a point. He shifted again in his torture chair.

"All right, good," Dre added. "I've got your wheels spinning."

The screenwriter brooded for a moment. "I'm not sure I understand. What're we talking about here?"

"He *works* in Hollywood, Marshall. He's here. One of *us*. I called Lindsay last night to congratulate her after the interview and we got to talking about who this guy is, what kind of person he might be, and so on, and she confided this to me. He *works* here, though Lindsay swears she has no idea in what capacity. And she won't tell me how she found out, either."

"I thought she was blindfolded during the interview."

"I believe she was."

There was a pause. "So how could she have seen anything?"

Dre shrugged his shoulders. "She might not have; maybe it was a slip of the tongue that convinced her. I just don't know. Mum's the word from this woman. And believe me, I pushed for it. You *know* I did."

Marshall couldn't help it — his eyes cut quickly to the painting to see if it had changed. It had not.

"Come on, admit it," Dre said. "It makes my theory about Dick just a little bit more interesting."

"Does it?"

"Sure it does," Dre said indignantly. "How could it not?"

"Well, for one, Dre, you can't corroborate the information. This could be another of Mr. Black's mirrors. He may *want*

Lindsay to think he works in Hollywood, just so people like you and me will have confusing conversations like this one."

Dre waved his hand, playfully dismissive. "You're giving this guy way too much credit, Marshall. I don't believe he's that clever." When Marshall didn't comment, he continued: "Anyway, I think Lindsay's going to call you. You can ask her about these things yourself."

"Me? What for?"

"She asked me for your number. She *likes* you, Marshall, though God knows why. I think there might even be a little crush." He noticed the unease on the screenwriter's face. "What, you suddenly have a problem getting calls from beautiful women?"

"She probably wants gossip about Colt, for a story or something. I just don't need the hassle right now."

"Actually, no, I don't believe that's *all* she wants. But that's fine. You're obviously under no obligation to talk to her."

Marshall was suddenly distracted by something over Dre's shoulder.

The agent turned. Past the angled windows they both watched as the dead MIB flickered on, then suddenly off again, then back on. Finally, after another quick fade-out, it stayed on for good, and they observed Cary Grant's chagrin at some unexpected flatulence, a ReStars commercial for Gas-X.

Then Colt appeared. He was seated sideways, cowboy hat pitched at a stylish angle, two fingers held up like a pistol to the camera.

This Fall Colt Reston Is Gunning for YOU, said the billboard, Colt flicking his thumb like a hammer and blowing imaginary smoke off his index finger.

"Well, I'll be damned," Dre said, "back in business." He began to clap, slowly and spitefully, while Marshall looked on in silence. "And you know the best part about all this?" the agent asked. "I'll bet you Dick Vale is looking out his window this very moment, right across the street, big Waspy face flushed with anger." He turned back to Marshall with a smirk. "Let's hope he chokes on it, shall we?"

SEVEN

As she sat waiting at the bar, smoking her cigarette, a warm, briny Pacific breeze drifting through the restaurant, she thought, *I'm smoking and they won't say anything. They're afraid to tell me to put it out.*

Damn, I could get used to this.

The bistro was in Venice, two blocks from the beach. The place hadn't been fashionable for more than a year, but she liked it for that very reason, because it was half-empty, and because it was dark — pitch black, with votive candles and black-and-white Italian cinema classics thrown silently against the four opposing walls. She had ordered her Gibson and then, without thinking — because she was nervous and suddenly excited about her career and the possibility of sex tonight — lit up a cigarette. She was three puffs into it when the bartender slipped a demitasse saucer in front of her as a makeshift ashtray and she realized, *Shit, I'm smoking in here and they won't say anything.*

They won't say no to Lindsay Williams.

The aftershock of the Mr. Black interview was something that she pretended had unsettled her. There were the furtive whispers as she entered rooms, the entertainment-television mentions, the subtle new deference in banks and shops—*Feeble bullshit,* she'd told herself, but in fact she was enjoying it. Celebrity suited her, she'd discovered. Lindsay had felt lighter these past few days, less in her own head. And if truth be told, a little high. They didn't tell you that, did they? Fame, even a modest serving, was like one high-quality joint, savored slowly and intermittently throughout the day.

She wanted desperately to be ashamed of herself but then kept thinking of the years at that morning show in Cleveland, 4 A.M. call times and obligatory dinner dates with the executive producer (a cyst-backed gibbon, as she remembered). Then, more poignantly, of her father selling shoes back in Bellville. He'd driven a cab during the day, a rickety station wagon with a little light on the top that didn't work, taking people to and from the rail station or, at the start of the morning shift, picking up drunks who couldn't drive home. Then at night he sold shoes. She went to see him at the store once, when she was seven, and she had never forgotten what she'd seen there: Her father on his knees, filthy sock dangling in his face, the teenage customer unappeasable as her father returned repeatedly to the stockroom for more shoes. And then back to his knees.

Lindsay knew that the vision was traumatic mostly because of her age—the first time you realized that your father was not a hero. And although she felt that enjoying a smoke at a bar more than twenty years later was a petty revenge, not at all what her father would have wanted, she had no intention of putting it out.

Let them *bow a little,* she'd thought.

She'd signed with Dre the previous afternoon and by nine o'clock heard that she'd had seven-figure offers from *Newsline* and *Monday Night Football,* not to mention a small part in a film touted as "the black *Big Chill.*" None of them a fit, Dre had pronounced—though somewhat presumptuously, as far as Lindsay was concerned, seven figures sure sounding like a fit to her. Still, it was all a little dizzying. To calm herself she went AWOL from work (she'd given notice) and went shopping in Beverly Hills, not declining the glasses of chardonnay she was offered from the silver trays in the lobbies. She took the Diva to a grotesquely priced lunch on Rodeo Drive, shopped seriously for a hydrogen-powered Mercedes, and tried Bliss for the first time at a party on one of the bird streets, not entirely surprised to find that she enjoyed it.

Then, remembering that she liked to celebrate moments like these with sex, she made a few calls, one of them a nervous, can't-believe-I'm-doing-this digression to Marshall Reed.

Her crush was now ten years running, and though he was not as good looking as he had once been (the original stills of him from the set of *CV*—in gesticulating argument with the director, bedraggled beard and desert-mussed hair—were like pornographic trading cards for women of a certain sensibility), he had retained a good deal of the gritty sex appeal that had always separated him from Colt. She remembered seeing on the *Chula Vista* fan site the succinct difference between the two: it was Colt Reston whom you wanted to marry, and Marshall Reed whom you wanted to fuck.

It had been a low-pulsing but surprisingly enduring crush, one that seemed to fluctuate between Marshall Reed the distant erotic figure in her mind and Marshall Reed the writer of *Chula Vista,* from whom she simply wanted to see more movies. To ever get near him romantically seemed an adolescent absurdity (an A.M. TV personality from Cleveland!). But then she *could* reasonably hope for another film, or so she'd once thought, and so let her obsession settle there. She would glance through the trades, looking for mention of him, discovering his name only as a footnote to recent Colt Reston projects, or google him with the subsearch "new movie," coming up empty except for phrases like "two-week polish" and "rewrite on the troubled film . . ."

He had been married once, Lindsay discovered amid the Net's autobiographical crumbs. Strangely, this bothered her.

After coming to L.A., she cultivated a friendship with a woman in development at Panoramic, primarily to build up to the question, *Ever see that screenwriter around named . . . ?* and was disappointed to hear that Marshall was a murky presence around the studio at best, known primarily for being Colt Reston's boy, untouchable and with great Bliss connections (and also for keeping the door to his bungalow closed, the open-door policy being de rigueur).

She bought the collector's edition of *Chula Vista* and watched him talk about the "making of" with an eerie dispassion. His face had hardened and grown hollow a bit, his look slightly depraved now, she thought, a dying boyishness struggling to hold on.

Lindsay flicked ash off her cigarette now, recalling her breakfast with Dre—the agent offhandedly mentioning his next appointment and she quivering slightly with excitement at the name, thinking of ways to extend their conversation in hopes of running into the screenwriter—when she realized that the man who had this moment slipped in next to her at the bar ("Bushmills, two cubes") was none other than Marshall himself. He slapped some bills down on the zinc and, without preamble or even "hello," launched into a bizarre divagation that immediately left her with the impression he was completely zonked.

"Makes you wonder, doesn't it?" he began, gesturing to the screen behind the bar, where a silent, dispirited, Marcello Mastroianni shuffled along the outskirts of Rome at dawn. "These old film stars seem to have such great, complicated faces, you know, with so much emblazoned there: charm, sadness, disillusion, weakness, humor, dignity, and so on, whereas now there's not a single contemporary movie star who doesn't look like a high school senior in need of a good backhand." His drink arrived and he immediately took a deep, tremulous sip. "There's nothing to discover in these new faces, Lindsay. Nothing to hold your interest. At worst there's almost a sort of blank meanness to them. Makes you sad, or at least that's what it does to me. So here's the question: What happened to all the great faces?"

Surprised to see that she was smoking, he looked around like someone in front of an unguarded bank vault and took a cigarette out of her pack on the bar. He stuck it in his mouth and was off again before she could reply.

"And you can't say, 'What about Colt Reston?' Colt is the exception to everything. Nothing about him makes sense. He's got lousy skin, can't act, he's dyslexic—did you know that he can barely read? But when you light the guy and turn a camera on him, you can't pull your eyes away. 'Unturnawayable,' that's how Dre describes it, which isn't even a word, of course, but he's absolutely right. Do you know the story about Colt and the director Pedro Orlavio?" She shook her head as though Marshall had bothered to look. "This was about six years ago, when they were making *The Ruins*. I was there on location making little tweaks in the script. Did you see the movie? I'm talking about that scene, that famous love scene, where Colt and Linda Beck are on the bed in that hotel room by the ocean. It was a closed set, so Orlavio himself was doing the camera work, all handheld stuff, shooting Linda naked from the waist up. Naturally she was the centerpiece of the shot, she and her breasts, which were her claim to fame, after all. But the remarkable thing was when we went over the dailies that night, you couldn't help noticing how the camera kept listing toward Colt's face. It was a simple two-shot, with Linda more centered, but then the camera would slowly start to drag. Take after take after take, it was all Colt! Naturally Orlavio was furious, just beside himself. Linda was getting millions to take her shirt off for one day and he'd blown the shot. I remember him stomping around the hotel that night, screaming, '*Teets out to here,*' "—Lindsay smiled as Marshall cupped his hands in front of his chest in imitation—" '*and I'm looking at deez fucking guy!*' But that's just Colt, you know. Once in a lifetime."

Marshall held up his drink, Lindsay taking an extra second to realize he was offering a toast. They clinked glasses, though the soliloquy was still incomplete.

"Or hell, maybe I'm just full of shit, you know, romanticizing the old stars. Maybe it's just the lighting, that old black-and-white stock that gave them the *illusion* of character, those great silver and gray shadings." He looked back toward the screen again to find Mastroianni in close-up. "I mean, Marcello was never as good in color, was he?"

Marshall gestured to the screen with his drink, but Lindsay was looking at his eyes, the two sets of bloody fish lips, moist and slow to blink.

"No, I think you're absolutely right," she commented, taking an overdue sip from her Gibson. "About the faces, I mean. But I don't believe it has anything to do with film stock, the texture of celluloid, any of that."

"Please," he said, apparently happy to relinquish center stage, "go on." He leaned forward and lit his cigarette off Lindsay's, nose to nose, a gesture of intimacy she found erotic.

"Well, there's no arc to people's lives now," she told him as he backed away to take a drag. "We don't have the kind of experiences anymore that mark a face with something interesting. It's the corporate century: we all have these safe, mundane lives, played out on this completely sterile commercial landscape."

Encouraged by Marshall's apparent attentiveness, she kept going.

"Which is one of the reasons we like these screens everywhere, I think. There's no personal narrative, so we surround ourselves with these facsimiles of what life once was. Advertisements for a glamour and adventure we'll never experience. Not that people like you and I don't contribute to this in a big way."

Marshall was leaning back now to get a wide-lens view of her, looking simultaneously amused and taken aback. "Wow," he said.

"What?" Her eyes narrowed warily.

He seemed to shrug, dragging again on his cigarette. "It just never occurred to me that Mr. Black was a woman, that's all."

She smiled, pleased by the quip.

"Yeah, that actually pissed me off," she confided. "How everybody assumed it was a man right from the beginning. *Mister* Black. Of course it did turn out to be a man, so I should probably just shut up."

"So what's he like?" Marshall asked, purposefully looking away for his drink. "Did you get a look at him?"

"Wow, you work fast." She reached for her cigarette, her face showing the coy satisfaction of knowing she had something he wanted. "I guess you talked to Dre."

He nodded over the rim of his glass.

"And so you think I got a look at him?"

"I don't know," he said. "That's why I'm here."

"I thought you were here because I asked you to dinner."

There was a pause. "Well, sure. That too."

Now Lindsay nodded, openly acknowledging a certain disappointment. Had it been too optimistic to think he'd come just for her? Breathing deeply, she drained off the rest of her Gibson and gobbled an onion off the skewer.

Her voice had a slight edge to it now. "What do you care what he looks like anyway?"

"Dre said you think he works in Hollywood."

"That's what I believe, yes."

"Well, I'd like to know why you think that," he said. "I want to find out who this guy is."

"Why?"

He dragged on his cigarette again, Lindsay deciding he was not really a smoker. Just something to do with his hands.

He was nervous, too, she thought.

"Somebody tried to kill Colt the other day," he reminded her. "I'd think it would be interesting to chat with Mr. Black about it."

"You think he's involved? He's just a *writer,* Marshall."

"He's been pretty tough on Colt . . . I mean, come on, you met the guy in a *blindfold,* for God sakes. You can't pretend that this is a completely sane person."

The bartender walked by and Marshall signaled for another round.

Lindsay leaned back against her stool. "All right, fine," she said, continuing on in her more businesslike manner. "But it's going to cost you."

Marshall laughed. "You can't mean money?"

"No, of course not," she said defensively. "Information. I ask you and then you ask me. Tit for tat. And no dodging questions or fuzzy answers."

He thought about this. "I have things you want to know?"

"Sure."

"Like what?"

"Like" — she leaned to him, coming closer than she'd wanted. She'd drunk her Gibson too quickly — "I tried Bliss for the first time the other night, and . . ." She waited for him to finish the thought, but he only gazed sternly at her. "I wouldn't mind trying it again."

"*No,*" he said then without hesitation, immediately backing off a step. "Absolutely not. I never turn people on, okay? Never."

Chagrined, Lindsay faced the bar.

"Now, it's my turn," he announced. "Did you or did you not get a look at Mr. Black?"

She paused, alarmed by the urgency in his voice.

"No dodging or fuzzy answers, Lindsay."

"*Yes,*" she said finally, glancing up at him. "Okay? Yes, I saw him."

Marshall nodded slightly, watching her eyes. "Good," he said. "Now keep going. How did you see him? What did he look like?"

"Nope, my turn now," she countered, the edge returning to her voice. Marshall did not hide his irritation, but at this point, she thought, who gave a shit? The "date," at least as she had imagined it, was pretty much in the toilet. "I want the answer to the big question. The one everyone's afraid to ask."

"And I have the answer to this?"

"Yes, I believe you do."

"All right, then," he replied skeptically. He took a hearty sip of his drink. "This ought to be good."

"I want to know if Colt is gay."

Lindsay's heart sank as she watched Marshall's body slacken against the bar. "That's the *big* question?" he asked. He laughed without humor—another mortal jab. "Come on, Lindsay, for chrissakes. You're better than this."

"Enquiring minds want to know, Marshall."

"Well, I'm not answering it."

"You don't understand the curiosity?"

"Sure I do. It's the kind of thing bored people with no sex lives want to know so they can feel superior to someone they're very jealous of. Jesus, you really think your viewers are interested in this crap?"

Lindsay was offended. "It's not for my *viewers,* smart-ass. Just personal curiosity. Which I think is only natural, given that I can't take a pee in a public toilet without Colt Reston shoving himself down my throat."

"Well, that's too bad. I'm not answering it."

"Fine," she said, "I'll take that as a yes." She looked down at her new drink, which seemed suddenly daunting, and consulted her watch. "Anyway, it's getting late," she said, taking a step off her stool.

"You're right. We'd better get a table if we're going to eat."

She paused, her head bobbing with surprise. "You mean you still want to have dinner?"

"Sure, why not?" he said. "What, you don't want to now?"

"Hell, I don't know." Lindsay looked around the thinning dining room. "You're very strange, you know that?"

"What's the problem? You asked me here."

"Yes, but maybe you've noticed a little *tension* tonight, Marshall?"

"Tension's good," he replied, finally now with the flirtatious energy she'd been hoping for. "And anyway, I'm starving. Aren't you?"

She paused then, measuring him with her eyes, quickly concluding that he was full of shit. His motivation was obvious: he wanted more about Mr. Black. For pride's sake she knew she should get the hell out of there, pack it in and go home. But then home was nowhere. Home was one glass of wine too many and the dull glim of the plasma. Home was the Diva calling to say they'd mentioned Lindsay's name on *Hollywood Insider.*

Home was death.

"All right, fine," Lindsay said. She got up off the stool and slung her pocketbook over her shoulder. "But there's been a slight change in plans."

"What's that?" he asked.

"You're buying."

That September of their first year with the Angels, Marshall and Colt cleaned out their lockers, which naturally were adjacent, leaving the contents in a local storage depot somewhere between Indio and Palm Springs. What little they were going to need, they put into Marshall's convertible: swimming trunks, espadrilles, two gloves and a ball, a few cases of bottled water, and the old milk crate with Marshall's books. There was sadness, but also a relief at the season's being over. They were exhausted, for one thing, their bodies battered by the grueling travel schedule and cramped cots in shitty motels. And for Marshall there was the deep longing for solitude and books. Someone had once asked him what he'd liked least about his playing days, and he had answered, without hesitation, "Having no one to talk to." There was a side to Marshall that could never be satisfied by a life in baseball. Stanford had been the exception; at college there was still an intellectual camaraderie to be had. But the professional ballplayer was a different breed entirely. They were a fun-loving, good-natured, even honorable bunch, and Marshall welcomed the loyalty and occasional friendship that went along with playing by their side. He battled with them on the field, drank with them afterward, laughed at their jokes, went to their weddings, played with their children. But their simplicity — a quality to which he aspired and that he believed was a virtue — left him lonely. And he knew that no matter how successful he became in baseball, this would never change. If intelligence was, to some degree, the capacity for doubt, then Marshall suspected he was not wired to be a pro athlete: that person for whom confidence is essential, and doubt a deformity.

Colt was his lone refuge in those days; it was a peculiar chemistry they shared. Mostly he listened to Marshall talk, in the dive bars and on long bus rides and through depressed nights in strange motels (they were roomies, of course). Colt was embarrassed about not having finished high school, anxious to shed his small-town provincialism, and he found himself swept up in the pitcher's enthusiasms. With Marshall it was all books and movies, movies and books, and he seemed to have a hard-bitten outlook on life, which Colt found appealing. He was secretly astonished to find that a pitcher as talented as Marshall could have such intense passions outside the game, just as the pitcher marveled at Colt's lack of self-consciousness or uncertainty, the man for whom the bucolic paradise of a ball field was all he could ever want from life.

So, even after rooming with each other for eight months and spending a majority of their time together off the field, Marshall and Colt left in late September for La Fonda Beach, Mexico. It was there, during the previous winter, that the pitcher had bought a rickety bungalow near the ocean with a chunk of his bonus-baby money. The isolation of the bungalow was either exhilarating or harrowing, depending on your taste. Owing to the Day of Terror, the border checkpoint was a four-hour headache minimum, with admission during daylight hours only. By the time they passed into Baja, it was night, battered Route 1 getting worse with every mile until it became like a Road to Hell in one of Peckinpah's neowesterns, a dark highway with packs of vagrants waiting for cars to break down in the cavernous potholes they'd made with shovels and pickaxes. The house itself wasn't much, either. It sat on a short bluff above a neglected beach, completely isolated but for a mobile home or two in the distance. When they arrived, they found it had been "borrowed" during the summer: a broken window by the doorknob, dishes in the sink, empty tequila bottles strewn about. They couldn't have cared less. They fixed it up, and, for a few weeks at least, it was a kind of Arcadia. They slept (the first few days they spent almost entirely comatose, still exhausted from the season), drank, bodysurfed, and read. At night they had dinners in town at the honky-tonk seafood shacks, trying to make time with the Mexican waitresses.

It was during that second week at La Fonda that an incident passed between them—one that would either destroy their friendship or bond them together forever. A short walk from the bungalow was a higher bluff with a wooden deck, a "scenic overlook," and it was there that a local tradition called Sevenish took place. Around that time every evening, the people of La Fonda, both locals and tourists alike, would take their drinks to the overlook to wait for the stunning Pacific sunset. Every so often, just as the last wedge of sun disappeared on the horizon, there would occur what was known as the green flash — an unexplained blaze of disk-shaped, aquamarine illumination. Though it lasted only a second, witnesses became infatuated, returning to the coast year after year just on the chance of seeing it again.

On this evening, however, there'd been a light rain shower as Marshall and Colt were heading to the overlook, and when they arrived they found themselves alone. Eschewing the deck, they saw that erosion had created a small shelf high up on the bluff, and not caring at all about the wet sand (they had been drinking margaritas most of the day), they stretched themselves out on it. Suddenly the clouds broke, the way they do in an instant in Mexico, and the beach was covered in a gaudy coral blush, the colors so rich and painterly that Marshall felt a welling in his eyes. As to what happened next, it was hard to know what to attribute it to — whether it was the distraction of a sublime moment, a drunken sentimentality, or just the relaxed openness that long, lazy days in Mexico can bring forth. But the fact remains that Colt's hand came to rest just above Marshall's kneecap and then, unchallenged there, made its slow but determined way up along his thigh to the button of his shorts.

"My God, so it *is* true," Lindsay exclaimed now with garish excitement.

The journalist and the screenwriter lay on the couch in the dark, their naked bodies strafed by the digital lighting of an extravagant entertainment center, the gelled screens of the six dormant plasmas swimming like aquariums. Despite their lack of clothing, an air of embarrassment hung between them. Dinner had gone much better than the drinks, and afterward they had found themselves sitting together in Marshall's car, where Lindsay discovered a sizable packet of Bliss inside the armrest. Too drunk to put up a fight, Marshall was bullied into giving her some, then ended up indulging himself.

They had wound up here, in her apartment, only to spend a furious hour trying to bring each other off. Eventually they had given up. To fill the awkward aftermath — and probably to create a segue to Mr. Black — Marshall began telling her more about Colt Reston than he had anyone else before.

"Then what happened?"

"He kept going."

"Oh my *Lord,*" she squealed. "What did you do? You didn't punch him, did you?"

He seemed surprised at this. "Of course not."

"So what happened? *What did you do, Marshall?*"

Marshall tried to adjust his leg; Lindsay had laid her head on his lap and he was going numb below the thigh. It was chilly in the room and he wanted badly to get dressed (as he believed she did too) but knew it would only highlight the awkwardness of their misfire.

"Nothing," he said.

"What do you mean, *nothing?* He was . . . You did *something,* Marshall."

"No, nothing," he told her. "I just leaned back, put my hands behind my head, and watched for the green flash."

Lindsay propped herself on an elbow to look at him.

"You didn't," she said.

"I did," he said, returning the look. "Is it really that big of a deal?"

"Are you *kidding?*" She let out a breathy, astonished sound, then forced herself to show more composure. "I mean, I guess I shouldn't be so surprised, with the rumors all these years, but . . . wow. *Holy shit.* He's such a male icon, you know. All those movies."

Marshall watched closely as her astonishment began to yield to a wistful disappointment. He realized he'd made a terrible mistake. Over the years, Colt's secret had slipped out here and there, and this had been the common reaction: an initial exhilaration giving way to melancholy, even anger, the feeling of having somehow been cheated. The public didn't *really* want to know, he reminded himself. They thought they did, but they didn't. They wanted their illusions intact, and for those unlucky enough to discover the truth, something was spoiled forever.

She leaned over to the coffee table and lit a cigarette from the pack lying there.

"And what about you?" she asked.

"Me?"

"Yeah." She was trying to figure out how to articulate this even as she spoke. "I mean, you know. Do you and Colt still—"

"No," he cut in with a laugh.

"No?"

"*No,*" he repeated. He moved his leg again, and now she got the hint and sat up straight with him on the sofa. "Look, afterward I told Colt that I thought it was presumptuous of him and that it was never going to happen again. He apologized and we left it at that. It's never been mentioned since."

"Never?"

"*Never,*" Marshall insisted. "And it's not something I ever explored again, or ever wanted to. I'm not even sure how it happened in the first place. The only way I can explain it is to say that it was for friendship."

"Friendship," she repeated, the word suddenly foreign to her.

"That's right. I didn't know he was gay; it was a total surprise to me. And I realized how difficult it must have been for him to live with that secret. If any of the guys on the team had found out, it would have been a disaster. These are not sophisticated people we're talking about here. So in that moment, I realized the whole time I'd known him he'd been hiding a big part of his life, and I felt bad for him. I didn't want to embarrass him or make him feel rejected. I was drunk. It didn't seem like a big deal. Still doesn't."

She dragged on her cigarette, looking at him with a grudging admiration. "Well, you're one hell of a friend, I'll say that much."

"We're best friends," he said. "We love each other. We've grown apart lately, but it's been a great friendship. A rare thing."

He sat forward to the edge of the couch, reaching for a glass of water.

"I'm sorry about what happened between us tonight," he added then. "Or *didn't* happen. But it has nothing to do with what went on between me and Colt."

"I was a little embarrassed, I have to say."

"Let me be embarrassed, Lindsay. You don't have to be."

"Actually, you don't seem embarrassed at all."

"Well, it's really nobody's fault." He took a sip of the water and saw the odd look on her face. "Come on, you're telling me you're living in Hollywood and haven't slept with a guy on Bliss before? There's almost zero chance of a happy ending, sweetheart. And that goes for *both* participants." He smiled then. "I think we gave it a hell of a try, though, don't you?"

She stared past him, confused now and maybe a little unhappy with herself.

"Really, you should punch me in the face for giving you some," he continued. "That was a stupid thing to do." He sipped the water and then reached out for her elbow, gripping her with a surprising firmness. "Stay away from this shit, Lindsay, please. It's bad fucking news. Take it from me."

Lindsay nodded slightly and then stood up; something seemed to have ended. Most of her clothes were strewn on a nearby ottoman, and she began to dress. Taking his cue, Marshall found his pants on the floor by the plasma, hopping a little as he climbed into them.

She walked toward the hall, then stopped and gestured with her head for him to follow her.

"Aren't you coming?" she asked.

"Where?"

"My office. I have something I think you'll want to see."

EIGHT

Fully dressed now, Marshall followed Lindsay down the hall to a second bedroom, which she had remade into a study. Inside was a black graphite desk with a very sleek home Pod and some industrial bookshelves along the walls. Saying nothing, she pulled a dog-eared novel from one of the shelves and took out a key that was resting in its pages. Then she bent down to unlock one of the desk drawers, pulling out a black folder and tossing it matter-of-factly on the desk in front of him.

"There," Lindsay said, dropping herself into a chair behind the desk.

He looked at her, wondering if what was inside could possibly be what she'd implied.

"Go on, you're dying to," she told him. "I can hear your heart beating from over here."

He opened the folder slowly, heart thumping nearly as loudly as she'd described. Inside were a series of large photos, six color shots of extraordinary quality. In one you could actually see the whitecaps of the ocean in the distance behind him.

The photos were from the interview at Mr. Black's house.

His first impression, looking at the photos, was that this was exactly who one would've cast for the role. Early forties, bespectacled, with a slightly puffy face (from sedentary living?), the eyes possessing both mischief and a lucid clarity. His forehead was wide and pale, his hair uncombed and in need of a wash in the style of geniuses too engaged for the trivia of hygiene. Then Marshall noticed the grease stain on the pocket and smiled, a detail right out of Panoramic wardrobe.

"Recognize him?" Lindsay asked.

Marshall neither answered nor looked up, going over the photos very meticulously. "How did you get these?" he asked after a moment.

"I had a pin camera on the cuff of my field jacket. I was actually surprised he didn't check me more thoroughly. It was sort of a crazy thing to do . . . What's the matter?" she asked, seeing something in Marshall's face.

He closed the folder, looking down.

"Did you stay blindfolded the whole time?" he asked, thumbing the edge of the desk.

"Yes."

"So this is all you saw—what you photographed?"

"Yes," she replied. "Marshall, what's going on? Why won't you look at me?"

He glanced up now. "Why did you tell Dre you think he works in Hollywood?"

Lindsay reached for the folder and opened it intently, as if trying to make amends. There she removed a photo that had obviously been taken inside the house. The shot was of a cluttered cottage living room, chaotic but somehow warm, Mr. Black standing in profile at a sideboard pouring two iced teas.

"Down there, you see?" She circled an area with her finger at the bottom left of the photo. "That table there, on the right-hand side."

He looked. Resting on the corner of a paper-strewn coffee table was a laminated card that looked like a name tag or the inside of a passport. He pulled the picture closer.

"I don't know what I'm seeing," he remarked.

From the desktop she pulled a pair of glasses out of a leather pouch.

"Nearsighted?" she guessed.

Nodding, he accepted the glasses. They barely fit around his head, but he put them on without embarrassment and looked more closely at the photo.

"You see it now?"

After a long beat, he said, "Yes, I think so."

"It's a Panoramic studio pass, isn't it?" Lindsay asked. "I did a little research. I'm pretty sure it's not a visitor's pass. It looks green to me, which is what they give employees. Am I right?"

After another pause, he said, "Yes, that's true." He looked up at her. "I don't know if I would make too much of it, though."

She was very surprised. "How do you mean?"

"Well, whose is it, first of all? The pass is upside down. You can't make out the face or the name on it."

"Who else's would it be, Marshall?"

"How about a friend's? How about a forgery? How about you've been set up?" He saw her getting agitated. "What I'm saying, Lindsay, is that we have a very clever guy here. You don't know what you're meant to see and what you're not. Maybe he knew you had a camera all along. Maybe that's why he didn't check you more thoroughly. You don't know anything for sure."

"I asked you before if you recognized him."

He took a last glance and removed the glasses. "No, I don't," he told her. His voice was very far away now, Lindsay noticed. He seemed either exhausted or angry, or both.

"But you admit that doesn't mean I'm wrong?"

"No," he conceded. "Panoramic's a huge place. If he's there, I wouldn't necessarily have run into him." He laid the picture back on the desk. "Basically what we have here is a labyrinth of possibilities that don't add up to very much."

Lindsay pushed the chair away from the desk, looking frustrated. "What the hell is this, Marshall?" she demanded.

"I don't know what you mean."

"I give you Mr. Black on a silver platter and you dismiss it with this convoluted . . . *horseshit*. Then at the same time you act pissed off at me for showing you. I mean, where's the goddamned appreciation?"

"Appreciation!"

"That's right. I took a hell of a chance getting those pictures, and I was under no obligation to show them to you."

Marshall looked ready to get into something with her and then backed off, taking a deep breath. "Look, the pictures are interesting, okay?" he told her. "I'm glad I saw them. It's a start, at least. But at the same time I'm a little put off by the means."

"The means?"

"You ambushed this guy, Lindsay. You betrayed his confidence . . . I'm a little shocked at the deviousness, I have to say."

Lindsay was dumbfounded by this. "Well, aren't you a hypo-critical son of a bitch!" she said, wheeling the chair back toward the desk. "The biggest sellout in Hollywood history is giving *me* shit about personal integrity. *Marshall Reed,* of all people."

"All right, all right, take it easy." Marshall pretended to gri-mace, though the sellout tag was so old and boring to him now it no longer had much traction.

"Anyway, asshole," she said, "taking the picture wasn't my idea. I did it, yes, and I take responsibility for it, but I can't say it was something I thought of doing or particularly *wanted* to do."

"So it was Mr. Black's idea."

"No. It was Dre's."

That got his attention. He found his body weight drifting back toward his heels and had to rock slightly forward again to hold his balance.

"All right," he said, "let's have it."

"We had a deal," Lindsay explained; she was looking past him, her eyes grazing the bindings in the bookcases, registering nothing. "I was going to sign with NetTalent anyway, but Dre said if I'd take the picture, he'd represent me personally. Now, you know what that means as well as anyone, to have Dre on your side. He basically guaranteed me a two-million-dollar-a-year job. I don't know where you come from, Marshall, but that's a serious upgrade for me and for my family back home."

He nodded without comment.

"Dre's obsessed with the identity of this fucking Mr. Black even more than you are, Marshall. You should hear him; he's gone bonkers with this thing."

"I'm aware, believe me. So what did he say when he saw the picture?"

"Nothing."

"*Nothing?* I find that hard to believe."

"Nothing," Lindsay repeated, more aggressively now, "because I didn't show him."

Marshall waited, measuring her.

"Screw you with that *look*," she told him. "I didn't show him — take it or leave it."

"Why?"

"Because, I regretted it. I told Dre I took the pictures but they didn't come out right. I gave him the ones that didn't make it, the blurry ones. You should see him with these things; he's going over them like the Zapruder film."

"He believed you?"

She shrugged. "What choice did he have?"

Marshall turned away, trying to understand all this, until his vidphone began to glow like a firefly in his breast pocket. He looked immediately to the clock on the desk: 3:23. The hour made him shudder. Even *he* didn't get calls at 3:23 in the morning.

The glowing stopped just as he reached for it, and he turned back to Lindsay. "Why did you show me the pictures, by the way, if you didn't feel right about giving them to Dre?"

"Because you seemed so convinced Mr. Black might be trying to hurt Colt." She looked hard at him again, searching the angles of his face. "Obviously it was a big mistake. This whole night was a big mistake."

Before he could reply, the phone started to flash again. Something was definitely wrong. He shrugged apologetically and retreated to the hallway to take the call.

When he opened his vidphone, he found that the line was connected but that the tiny screen was dark — "caller's choice," the phone informed him. The voice on the other end, however, could not have been more familiar.

"Marsh?" said Colt Reston plaintively. "Marsh, you there?"

"Hey, what's going on? How come your vid's down?"

"Forget that. Just get the hell over here."

"*Now?*" Marshall laughed dismissively. "You're crazy. It's almost three thir—"

"Marsh, listen to me, okay? Please. This is no fucking around. You gotta get over here. You gotta come to the house *immediately.*" There was a panic in Colt that he could never remember hearing before. There were tears in his voice. "I'm mean *now,* Marsh."

"All right, I'll be there in a few minutes," the screenwriter replied, the line suddenly going dead.

When he looked up, he saw Lindsay watching him in the hallway.

"Something wrong?" she asked.

"Nah, just my dealer," he said, trying to hide his unease. "She likes to prey on me in the wee hours. See how great Bliss is? Big fun, twenty-four seven." He went to the living room and began putting on his shoes, his fingers now trembling with anxiety.

She followed him in.

"Sorry it was such a crazy night," he added. "It was my fault, really."

She stood there, not caring to argue. Marshall saw the hurt in her face, and an old desolation seemed to sneak up on him. He'd thought he'd sworn off this kind of night for good: bad sex, embarrassing confessions, anger, drugs—the *works.* But here it was all over again.

"Good-bye, then," Lindsay said. She went to the door and held it open for him. Marshall was silent as he passed her; no last words could save the evening.

As the door closed behind him and he took his first steps down the hall, he could still hear the muffled voice from inside the apartment. "Don't come back," she said.

The ride was less than ten minutes. Marshall didn't know if it was the eerie phone call, but the night suddenly seemed to have a mood, that old noir shiver he hadn't felt in L.A. since the years before the MIBs. Streets deserted, the bedroom town locked up, shut tight. *Afraid.* He'd thought the MIBs had changed all that, brightening all the dark, sordid corners of the city, but then a few more billboards were down tonight, completely dark, and somehow their malfunctioning made the other, working MIBs all the more tawdry and intrusive. Marshall saw a desperation in them tonight that was unsettling.

On his thumb he imprinted some Bliss residue left on the shifting console, stuffing each nostril with the spoils.

Finally turning onto Colt's cul-de-sac, he discovered a surprising number of media diehards still hanging on. The trucks were lined up all along the curbs, illuminated in the beams of the upturned floodlights that lit the hedges of the Spanish-style mansions, neighbors whom Colt had never spoken to or even seen. A few of the truck's interior lights flickered as Marshall drove by, but none could rouse themselves quickly enough to make a move.

Marshall pulled up to the buzzer at the front gate and was admitted swiftly, curling the car slowly around the circular driveway until he found his usual niche near the guest cottages. Stepping out into the night air, he felt that his senses had become especially keen at this hour, hearing the crunch of the marble chips under his feet and smelling the flora of the compound's effusive grounds: ficus, bougainvillea, and orange blossom, eucalyptus, and fern. It was at least partly about exhaustion, he thought, these perceptions sharpening to combat his fatigue. And all the Bliss he had done today gave the whole thing an extra hum: for a moment he actually thought he could hear the sluicing of his own brain fluid, until he noticed the spewing water nymphs behind him.

The floodlights came on and Marshall spied a figure waiting for him on the front steps of the house: Ben Grimsley stood scratching his coarse gray beard, awaiting Marshall's approach. Ben had been the Angels' clubhouse manager back in the day, and Colt had recruited him, even as Ben pushed seventy, to be the majordomo of the compound. If he was not particularly good at his job (he was a drinker, and as in the many clubhouses he had taken care of over the years, there were areas of the estate that betrayed neglect), he did provide Colt with what he wanted most from the people around him: camaraderie and a sense of nostalgia—the illusion that life was a team sport, another larkish season just around the corner.

Ben embraced him as they met on the top step, and the gesture officially put Marshall in a state of alarm. This was not Ben's style. The man was a wiry old sourpuss, physically standoffish. A swapping of genial locker-room insults was as close as he got to tenderness. The embrace meant that something dire was going on inside the house.

"Where is he?" Marshall asked, the words slightly malformed. His mouth was suddenly tight from panic.

Ben flipped a thumb skyward. "Upstairs," he said.

Marshall waited in vain for something more, some account of what was happening. Why wasn't Ben saying anything? Did he assume the screenwriter had already been told, or was there something else preventing him? Marshall decided to quit torturing himself with this speculation and reached for the doorknob.

"Marsh?"

He stopped as the old man's hand landed on his shoulder.

"Be ready," Ben warned in his gravelly voice.

"Now what does that mean?" When the old man looked away from him, Marshall added, "Ben, nobody's told me what's happening."

"Just . . . try not to be shocked when you go up there, okay? Play it down, Marsh, whatever you do. Tell him it's not that bad."

Marshall broke from Ben's grip and headed anxiously into the lobby. Turning right, he entered the sprawling living room, large as the deck of a cruise ship. It was empty except for Rip, standing guard at the bottom of the wide marble staircase, despondently stroking his goatee. Marshall nodded to him with searching eyes, the solemn bodyguard nodding back and . . . that was all. Apparently he wasn't talking, either.

Taking a breath for stamina, Marshall headed up the stairs to Colt's room.

He took the steps quickly, realizing almost too late that the light was becoming dimmer as he climbed, until by the last few steps he had to hold on to the rail for direction. Marshall paused at the second-floor landing, letting his eyes adjust to the darkness. Finally he discovered some faint illumination coming from Colt's bedroom. The door was ajar, and he could see soft light flickering from inside.

He headed down the hall and pushed the door open slowly. "Colt?" he asked in a hushed voice. A low firelight glowed from a hearth across the room, and he could see Colt at the vanity, face buried in the crook of his arm, shoulder blades twitching as he sobbed. Marshall remained in the doorway, not knowing what to do. Reminding himself he had been summoned here, he rapped his knuckles hard against the doorframe, calling his friend's name louder this time.

"I heard you," Colt said with some irritation. "Come on in — I don't bite. Not yet, anyway." He raised his head without turning, discreetly wiping the tears from his eyes.

Marshall felt his pulse pound once more tonight as he took a few tentative steps into the bedroom. He didn't know how close to come; he wasn't really sure why there should be any distance at all. But as he continued cautiously toward Colt, the angle of the mirror brought the countenance into view.

Even in the soft firelight, Marshall was startled by what he saw. Slightly woozy, he made a move to sit down on the edge of the canopied bed, then recalled Ben's warning about showing alarm. Summoning what little energy he had left tonight, he forced himself to remain on his feet while he tried to clear his own face of its spooked expression.

"I told you, didn't I?" Colt snapped, lifting his eyes to meet Marshall's in the reflection. "Goddammit, what did I say? I told you there was something wrong with me, and what did you do? You *laughed*. You laughed at me and made it into a fucking joke!"

Marshall didn't think he had laughed at all, but he accepted the cut without protest. How could he argue with a man in this condition? *His face* . . . the only way to describe it was to say that Colt appeared to have gotten dramatically older. There was the sudden flaccidity in the skin, a subtle but striking lag of flesh on bone, along with a number of darker markings, like liver spots, which had broken out on the surface. The actor's eyes seemed sunken and weary tonight, somewhere beyond fatigue, and not even the muted light could hide the new shininess of his cheeks and forehead, the skin having taken on the slightly stretched, onion-skin texture of the aged.

"I was asleep for almost fifteen hours," Colt started to say, his voice uneasy but less angry now. "I don't know why they let me go so long. I guess they thought I needed it. Anyhow, I wake up to take a piss and see my face in the mirror and I figure I must be dreaming—I *have* to think that, Marsh, you know? And so I'm laughing at myself in the mirror, saying out loud, 'Okay, very scary, you can wake up now,' and then I turn and see Ben standing at the bathroom door next to me, and he lets go this absolutely *bloodcurdling* fucking scream, and I suddenly realize this is no dream. My face is *real*. This is happening! And so then I start screaming with him, like you do when you're trying to pull yourself out of a nightmare. It sounded like an opera from hell, Marsh, I swear to God. Rip was downstairs and he said even *he* almost shit his pants . . . Hey, what's the matter? Why aren't you saying anything?"

Perhaps unconsciously, Colt turned from the mirror to look squarely at Marshall as he was telling his story, and the sight of his face, without reflection, was somehow even more paralyzing to the viewer. In the mirror there had still been hope of transmutation, Marshall believed, the possibility of exaggeration or distortion through another medium. But no, he saw now. It was *real*.

Colt's voice had taken on a reedy desperation. "I'm counting on you, Marsh, you know that. I'm going to need your help. I'm going to need . . . Christ, I need you to *say something!*"

"Why aren't you in the hospital?" Marshall managed to ask.

"It's being taken care of," Colt replied. Out of the corner of his eye he seemed to catch a glimpse of himself in the mirror, then immediately turned away with a pained expression. "They're clearing a wing for me at Cedars, with a private entrance, everything confidential. Nobody can see me like this, Marsh, or I won't go. I told them that. Not a single person can see me. I'd rather die, I swear to God."

"You should be there *now*," Marshall said anxiously. "Somebody should be looking at you *now*."

"Dr. Heilman's here."

"And?"

Marshall looked at Colt's neck and hands, noting the same flaccidity, the dark markings. Clearly the whole body was afflicted.

"He's frightened, Marsh. He hardly looked at me, the son of a bitch. I think he's actually afraid to touch me. My own doctor, and I'm scaring the shit out of him. I'm *dying*, Marsh."

"No."

"Yes, I am."

"They're gonna make you better," Marshall countered. "I'm *telling* you they will."

Of course Marshall hardly believed this himself but in fact was desperately trying to conjure some glimmer of hope. He told himself that no matter how terrible the actor looked, it was still Colt Reston there, somewhere, the face still unmistakably his. There were no wrinkles, for example, beyond what Colt had already accrued at forty. And the actor's motor skills, the way he moved in his chair with the usual fluidity—in fact rising this very moment to stand in front of Marshall—seemed as sharp as ever. These had to be good signs, he told himself. Marshall was no doctor, but to him there seemed something almost *topical* about the whole thing, something explicitly *superficial*. If it were a makeup job, Ray Manuel would have condemned it as half-assed, incomplete.

"You'll get the best care in the world," he added, trying to impress his optimism on Colt. "Whatever doctor you need, from wherever — "

"I'm dying, Marshall."

"Stop it."

"I'm *dying*. I am."

"Shut up."

"I can *feel* it. I feel like I look, if you can imagine. It's not pain exactly, but I don't feel right. I'm sick as a dog. I got fucking nausea like you can't believe . . ."

Suddenly Colt's eyelids began to flutter, and he grabbed Marshall by the collar of his jacket as if to pull him to the floor. Then, just as abruptly, he let go and crumpled to one knee. Marshall bent down to help him, begging him to say what was wrong, and then quickly pulled away as Colt vomited with a heaving, spasmodic violence onto the carpet and across the writer's shoes.

"*Doctor, Dr. Heilman!*" Marshall shouted now, turning to project his voice out the door. He noticed Colt's breathing had become more labored, his body increasingly limp as he slipped through Marshall's grasp and lay prostrate on the carpet.

"BEN! DR. HEILMAN!" He looked at Colt's eyes to see if he was still lucid, but the firelight was fading in the hearth, the room slipping into darkness.

Finally there was the muffled sound of voices and pounding footsteps in the hallway.

Marshall turned back and saw Rip at the door, his large silhouette frozen by the scene on the carpet, and then an even darker figure behind him, a man eagerly trying to get by the bodyguard and into the room. Colt heaved again, Marshall bracing him till the episode passed. Now when he looked back at the two men, Marshall saw the darker figure approaching — his walk the unstable gait of grief, whinnying cry at his lips, arms splayed and then pulled distraughtly to his bald pate — Dre McDonald shaking his head and murmuring, *"Good God, no!"* through unhinged tears.

NINE

I want the best doctors in the world," Dre was explaining later. "I want *teams* of doctors, fucking *legions,* flown here from every ass crack of the world, for which I will pay the tab personally at whatever the price, I don't give a goddamned shit."

Colt had left, ushered by stretcher to an anonymous car, undoubtedly at the hospital by now. And he had gone alone, the rest to follow later once the actor was situated. Marshall had protested at first and then relented, knowing this was per Colt's instructions, in the hope that he would not be followed.

The rest had been left here to worry: Marshall, Dre, Rip, Ben, and Dr. Heilman. They had assembled in Colt's library for an emergency meeting, exchanging fragmentary utterances of disbelief and swearing silence about what they had witnessed. Naturally, the doctor endured a fusillade of questions, and it soon became obvious the poor man was in over his head. Nearing seventy now, he had been Colt's physician for no less than fifteen years, but his boutique family practice in Holmby Hills left him unprepared for the deviant malady he'd been confronted with on this night. The doctor admitted to a cursory examination (there was the chance that Colt might be contagious, he felt, which worried Marshall) but thought he detected hints of progeria, the rare child-aging disease, while other symptoms pointed to nothing short of leprosy, an illness now all but unheard of. And the speed and severity of the symptoms were unprecedented as far as the doctor knew.

Assignments were given. Dr. Heilman would make some calls, beginning the process of assembling the specialists. Meanwhile Rip would remain in contact with the hospital, and Ben would get ready to stave off the morning media blitz.

When the library cleared, Marshall found himself alone with Dre. They stood looking at each other, shaking their heads in a show of confusion and heartbreak. The possibility that Colt Reston could die—once an idea as preposterous as the end of Hollywood itself—was now palpable, a notion that bore down on them with real force.

It was Marshall who broke the silence.

"I need some answers," he announced as Dre lifted his large, exhausted eyes. "I need you to explain to me *specifically* how things will change around here, business-wise, if he goes. What happens at the agencies, for example? Your relationship with Panoramic. Who gains, who loses? All of it."

The agent sighed histrionically. "Haven't I told you all this a hundred times before?"

"Tell it to me again," Marshall said firmly. "I'm not too bright. I need you to spell it out one more time."

"Dick *buries* me," pronounced the agent in a splenetic tone. "Okay? You got that? Dick *eviscerates* me. He takes everything. Without Colt I lose my leverage with Panoramic, first of all;

Talent United takes over the exclusive packaging deal I have with the studio. Then the dominoes really start to fall. The networks begin to look at us differently, along with the major cable stations. Suddenly we're not the agency with Colt Reston anymore, we're not so attractive, and I can't place my people. My big stars, the few I have left, will all defect. Then what? Dick Vale burns down my house, fucks my wife, eats my children."

Marshall felt for the keys in his pocket, knowing now what he needed to do. He checked the light outside, then his watch, to confirm his guess: half hour till dawn.

"By the way," Dre said, "I've got my hands on some interesting pictures. Maybe you've heard?"

"Lindsay told me," Marshall replied. Obviously now there was no use in denying he had spoken to her. "That was a risky situation to put somebody in, don't you think?"

Dre nodded in agreement. "Yes, there was some risk, for which Lindsay will be well compensated." A thin smile came to the agent's lips. "Actually, I'm a little pissed off at our girl."

"Why's that?"

"Well, she hands me these lousy, blurry pictures. Basically useless. Meanwhile, my tech guys just reminded me that the camera we gave her fires off three quarter-second bursts — bang, bang, bang. But not all of the pictures she turned in to me are in succession. Does this sound at all strange to you?"

"Dre, what do I know from cameras?" Marshall asked innocently. "Maybe those were the best shots she had. You'll have to ask her."

"You were out with her this evening, were you not?"

The writer stared at him for a moment. "So what?"

"You realize, don't you, Marshall, that knowing who this

writer is could help us with Colt? There could be important connections here."

"You think I don't know that, especially after what went down at the studio? I want to know who this guy is as much as anyone." Marshall glanced out the window again, seeing blue light breaking through the night. "Look, I have to go."

"At this hour? Where to?"

"The beach."

"*The beach?*" Dre looked at him, clearly appalled. "With everything that's going on?"

Ignoring this, Marshall headed toward the door.

"So what the hell's at the beach?" Dre called out before suddenly comprehending. "Don't tell me Zuma?"

"You got it," Marshall said, taking a last look back. "Surfing with Dick and the boys."

Marshall found Rip on the back patio, having just spoken with the hospital. Colt was safely ensconced, the bodyguard explained, condition stable. The vomiting had subsided. They were preparing him for tests; specialists were flying in. Help was on the way.

Marshall nodded, showing pleasure at the news. Then he put a hand on Rip's shoulder, pushing him gently against the side of the house.

"Gimme your gun," he said in Rip's ear.

"What? No way." Marshall was blocked as he reached around the bodyguard for his holster.

"Rip, I need it. I'm serious."

He reached again and this time the arm was chopped away hard. Rip assumed some sort of military stance, and Marshall took a step back. The next strike, the writer understood, would be something he wouldn't walk away from.

He tried a different tack. "All right, Rip, tell you what. Go home. You're fired."

"What?" Rip's fighting stance went slack.

"You deaf? I said *get out*. Get your shit and go home."

"You can't do that."

"The fuck I can't," Marshall told him. "I'm in charge now and I say you're fired. Go home, Rip. Don't call to ask how Colt's doing; no one will talk to you. You're officially banned. In fact, here: let me go write you your last check. How much do you want?"

He'd taken a step toward the house when Rip grabbed his hand.

"Marsh, what are you doing?" he asked, his voice stricken with panic. "Don't do this, please. *What are you doing?*" Rip and Colt had once been lovers, and though the affair had ended years ago, it was clear to everyone that the bodyguard was still holding out hope. He would sooner relinquish his life than his proximity to Colt.

"Then give me your gun," Marshall insisted. "Give me *any* gun, I don't give a shit. Just do it quick."

Rip took a deep breath, looking around desperately. Hating himself, he reached into his jacket and handed over his pistol. Marshall pulled it from the small leather hip holster and held it up distastefully.

"What the hell is *this*?"

"A Kraecher, German made. It's a compound weapon — fiberglass with some wood and plastic, to get through detectors." Marshall began waving the weapon around, as if he didn't quite believe in it, and Rip had to still his hand. "Highly illegal, by the way. You get caught with that, I'll be seeing you in the next life."

Marshall kept looking at it, turning it over in his hand. "Can it do any damage?"

"If you have to ask that question, you shouldn't be holding it."

"What about the bullets?"

"Fiberglass. They explode on contact. It's not pleasant."

They heard a helicopter approach from a distance; the daily haunting had begun. Marshall attached the holstered weapon to his belt and covered it with his jacket. Then he looked up at Rip affectionately, pinching his cheek. "Thanks."

"Marsh?"

Once again the writer took a step and stopped.

"Don't do this," Rip implored. "Let me take care of it, whatever it is. This is why I'm here. This is what I get paid for."

"Don't worry," Marshall said, shaking him off. "I'm just going to wave it around a little. Make some people nervous."

"You make people nervous anyway."

"You see? Nothing new to worry about."

TEN

They're onto you; it's important you know this. They already know we're all sick of it, so they'll find a way to market exactly *to* that. The *I'm-sick-of-big-media-and-corporate-advertising* market, the *I'm-too-smart-to-be-marketed-to* market. Huge market, they tell themselves. And so media will become more and more self-conscious, making fun of itself, buddying up, flattering you as the "smart" public. There are think tanks at work, the best and brightest on the case, corporate manifestos being written, sales conferences all dedicated to the new challenge. This is what they're going to sell to you now: the public's savvy and brilliance via marketing. "*You're all too smart for us . . .*" That is the new market. You are it.

Forty-five minutes later Marshall was pulling into the parking lot at Zuma Beach. The twenty-first century had hit Los Angeles hard, but the lot at Zuma seemed much the same as ever. The sand-swept expanse of parking spaces, empty at this hour, the sagging chain-link fence, a huddle of cement barriers and pylons sprayed with gang tags, and a beach-patrol station with a singular nod to modernity: an MIB for baby food, glowing mutely in the fog. In fact, the beach was almost completely obscured in the mist, though relief was on the way — a melted-butter sun rising at eye level, sliding in and out of vaporous clouds.

Battling a wave of fatigue as he exited the car, Marshall turned to let the fog dampen his face, refreshing him slightly. He headed off toward the beach, turning south as he hit the sand, trying to recall the distance from memory. After a quarter mile of trudging, he became discouraged; there was no sign of anyone, and the fog was limiting his visibility, thirty feet at the most. The only way to see if they were out here was to keep walking.

He kept walking.

A few more minutes, and he thought he began to hear voices — bits of broken chatter carried on the brume. Then there was the telltale sign: the glow of a cigar tip, faint and halolike in the fog. Here they were at last.

Marshall walked up to the camp. They were just finishing up. A lacquered Japanese tea table lay studded with handleless cups, the briefcases all in a row, surfboards sticking out of the sand like gravestones. Dick Vale and some of his younger lieutenants were toweling off, Dick with a morning Corona glowing from the side of his face. It was he who noticed the writer first.

"Marshall?" The agent stood dumbfounded, taking the cigar from his mouth and cocking his head to check if what he was seeing was real. "It is you. Jesus, thought I was having some sort of vision for a moment. Gondolier on the river Styx, that sort of thing. You look like death warmed over, my friend. What gives?"

"I had a long night."

Amused, he looked back toward his other lieutenants. "He had a long night, he says."

"Listen, can we talk?" Marshall gestured behind him toward a thickly fogged stretch of beach. He wanted to take a walk, get the man alone.

"Sure," the agent replied after a short hesitation. "Give me a second here."

Dick finished toweling off as an assistant pulled an impeccably folded suit from a briefcase. The man then laid the pants across his arm, draped the jacket on his shoulder, hooked the hangered shirt through a belt loop, and dangled the boxer briefs from his fingertips: a human clothes tree, ready for service. The precision with which this was carried out (Dick already slipping smoothly into his slacks) spoke to the repetition of a highly rehearsed act. Of course, this had been Dick Vale's famous ritual now for twenty years and counting: the morning surf. He swore by it as the ultimate business wake-me-up, citing the holistic benefits of saltwater, the brisk, invigorating temperatures, the competitive challenges of the rough Pacific tides—all providing TU employees with whatever advantages they might need for their day of agenting. (And woe to the budding executive who suggested a wet suit.)

Marshall himself had been summoned here approximately three years ago, when Dick had begun his poaching frenzy. After Colt had turned him down repeatedly, Dick had made an overture to Marshall, hoping to get at the star through the back door. The writer had come to the beach at dawn and was given the usual routine: absurd promises, a "vision" of a career trajectory, smoke blown far up the ass—everything contingent, naturally, on Colt's joining the agency. Marshall had turned him down but had gotten a close look at Dick Vale the man and his methods.

Dick had started out as an actor in the 1980s—Richard C. Vale, six film credits—but his uncanny resemblance to Burt

Lancaster, which had only increased with age, had handicapped his chances. The similarities were too spooky to overlook: the same ironic smile, the chilling gaze, the *voice*. He was like a ghost, or a reincarnation. This morning, in fact, as Marshall came upon Dick in his swim trunks, the writer had half expected to see Deborah Kerr come loping along to roil with him in the surf.

The affinity had hurt Dick as an actor, but he had found its advantage as an agent. First with NetTalent and then with TU, he had used his looks as a subconscious talisman, saying, in effect, *This is where the stars are. You coming aboard or not?* His aspect awakened a sense of nostalgia, harkening to an era whose golden shimmer had probably been half an illusion but had to be better than the *now,* Dick embodying that age before ReStars and the MIBs, before Bliss, before the dominance of the talent agencies and Colt Reston, before the half-billion-dollar opening weekends. The age before movies had been completely deforested of ideas, then character, then nearly dialogue itself.

Of course the reality was that Dick was not really Old Hollywood at all, nor was he the anti–Dre McDonald. Dick and his agencies had contributed heartily to the current state of things and had done so without remorse, were in fact kicking and scratching to contribute *more,* and by whatever means possible. Marshall had experienced this firsthand that morning three years ago. Sensing his resistance to a defection—or more important, his resistance to influencing Colt—Dick had reverted to cheap bullying. As they walked through the sand in the dawn light, he had suddenly stepped in front of the screenwriter, blocking his path. Then, leaning his rugged frame against him, Dick spoke in a low, threatening voice: if Marshall wasn't interested in helping him, the agent warned, then he, in turn, might not be able to help the writer with the LAPD, who had become interested in Hollywood's fascination with a new drug called Bliss. Perhaps Marshall didn't know that he and Hollywood vice detective Frank Borsalo had grown up in Newport Beach together, or that Frank joined him here to surf Zuma every Friday morning, for old times' sake.

This pulpy threat had turned out to be an idle one, but Marshall had thought about the incident quite a bit during the past few days. It *resonated,* to say the least. There was one man standing in the way of Dick Vale's reclaiming his kingship in Hollywood, and his name was not Dre McDonald. It was Colt Reston.

Dressed now, Dick joined him along the path at the top of the surf, the agent favoring the wet, firm sand that would be easier for him to walk on in his loafers. Marshall waited to say something, seeing if he could make Dick uneasy, get him a little off-balance, but the agent would have none of it.

"Thanks for coming," Dick began heartily, as if it were *he* who'd invited Marshall. The agent added something to this but was drowned out, the waves booming just off to their left; they were going to have to speak up. "I was just about to give you a call," he said, louder this time, "you know, given everything that's been going on lately."

"Sure," Marshall murmured.

Dick took a long pull on his cigar. "I think it was just the other day at TU we were sitting around, sort of lamenting the current state of cinema. And someone pointed out that *Chula Vista* was probably the last great American film. Of course we all agreed."

"That was a long time ago," Marshall countered, careful not to let Dick soften him up with stale compliments. He snuck a look behind them to make sure they weren't being followed. It was hard to tell in the mist. "Almost a decade."

"I know." Dick shook his head. "Something needs to be done around here, don't you think? It's just too sad."

"Not really."

"No?" Dick smiled, familiar with Marshall's contentious reputation.

"You want to know what I think is really sad?" the screenwriter told him. "Carmela Montoya dying at twenty-nine. That was sad."

"Well, of course," the agent replied, obviously taken aback. "I wasn't suggesting—"

"Beautiful woman like that. She had a daughter, Dick, did you know? She'd just adopted a little girl. You hardly heard anything about it when she died. They think of all the movies she'll never make; they never think about the person."

"Hell, I knew about the girl. Of course I did. You don't think I thought the whole thing was sad?" Dick grimaced now, growing agitated. "Where are you going with this, anyway?"

"Funny, I don't remember seeing you at the funeral, Dick."

"How could I?" the agent asked, lowering his voice again as if he might be overheard. "Given what was going on?" Dick stopped short, throwing his cigar into the ocean. "What the hell is this, Marshall? I told you I owed you a call. I blew it, okay? I'm sorry. What the hell else do you want me to say? I guess I just wanted to wait until things were more . . . in motion."

"*In motion?* What the fuck are you talking about, Dick?" Marshall looked behind them again. They definitely seemed to be alone.

"Come on, you know what. Stop the coy routine, Marshall. What's on your mind? Cut it loose."

Marshall took a step forward. Close up now, Dick Vale seemed less intimidating than he once had. His suit looked a little big on him, and age had dulled some of the chiseled edges of his face — the exhaustion and stress of being an acting general in the fatuous talent wars.

When they started to walk again, Marshall hung back for a second, letting Dick get ahead about a half step, then struck the agent as hard as he could in the lower back, the blow landing deep and flush and driving Dick to the wet sand.

"*Ughnnnn,*" the agent exclaimed, doubling over on his knees. Then he groaned again, a second wave of pain coming on. "Kidney shot . . . Jesus, fuck." He took a short breath. "Where'd you learn that one?"

"The movies," Marshall said.

"Funny." Dick tried to stand up and then exhaled in defeat. Through a tight grimace he said, "You want to tell me what's going on here, already? That way I can explain how wrong you are and get up and kick your spindly little ass?"

"Someone tried to kill Colt the other day, and now suddenly he's not feeling very good. I thought you could tell me about it."

"Colt's sick?" Despite the lingering pain, Dick managed to look up. "What do you mean? What's wrong with him? Why hasn't he called me?"

"*Called you?*" Marshall laughed angrily. "Why the hell would he call *you?*" He took out the gun he'd been given and pointed it at Dick's chest. The act sickened him — the weapon shook wildly in his hand — but he was fully prepared to use it. He would cut Dick Vale down like a dog if he had to.

"Whoa, *easy,* cowboy," the agent said, flashing the confident, Lancasterish glint. The old actor didn't believe the man with the gun.

Marshall raised the Kraecher now and pointed it at the agent's head. "Colt is sick. It's very serious. Nobody knows what it is or what's going on. I figured I'd come talk to the person who has the most to gain if, say, he were to die."

"*Die?* Are you kidding me?" Dick seemed genuinely startled, deeply concerned. "Are you *high?* Don't you know what's going on?" The gun was wavering close to Dick's head now, and he grimaced at its proximity. "Marshall, will you *please* point that fucking thing somewhere else? You don't know shit about what's happening. You've been kept in the dark."

"You're telling me you don't clean up around here if Colt goes, you greedy bastard?" Marshall came closer, the gun just inches now from the agent's forehead. Again he laughed. "And this from the guy who throws a party over at his agency when an actress dies."

"Party?" Dick looked past the gun muzzle at Marshall now with a sad, patronizing gaze. "Okay, first of all," the agent said, "you're a cocksucker for accusing me of celebrating Carmela's death. Who told you that? That's demented, Marshall. Your mind's completely blown from that powder, my friend. You need help." Suddenly, without invitation, Dick hauled his body up off the ground, knocking sand from the shins of his pant legs, while Marshall backed up a step, keeping the gun pointed. "Second of all," Dick continued, standing straight now, "you've got your facts all fucked up. Colt's left you out of the loop, though I'm not sure why. Have you guys been talking lately? Has there been a rift?"

Gun still shaking, Marshall tried to decide whether Dick was simply playing to the rumors, setting up distractions till he could wriggle free, or whether there was some void in the facts as the screenwriter knew them.

"Marshall, put the gun down and talk to me," Dick implored.

"You need to hear what's going on. You're going to feel fool-ish when I'm through with you, you dumb bastard. Now put it *down*."

Marshall fingered the trigger for a moment and then slowly lowered the gun to his side. Something told him he needed to take a step back, that he'd lost his bearings. He decided to engage Dick until he felt lucid again.

"We haven't been as close lately, not for a few months," Marshall volunteered. "Then I was in Vancouver. Soon as I got back, all this other crap started going down."

Dick was nodding before he could finish. "You see? You don't know shit. I thought Colt might have told you, but obviously he didn't."

"What is it?" Marshall said anxiously. "*Will you fucking tell me, already?*"

"My friend, this whole town's about to be turned upside down." Dick looked around again, still concerned about the pri-vacy of the desolate beach. "Now, I'll tell you everything, but you have to put that little peashooter away, Marshall. My bodyguard's gonna check on me, and if he sees you holding that thing he'll take you out from a hundred yards flat."

Turning warily now to peer through the mist, Marshall tucked the gun in his belt.

"Thank you," Dick said with relief. "Now, are you ready for this? Take a deep breath, my friend: Carmela Montoya was com-ing to Talent United." He paused again, waiting for a reaction. "Did you get that, Marshall? Did you hear me? There was no damned party when she died, okay? We were devastated by her death over at TU. We were *inconsolable*. Yes, probably for selfish reasons, but we loved her, too, in the way everybody did. And we were excited about the future. Anyway, the point is, she was going to defect. And Colt was going to follow."

This last remark seemed to stagger Marshall, to sap him of what little resolve he had left. He lowered himself to the sand, sitting back on his heels and looking out at the surf.

"Is that true?" he asked, his voice numb.

"Marshall, I have signed letters of intent from both actors sitting in my office. We can go there right now if you want. Or call Colt yourself, I don't care. Just believe it—he's coming over. We've been secretly flirting with each other for about six months now, and he finally pulled the trigger."

"How? How did you get him to do it?"

"The MIBs," Dick said. "What else? He hates them. So did Carmela. In fact it was Carmela who decided to leave NetTalent first, and I think she helped sell the idea to Colt. He'd been wavering, as usual. He's a loyal guy. He and Dre go way back— obviously you know this—and it made the decision that much harder for him. Carmela, on the other hand, just hated Dre. Always had. She finally convinced Colt that the MIBs were killing their careers."

Marshall was still staring off into the surf, and so Dick, in a gesture of truce, sat down on the beach next to him.

"You're wondering why he didn't tell you," the agent said, digging his buttocks into the sand. "I'm surprised myself; I took it for granted this morning that you knew. I can tell you this much, though: Colt was nervous as hell about Dre finding out. His contract with NetTalent runs through the summer, so he'd decided to finish that out, for old times' sake." He waited for Marshall to react to this, but there was nothing, the writer staring out at the ocean. "Now," Dick continued, "you want to tell me what's wrong with him? You can quit the histrionics. I talked to him by vidphone just a few days ago, so I know it's nothing too serious."

Marshall ignored the question, his mind still trying to wrap itself around Dick's bombshell. What little he was able to put together seemed to quickly dissolve in the surf.

"Dre doesn't know about any of this? About Carmela? Nothing?"

"No," Dick told him.

"You sure?"

"Yes," he said. "And you want to know how I know? Because whenever I steal somebody from Dre, I always get that nasty vidcall where he threatens my life at the top of his lungs, and then I tell him the whole thing's being recorded and will be turned over to the police in the morning. Both idle threats, incidentally." Dick smiled. "But let's just say if he knew anything about Carmela or Colt's defection, I would definitely have heard from him by now. We *all* would have."

Marshall nodded, suddenly shielding his eyes — there was a sharp glare cutting through the fog. He would need to get to one of the public sunscreen bays in the next few minutes before his face turned to cinders.

Dick's voice became rueful. "Damned thing was, Carmela was just a few days from telling Dre. Of course I was *dying* to hear about that. I made her promise to remember every detail — the words, the look on his face, everything. This was going to rock Dre to the fucking core, same way he'd rocked me once upon a time. But then what happens? Two nights later she wakes me up with a vidcall at four o'clock in the morning, crying hysterically. She was scared, she said. She felt sick and had a bad feeling about it. Poor girl."

Marshall's head slowly turned from the ocean to face Dick.

"The cancer?" he said.

"No," Dick said. "Well, yes, that was the unofficial word. I don't think they ever really did get a proper diagnosis. But apparently it was a very strange, very gruesome illness. Went through her like lightning."

Marshall was staring at Dick now, trembling in the sand. He said something but the words crumbled in his throat.

Finally he managed to murmur, "What happened?"

"Nobody knows," Dick answered. "I never saw her again after that. There were rumors galore, of course. Gruesome stuff about new AIDS strains and skin-eating diseases, that sort of thing. Jim Quartus kept it all very hush-hush, which is exactly what a husband should do, of course. But then you saw the closed casket yourself, so that tells you right there—"

Marshall had suddenly spun away, inadvertently kicking sand into Dick's face. Then he screamed something as he rose to his feet but was drowned out by the crash of a toppling wave.

"What is it?" Dick asked.

"It's the same thing," Marshall said, his eyes wide now and burning with alarm. "Colt. He's got it. It's the *same thing*."

"You mean the sickness?"

"Yes . . . *yes!*"

"Marshall?" Dick stood to grab the writer by his jacket. "Where is Colt now?"

"The hospital," came the absent reply, Marshall already lost in his thoughts. He broke away now from Dick and held his head with both hands, as if to try and keep all this information from spilling out before he could make sense of it. "It's his face. He looked older suddenly—it was fucking weird. And then he was flipped out by all this Mr. Black stuff recently. It's like he knew what was going on before it even happened . . ." Marshall paced again and suddenly stopped, turning to face the agent. "Dick, how did Carmela look on the vidphone that last time? When she called you to say she was sick? How did she look?"

Dick shrugged, trying to remember. "Tired, I guess. I don't know. Run down." He could see the writer already nodding in confirmation. "She didn't look at the camera much. I think she was embarrassed."

Seeing something over the agent's shoulder in the distance, Marshall went for his gun—then pulled back at the last second. It was Dick's bodyguard, he understood now, looking ghostly in the thinning mist. Marshall wondered why he was carrying a rifle big enough to take down an elephant, and then he remembered the lions.

"So what happens now? What do we do?" Dick wanted to know, bodyguard still looming.

Marshall still seemed a little dazed. "I'm not sure," he replied. "I'll call the hospital, I guess. I've got to tell them about Carmela."

"Cedars?"

"Yeah."

"He's really in bad shape? You're not exaggerating?"

Marshall's eyes turned slowly up toward the agent.

Dick nodded, looking away. After a long pause, he said, "You should probably talk to Jim Quartus, don't you think?"

Quartus, as he was more simply known, was the widower of Carmela Montoya. He had also been a classmate of Marshall's at Stanford, so they knew each other a bit. The latest reports were that he had gone into total seclusion since the death of his wife.

"You think he'd speak to me?" Marshall asked. "I hear he's pretty out of it."

"If he hears what you have to say about Colt, you bet your ass he would." The bodyguard must have noticed the gun in Marshall's belt and had begun to wander closer; Dick waved him off brusquely. "Maybe you could ask him about some of this *Black Book* stuff. See if there's any connection with Carmela and Colt."

Marshall held up both hands searchingly; his confusion seemed to be doubling itself every few minutes.

"You mean you don't know this, either?" Dick rolled his eyes. "Man, what do they keep you in, some kind of bubble over there at NetTalent?"

"Spit it out, Dick. There's no time."

"Word around town," the agent told him, "says Quartus is Mr. Black."

ELEVEN

To my mind, this will all end in terror. The future conflicts won't be East versus West, Jew versus Arab, or even jihad versus the infidel. It will be the people versus corporate media and advertising. Eventually, when the moon glows "Michelin" and the word "Trident" is etched onto our teeth in exchange for dental insurance and the Senate is the one hundred CEOs of the nation's top corporations, there will be a breakdown. Drunk, stoned on Bliss, or numbed from visual imagery, there will still be a rebellion and it will begin with terror. The irony is that you will see westerners employ jihadist stratagems, emulating the precise tactics we have feared and abhorred for so long: suicide bombers in the ad agencies, arson on the MIBs, planes flown into movie studios and television stations . . .

If it was September 11, 2001, that inaugurated the national debate over issues of privacy, immigration, and security, then it was July 12, 2010 (or the Day of Terror, as history had titled it), that basically ended the discussion forever. On this day, at approximately

12:02 P.M., EST, there were separate terrorist incidents in each
of the nation's fifty states save two—a cache of explosives that
failed to detonate along the pipelines of northern Alaska, and
a dirty-bomber near the levees of New Orleans with second
thoughts. The damage varied from city to city, arranged, it
seemed, in proportion to the state's size and profile. St. Louis,
for example, had its beloved Gateway Arch demolished by a
handheld SAM launcher, while Portland, Maine, lost a modest
Denny's to arson.

There were changes launched in its wake, in the country's
character and obsessions. A writer prone to hyperbole described it
as no less than "the end of ambiguity in America" and "the death
of complex thinking." But the point was made: an extreme moral
simplicity had taken hold.

It was into this void that Colt Reston had slid, headfirst, to
become the biggest star in the history of cinema.

After the Day of Terror, the country was looking for an el-
emental hero to fulfill its fantasies, someone quintessentially
American, guileless, utterly without irony. Someone to shut up
and shoot. After *Chula Vista* broke Colt, Dre moved him into less
complicated roles, shoot-'em-ups and bloody revenge dramas,
going where the big dollars roamed. The western had come back
into vogue (the American Indian providing the thinly disguised
stand-ins for terrorists), and Colt, with his carved-stone profile,
his honeyed Georgia accent, and, not least of all, his preposter-
ously evocative name, took the roles with all the ease of the mythic
Hollywood cowboys. Then western Europe's struggle with terrorists began to escalate, as it did in Indonesia, then the Far East and
northern Africa, until the hunger for Colt Reston's style of brutal
justice became a worldwide hankering, a universal yen. It was a

face blandly beautiful enough to know no borders, a face in which everyone, from no matter what corner of the globe, could find a launching point for their own fantasies and frustrations.

Geographically, however, things were closing down. The entire perimeter of the United States was sealed off, turning international travel into a nightmare and essentially putting an end to immigration. Soon American citizens found themselves at the mercy of the new HSCs, or Home Security Checkpoints — random security stops that could pop up anywhere, at any moment. These agents had been handed nearly unlimited powers, and encounters at an HSC stop were notoriously unpleasant. Travelers were subject to passport inspections, on-the-spot body searches, and ad hoc interrogations. Hit a checkpoint looking "suspicious," and you might have your car's interior slashed to ribbons during a search; antagonize an agent, and you might find a gloved finger and flashlight beam in your rectum.

Marshall knew the HSCs well. He had what he thought was an uncanny knack for running into them, an almost moth-to-flame sort of attraction, and he seemed to have hit another one now as he pulled his car toward the end of the Zuma Beach parking lot.

It was set up near the exit: the dark unmarked car, the scattering of traffic cones, and the large HSC banner that struck fear into the heart of the common commuter. The timing couldn't be worse. Marshall had never had a problem with drugs in his car (the agents seemed either uninterested or oblivious), but Rip's gun, which was still stuffed in his belt, could easily qualify as a terrorist weapon: unregistered, illegal, and invisible to security detectors — *precisely* the kind of thing they'd be looking for. Marshall actually thought about stepping on the gas and making a run for it, but he knew this would be akin to suicide. Checkpoint dodgers could be shot on sight. He'd get no more than a few miles before an HSC copter came swooping out of the sky to blow him to bits.

Marshall drove toward them slowly across the empty parking lot. He slapped his exhausted face, trying to shock himself awake, then wet his dry, hungry lips, understanding that the moment called for nothing less than his top-of-the-line, premium bullshit.

"How ya doin', guys?" he said, pulling up along the cones. He lowered the window halfway, showing a friendly, ex-ballplayer grin. "Listen, can you cut me some slack this morning? I've got a meeting in exactly twenty-five minutes at one of the big studios. Career-in-the-balance kind of thing, if you know what I mean." His foot was still off the brake, the car rolling infinitesimally. "I'd really appreciate—"

"Stop the vehicle and get out," announced a gloomy voice. There were two men, each wearing dark glasses and Yamori suits. The expensive clothes threw Marshall a bit; he'd never seen this before with the HSC. Just his luck, he thought, to have landed some agency higher-ups.

Then one of them stepped in front of the car, forcing Marshall to brake.

"Guys, please. I realize how important this sort of work is, believe me. I'm a big fan. But sometimes there are situations that—"

"Step *out* of the vehicle, sir," repeated the man by the window. "I'm not going to ask you again."

Marshall saw that the man had already drawn his gun, the metal glinting in the morning haze.

"Little quick on the hardware, don't you think?" he remarked. As soon as Marshall was out of the hybrid, the agent grabbed him hard by the back of his neck and slammed him up against the HSC's car, jabbing a gun into his back.

When Marshall looked behind him now, the second man was already rifling around inside the hybrid. Marshall looked away, feeling sick as the man began his search. They hadn't patted him down yet, but it hardly mattered: he'd forgotten the gun's leather holster in the glove compartment. They would find it in a matter of seconds.

"Got something here . . . ," the man said from inside the car.

Marshall spit over the front of the car, too furious to look. He thought about Rip's warning, seeing now how stupid it was to be packing an illegal gun he knew neither how to fire nor how to conceal. He was going to need one of Colt's bloodhound lawyers for this one, he told himself. Meanwhile the time to help his friend was rapidly slipping away.

Marshall was made to turn around, and then the man who had searched his car approached him. "Mr. Reed, do you recognize this?"

How does he know my name? Marshall wondered. They hadn't even asked him for ID.

He was just getting ready for the pat-down and the flat denial—*Never seen this before in my life*—when he looked up and saw what they had taken from his car: a small wedge of clay, a handful of wiring, and an old-fashioned cell phone.

Stunned, Marshall leaned back against the car, trying to look relaxed. He watched the men watching him, with their fifteen-thousand-dollar suits and the gun they had drawn too quickly, their obviously planted evidence and, on second look, unconvincing checkpoint sign behind them in the parking lot. This was not an HSC stop at all, Marshall understood now. And as the screenwriter finished the scene in his mind—the mock arrest, the savage beating, the long car ride to the secluded clearing—he slowly reached inside his jacket and began fingering the handle of the Kraecher.

"Face the car and put your hands behind your head," said the first man.

Forgoing caution or consequence—and knowing a second's delay might cost him both his own life and Colt's—Marshall pulled the gun from his hip and shot the man closest to him through the shoulder. The force of the blast spun the agent into his colleague, knocking the two of them to the pavement, where they collapsed in a heap of arms and legs.

The man on the bottom wriggled desperately to get the injured man off him and also to reach for his gun, which had fallen just beyond his grasp. The sight of this—a man reaching greedily for a weapon he intended to use without remorse— infuriated and then emboldened Marshall, and he stepped forward and began firing in a quick succession of bursts, surprising himself with his own ferocity. He fired at the man at point-blank range, missing—amazingly—and allowing the man to break free from his wounded friend and run like holy hell, diving over the heap of cement pylons near the exit and escaping across the highway.

Marshall looked back now at the wounded agent. The man had not been shot through the shoulder, as Marshall had first supposed, but slightly lower, near the top of his abdomen, a large radius of blood now sopping his shirt. His legs cycled slowly underneath him, as if he were riding an imaginary bicycle he thought would carry him away from the agony.

Marshall went over and reached into the bleeding man's

jacket, removing the gun he knew would be there and tossing it into the bushes that lined the exit.

He took a moment to scan the parking lot to see if anyone else was around—it was still empty—and tried to gather himself, tried to understand what was next. He knew he should probably be terrorizing the wounded agent right now, asking who had sent him, going through his pockets for some identification—but he just couldn't. Marshall was spent from the unexpected bloodshed, sickened by it, and now all the violence he had ever been asked to polish or stylize or "amp" came flooding back at him in the form of rage at himself and his own bottomless perversity.

Shot a man, he thought in amazement, and then, remembering Colt's wretched face, picked Rip's gun up off the ground and tucked it back in his belt.

Lindsay Williams sat lounging on a chaise by the apartment complex pool (drained, cleaned, and refilled since the lion incident, though some residents still swore to a feline scent). She'd spent the better part of an hour sipping sangria from an opaque plastic cup and trying to dislodge the Bliss in her nose, some granules of which had adhered themselves against the insides of her nostrils. Luckily the lion incident had turned people off, and the pool area was empty as Lindsay sniffled and sneezed, rubbing the edges of her nose raw like some pathetic Panoramic junior executive. She thought she should probably dive in and let the water wash them free but then decided against it. This shit was beyond expensive. Why waste it? She'd been thoroughly enjoying the half gram that Marshall had left behind at her apartment last night, and there was no telling when she would get her hands on some again.

The situation with Dre was beginning to worry her, she admitted. Just as his obsession with Mr. Black had begun to reveal itself, his excitement about her career seemed to have dissipated. What if it had all been a ruse to get his hands on a few pictures? She was inclined to think a black man wouldn't do that to her, on unspoken principle, but then Dre was so damned Wonder bread, with his light tweeds (weren't they illegal in L.A.?) and contrived Ivy League diction, that it seemed a hopeless thing to rely on.

And then, lastly: If she was as in demand as Dre McDonald had suggested, why hadn't she heard from Talent United or at least one of the second-tier agencies? Was everyone but Dre blind to the genius of Lindsay Williams?

She headed back up to the apartment, thinking she could use a refill on the sangria and whatever was left of the Bliss. A little more might free the passageways, help her think more clearly.

In the kitchen she poured the homemade sangria from the fridge and got down to business. She spread out the last of the gray powder on a mirrored serving tray and rolled up a canceled check. Within seconds she was already breathing in the first line, and this, she realized, was at least part of the drug's appeal: less than twenty-four hours, and already you were a pro.

Leaning down for the second hit, she jerked upright with the convulsion of an electric shock and let forth an earsplitting shriek.

There was a hand on her shoulder.

Lindsay immediately got to her feet, kicking the chair out from behind her and backing herself up against the kitchen cabinets. There she grabbed a steak knife from the sink and held it out, the blade quavering in her two hands.

The man she knew as Mr. Black said, calmly, "Whoa, love, take it easy."

He was wearing his khaki field jacket, which must have been stifling in the heat, and had his right hand in his pocket. Lindsay could see the outline of what looked clearly to be a gun against the fabric.

"Why don't you put that down, Lindsay, so we can talk. Otherwise things could get nasty."

"How did you get in here?" she demanded in a tremulous voice, the knife still quavering. "*How the fuck did you get in here?*"

"Now, what could that possibly matter?" he asked. "Come on, we have important things to discuss."

"Like what?"

"Like your sudden career turn as a photojournalist."

Bowed by this, Lindsay lowered the knife; it was exactly the sort of comment she had been dreading. She glanced at Mr. Black and then past him with a look of intense fright.

"It was stupid," she said, her chin bunching as if she might cry.

"Agreed," said Mr. Black.

"How did you find out?"

"I *told* you I would."

"Yes, but how?" Lindsay asked. "At least tell me that. Who snitched?"

Mr. Black leaned his large, balding pate against the doorjamb, his thick lips blubbering out a sigh. It was not a sound of fatigue, Lindsay observed, so much as a moral weariness. As if the world's cheap machinations left him melancholy.

He was one pretentious little bastard, Lindsay reminded herself, and she was almost more angry than scared that he was going to get to kill her now.

"I didn't give Dre anything he could use. You have to know that."

He nodded, head still heavy against the wall. "He speculates there were more photos. That's why I thought I'd drop in and take a peek. And, of course, to discuss this terrible decision you've made." He stood up straighter and exaggerated the bulge in his jacket. "Now put down your little steak knife and show me the rest."

Lindsay set the weapon in the sink, feeling his eyes on her in her bathing suit as she padded past him to the office. She was forced now to consider the possibility of rape, even though he didn't seem like the type (if there even was such a thing). He really was a jowly, piggy-looking fellow, she thought, and decided then that if he tried to touch her, she would die fighting. He could kill her, but he would not fuck her.

Lindsay got the key from the novel and opened the drawer. When she handed him the pictures, he perused them quickly, almost dispassionately, glancing at her after each one. Then he folded them into his pocket, quickly looking through the drawer to make sure there was nothing else. When he asked her for the pin camera she'd used, Lindsay handed it over without a word.

After this he told her to go take a seat in the living room.

He let her wrap a sarong around her waist, and they sat near each other: Lindsay on the couch, Mr. Black in a leather club chair. He kept his hand in his jacket pocket as they talked.

"Well, I can't tell you how disappointed I am about all this," he told her. "I was really shaken by it. I can't believe how wrong I was about you."

Lindsay tried to think of something reassuring to say, something that would express remorse, maybe even garner sympathy, but seemed at a loss. Even without the knife, she realized her hands were still shaking wildly.

"Then I come here and look around this apartment," he continued, "and I see what I'm dealing with."

"What does that mean?" Lindsay said, lifting up her eyes.

"I guess this is how people live now, isn't it?" he continued, eyes scanning the room. "In these dark little urban cells with pumped-in air and big plasmas to plug into when you come home and nobody's there to talk to."

Her eyes cut to him. "I live alone, so what? I work too hard to have a boyfriend . . . Fuck you, anyway." He was not going to kill her *and* humiliate her, Lindsay thought. "I'll bet you're a real hit with the ladies," she added.

Lindsay watched his pudgy cheeks break out in a small smile.

"Look, I'm sorry I took those pictures, okay?" she said. "I wish I never had. It was a shitty thing to do. I don't feel very good about it."

Mr. Black was quiet, eerily calm.

"I did it to get a better job, simple as that," she continued, somewhat desperately now. "Dre was going to help me upgrade my life in exchange for these photos—or at least what I consider to be an upgrade," she qualified. "But I'm beginning to think he's welshed on me."

"But you welshed on him first, no?"

"That's right," she said, encouraged by the logic. "I suppose I did."

Lindsay watched him nod, and just when she thought the momentum had turned in her favor and she might be forgiven, there ensued a long, agonized silence where he stared intently at something in front of him, as if summoning courage to complete an unpleasant mission.

"So, what happens now?" she asked finally, unable to bear another moment. "Is this your prelude to killing me, the woman who dared to take your picture? Friendly little chat before the deed? If it is, I say skip it and let's get on with it already." Lindsay couldn't believe she had risked such provocation, but then she was too frightened to stop.

Mr. Black finally lifted his eyes from the carpet. Then he stood — his hand still in the bulging pocket — and walked around the couch till he was behind her. Lindsay felt her heart ramming against her chest as she fought back tears.

"Don't worry, love," he said, leaning down now to her ear. "I'm not going to hurt you. I like you too much. Have for a while now." Lindsay felt him kiss the top of her head and then watched him come around the couch toward the kitchen. She didn't dare move a muscle, even as she saw him take the tray of Bliss toward the sink and heard him rinse it down. "I don't know what it is about you," he called out to the living room. "I guess you must have the special magic."

"What does that mean?" she asked, wiping tears on her sleeve.

"Star quality, making me care when there's no reason to." He returned from the kitchen, walking past her to the foyer and stopping there. "You'll be fine, Lindsay, with or without this guy who's supposed to help you. Believe me." He took the hand from his pocket and pointed to his head. "I know about these things."

Lindsay stared at the hand, realizing now there was no gun and never had been.

"You fucking son of a bitch," she said.

He smiled again. Furious, she followed him to the front door.

"Who are you?" she demanded. "I mean in real life, beyond all this Mr. Black bullshit. *Who the hell are you?*"

"*Real life,*" he repeated. He stopped and took his hand from the doorknob, the words confounding and amusing him at the same time. "I like that," he said, grinning to himself. "*Real life. That's a good one.*" Then he was gone.

TWELVE

If someone's trying to kill me, Marshall thought, *it might be time for a change of transportation.*

He had stopped by Colt's Malibu house on the way back from Zuma, deciding to trade in his hybrid for one of the two hydrogen-powered Mercedes atrophying in the garage—the cars used a few times by the actor and then discarded like a pair of old socks. He sat on Colt's deck for a few minutes, looking out at the choppy blue Pacific, and considered the wisdom of calling the police. Bad idea, he'd concluded. Though the agents were most likely phony, he had fired a highly illegal weapon—even in self-defense, any such admission would result in jail time, not only for him, but probably for Rip as well. And on the off chance that these were *real* HSC agents, turning himself in would be akin to suicide. He would most likely not live long enough to stand trial.

But the question still nagged at him: If these weren't HSC agents, then who the hell *were* they? Who had sent them?

With no more time to waste, Marshall hit the highway. He was still shaken from this morning, emotionally battered, though physically he was feeling a little better. He was alert now, at least (the terrible adrenaline of violence giving him a second wind), and his spirits were lifted by the clear roads back to L.A. He called Rip at the hospital to find out what was happening.

"He's okay; he's resting," the bodyguard told him. At a stop-light, Marshall looked down to see Rip on the vid standing in the waiting room.

"You sure?"

"They just did a bunch of tests; the doctors are having a big powwow. There's no diagnosis yet."

"He's stable, though?"

"Seems to be. They let me see him a few minutes ago. Colt looked all right . . ." Rip reconsidered. "You know, the same."

"Listen, you have to do something for me," Marshall told him. "And you have to promise me you'll get it done no matter what."

"Of course. What is it?"

"You have to tell the doctors that Colt has the same disease Carmela Montoya died from. All right? She didn't die of lung cancer. That was bullshit."

There was no reply.

"Hello?"

"What is it, Marsh? What's it called?"

"I wish I knew," the writer explained, his frustration evident. "I'm not even sure if there is a name for it. The point is, they need to find out more about Carmela. They need to see if she was treated there at Cedars, and if not, where. They have to find her doctors, locate the medical records, figure out which treatments worked for her and which didn't. Tell them to do this right away, do you understand? Are you hearing me?"

"Yes, yes," Rip said.

Approaching the city proper, Marshall looked up. There were a number of MIBs flickering, struggling to stay alight, while two others were blacked out altogether.

"What I'm saying is that there's a pattern that might help the doctors," Marshall continued. "That's all I really know. Meanwhile I've had a crazy morning and I haven't slept yet and I'm gonna fucking pass out at the wheel pretty soon if I don't watch it."

"You'll have a chance for a nap soon enough," Rip told him.

"Why's that?"

"You're about to hit the mother of all L.A. traffic jams."

Marshall looked down the boulevard, though the streets remained unusually clear. "What're you talking about? I don't see anything."

There was a pause. "Somebody leaked it, Marsh."

"Oh, no."

"Yup."

"Oh, shit."

Rip walked to the window and held out the vidphone so Marshall could see the parking lot. It looked like a rock concert, thousands of people on their feet, some standing on top of their cars, yelling, waving their arms, trying to summon Colt's attention. Somehow they knew the special wing he was staying in, the very room, and were calling out for him to show himself. Some were holding up desperate signs, others weeping openly. Marshall could see along the edges of the vid that the police were being overrun by the amount of people trying to pile into the lot.

"You can't get here now, not even close," Rip explained. "Even if you walked the rest of the way, they wouldn't allow it. You need to give it a few hours at least."

"Few hours!" Marshall held up the vidphone as if he might dash it against the windshield, then brought it back to his ear. "Do we even know that Colt has a few hours?"

Now Rip panned to show Marshall a view of the hospital entrance, the cars backed up for miles, hordes of pedestrians swarming over the fences and makeshift barricades, National Guardsmen spilling from the backs of canopied transport vehicles, and, above it all, the endless rows of MIBs flickering uncertainly over the scene.

It seemed very clear to Marshall that the world had gone completely mad.

"Go home and rest, Marsh. There's nothing you can do here. I'll tell the doctors about Carmela."

"You gotta tell them, Rip."

"Hey, I'll *make* them listen if I have to. You know I will. Now go rest."

It was late afternoon by the time Marshall made it back to the Ming. He ordered a club sandwich and some coffee from room service, both of which he craved but hardly touched. Then he lay back on the bed for a power nap and almost immediately fell into a torpid, bottomless slumber during which he had a series of disturbing dreams.

He finally awoke at 6 A.M. It took him a few moments to realize that his vidphone was ringing, but despite the current circumstances of his life, he was too tired to care.

He fell back asleep and then woke ten minutes later to find it ringing again. This time he roused himself, his eyelids hauled open like sealed crypts. When he finally checked the message, he thought it was another dream, since the voice was the last he had ever expected to hear. The call was without video, the voice so hushed that Marshall had to maximize the volume on his phone to hear the words: "Jim Quartus here. Got your call. Terrible news about Colt. Look, come see me, would you? I'm at Redding Brothers. Visiting hours nine till eleven . . . And Marsh, no trail, okay? Nobody can know I'm here. Pretty fragile right now . . . Not much has changed, eh?"

THIRTEEN

Marshall drove toward the Santa Monica mountains in the blue morning light, thinking of the ongoing mystery known as Jim Quartus. At Stanford, Jim had been two years ahead of Marshall, and although their acquaintance there had always skirted on the edges of friendship, it had somehow never quite made it. Quartus had been small, bespectacled, and wiry, with a mind like a scabbard that he waved wantonly and with extreme arrogance. Marshall was a freshman when he first encountered him, in a course on comparative religions. On the first day of class (Marshall's first five minutes of college, no less) he watched as Quartus upstaged his professor by launching into an unsolicited monologue on depression and the prophets: Jesus, Moses, Mohammed, the Buddha, et al., were really just manic depressives, Quartus posited, their teachings the manifestation of a euphoric upswing, accompanied by the usual messianic visions.

"Is that right?" asked the professor, who then made the mistake of asking the formidable Quartus (rumored to be one of the fifty highest IQs in the nation), "Please, regale us, Mr. . . . ?"

"Jim," came the casual reply, followed by sniggers from those students who already knew him. He elaborated on the "obvious" symptoms: a youthful wanderlust, followed by the seeking out of solitude and oblivion; missing years (the downward cycle); bursts of incendiary anger; the said messianic complex; the renouncing of social and religious norms, not to mention apocalyptic visions, suicidal tendencies, romance with martyrdom, and so on. As flawed and fanciful a diatribe as it was, it was also so lively that everything the poor professor said afterward seemed stale by comparison, and soon nearly two-thirds of the students had dropped the course. Marshall, though, kept coming back, if only to see what this crazy contrarian would say next. He was soon disappointed: Quartus attended the next two classes looking disheveled and morose, his face a mask of gloom, and was silent except for a few under-breath guffaws designed to let the professor know his lecture had hit a false note. Then he disappeared entirely, with Marshall left wondering if he would ever run into him again.

Imagine his surprise when several months later he spied a lone figure in the bleachers at Sunken Diamond Field, inexplicably on hand for Stanford baseball's dreary February workouts. The man was in the stands every day that first week, keenly watching practice from the opening stretches to the final wind sprints, until there was some speculation that he might actually be a spy for the USC Trojans. Marshall, however, quickly relieved his team's paranoia: the hunched and haunted observer was definitely the man he remembered as Jim Quartus, threat to no one save prosaic university lecturers. By then Marshall had done a little asking around on campus and was not entirely surprised to hear that Quartus was a figure of some notoriety, his knowledge of depression and the messianic complex no less than firsthand. He was known for taking classes and never showing up, only to reappear during finals week to ace the course despite having heard only a single lecture; or, in those classes he did attend, for suddenly lashing out at unsuspecting students and professors for what he liked to call their "brutish inanity." With Jim there were grim silences that could last whole weeks, or days when he wouldn't shut up for the merest second, walking the campus muttering to himself, then suddenly ascending a lecture hall's steps to deliver a spontaneous soliloquy on entropy or the evils of pharmaceutical medicine, often referring to himself in the third person. "It is Jim Quartus's contention that . . ." Publicly, he loved the romance of refusing all mood medications, preferring to ride the highs for energy and inspiration and to mine the lows for what he called a "peek into the crypt," but in fact he suffered from TRD, or treatment-resistant depression, which no amount of drugs, shock treatment, or electrical stimulation of area 25 of his brain could salve.

His dream, of course, was to be the greatest writer of his generation.

For reasons unknown even to him, live baseball (never on the plasma) chased away the furies, and that spring had been a particularly bad one for Quartus. He was on hand for every Cardinals workout and home game, immersing himself in the pastoral relief of the ball field. And like every other Stanford baseball fan, he became a huge admirer of Marshall Reed's blend of power and surgical precision on the mound. Not long after, when Marshall began attending free viewings of American Films of the 1970s at night in the commons and found Quartus running the projector, they finally spoke, if coolly at first, each pretending to know nothing of the other. In fact, they soon discovered they had more in common than either could have imagined. They were both budding writers (like Colt, Quartus was confounded to discover that baseball was not Marshall's first love) with a weakness for film. Their conversations continued over the next few months, in the bars and coffee chains and on the dusty secondhand couches of off-campus apartments. Soon Quartus began to acknowledge that Marshall Reed was not just an extraordinary athlete but a formidable mind to be reckoned with. Late one night, when the pitcher admitted to a secret ambivalence about visual media — specifically the prevalence of screens and moving images — a rare light seemed to bloom on the doleful countenance of Jim Quartus.

"You should meet some of my friends," he'd said.

Secretly, Quartus had fallen in with an antimedia cabal. This was a group of professors, students, and local intellectuals who gathered at various off-campus locations, exchanging ideas about corporate media, advertising, and the growing ubiquity of the transmitted image. Marshall attended three or four meetings, sometimes finding the rhetoric inspired, other times narrow and didactic. There was a splinter group within the ranks, an extreme and very vocal faction who saw themselves as 1960s-style radicals, millennial Weathermen. They took themselves awfully seriously, Marshall had thought, speaking in broad, ideological terms about "image fascism" and the "advertising plutocracy" and proclaiming a need for violent mischief in the name of liberation. Back then the group was getting its first reports about something called the moving image billboards, further stoking the flames of paranoia. When a scheme was presented for planting a bomb at the then nascent Mannix Corporation in Simi Valley ("something small, a wake-up call") and Quartus did nothing to denounce it, Marshall began to lose faith not only in the group but in Quartus himself. He immediately stopped going to meetings, and not coincidentally, their friendship fizzled. There were still the occasional stop-and-chats around campus, a few brief waves from the stands the following spring at Sunken Diamond Field. But the camaraderie had clearly died.

By the next fall they had both left the university. Stanford's certified genius never did graduate, though he still elicited a number of offers from the multinationals, all of which he rejected. Meanwhile its reluctant pitching hero accepted a $1.25 million signing bonus from the Los Angeles Angels and was designated for the single-A affiliate in Palm Springs. Years passed, the MIBs were slow in developing, a bomb never did appear in an advertising firm (the antimediaists likely trumped by the Day of Terror, a thunder with which they could never compete), and later, when Marshall was knocking on the door of Hollywood as a scriptwriter, he barely batted an eye to learn that Jim Quartus was currently the hottest gun in town. Naturally, Quartus would have an aptitude for anything he put his mind to, and Marshall remembered how passionate his friend had been during those long discussions about the architecture of scriptwriting. Quartus's quixotic dream back at Stanford had been to rid the paradigm from the screenwriter's palate, demolish it once and for all, and in Hollywood it seemed he'd almost pulled it off. Marshall read somewhere that Panoramic had bought both of Quartus's first two screenplays. The downside was that they were both regarded as unfilmable (particularly his three-hundred-page script for *Cortés and Montezuma,* a screenplay so phantasmagoric most producers couldn't follow it, while the few that could estimated its budget at around five hundred million). Panoramic, it turned out, just liked owning the scripts, not simply for the cachet, but also to prevent a rival studio from finding a way to actually *produce* these movies—which, if done correctly, they feared just might turn out to be legendary hits.

Battered by the experience, Quartus decided to leave the business entirely, ending up teaching a course in existential cinema at UCLA. There he was fired after just one semester for allowing students to roll dice for grades to demonstrate the arbitrariness of all things.

Eventually Quartus returned to Hollywood to write one last script, a rock opera called *The Bonzai Kittens,* only to have it rejected by every studio in town. Then he met Carmela Montoya, the buoyant, energetic actress who somehow fell in love with his irascible mind and suffered valiantly through his terrible mood swings. By now Marshall had struck big with *Chula Vista,* and though he and Quartus often found themselves in the same room together, they mostly avoided each other. It was not hostility that kept them apart, so much as a shared embarrassment. Despite the glow their work emitted in certain circles, they were each, in certain respects, kept men—attached to big stars who protected them financially. The great dream they had shared at Stanford, the need to challenge the encroaching world of acquisitive images, had been shrouded by their own weaknesses and desires.

And so now this, Marshall thought, driving through the empty canyons and winding roads of the Santa Monica Mountains, past the tasteful million-dollar bungalows, and up near the rapidly shrinking nature conservancy. The strangeness of his long trajectory with Quartus did not escape him, and like an ironic punctuation to their past, Marshall drove past his first-ever advert home—only to quickly turn back for a closer look. It was a rather large house for these hills, with eight or ten bedrooms, its size no doubt made affordable by sponsorship. He pulled the car to the base of the

driveway and saw that the roof's seven solar panels spelled out
S I L K S O Y, and that there were no less than four eight-by-five
MIBs along the front facade (though oddly black at the moment).
He found himself summoning a memory from those antimedia
meetings years ago, when it was Quartus himself who had pro-
posed the possibility of such domestic prostitution. The idea was
denounced, if Marshall remembered correctly, snickered at, the
concept too vulgar and outrageous even for that jaded set.

Marshall tried Rip on the vidphone, but there was no answer. Then he got back on the road, twice missing the turnoff for
the retreat, which was unassuming to a fault. Address in hand, he
circled around once again, cursing furiously, straining to read the
faded numbers on the mailboxes set back from the road. Eventually he found the small, hand-painted sign that read *Redding
Broth,* the final letters shrouded in the thick flora that somehow
still thrived in the hills.

He turned the car down the path, driving slowly along the
dirt track before encountering another hand-painted sign in-
structing him to stop. There was a gravel clearing off to Marshall's
left, and it was here that another sign commanded him to park
his vehicle and rid himself of "all pods, money, weapons, credit
cards, and sound or anxiety-making devices of any kind." He did
this, not unhappily, heading on foot down a path of blooming
flannelbush and St. Catherine's lace. Soon there were more hand-
painted signs, visitors now warned to "refrain from the humming
of musical lyrics, classical themes, or advertising jingles beyond
this point" and, farther on, against "discussion of media of any
sort with residents."

It was a conspicuous silence he encountered as he walked the
path, though a brighter, less sterile brand than at the Ming. The

breeze was soft, gently rustling the cypresses. And there was the trill of birds, whom Marshall gently shushed.

"Hey, keep it down, fellas. You oughtta know better."

Finally he approached a one-man gatehouse, where he was frisked by a quiet, saggy-faced old gentleman who plied his task with gentle good cheer. Marshall appeared clean except for his watch, which was removed and tucked into a numbered nook for pickup on his way out. Following another short walk, he saw a clearing beyond the foliage and came upon what looked like a slightly run-down summer camp. There didn't seem much to the place: thirty or so small wooden cabins spread out among the trees, an open-air dining area with a large cement barbecue, a seldom-used volleyball pit, and a squat, roofed building with latched doors that was presumably an outhouse. A man and a woman seemed to be washing pots in a large sink near the barbecue, but otherwise the retreat was empty.

He didn't know where to go next when someone startled him from behind.

"Welcome to Camp Silencio," quipped a low voice. "You just missed breakfast."

Marshall turned to face Jim Quartus. They stood silent for a moment, smiling awkwardly at each other. Quartus was wearing Birkenstocks, khaki shorts, and a battered white T-shirt that bulged at the abdomen, from under which peeked a thick slab of flesh; apparently media fasts did not extend to the kitchen, Marshall observed. Unfortunately the laid-back clothes did not speak to a more relaxed spirit, since there was the specter of doom on Quartus's face. Marshall knew that look all too well, Quartus's countenance a bellwether for his state of mind, the black half-moons under the eyes and pallor always prefacing a new period of darkness.

"How did you get my message?" Marshall finally asked, wondering if his voice was low enough. Not until he'd seen the signs on the path did it occur to him how difficult it would have been to contact anyone here.

Quartus leaned closer. "I cheated," he said matter-of-factly. "My brother-in-law's been checking messages for me. It's a disgusting habit, but it's been tough lately and . . . well, there you have it. When he told me what was going on, of course I knew I had to contact you."

"How?" Marshall whispered.

"I did what we do here. Borrowed a phone and went up on the Fringe."

Marshall shrugged as Quartus pointed toward a canyon peak in the distance above the high trees.

"It's where you go if you backslide," he explained. "If you just have to make a call, let's say, or hum a song to keep yourself sane. The staff doesn't mind; they don't expect miracles right away. In fact"—his eyes flashed toward a man wearing a staff T-shirt near the volleyball court, obviously eavesdropping—"why don't we go there now?"

They passed through the campgrounds and followed a narrow path along the side of the canyon, walking single file up the sharply pitched slope. During the vigorous jaunt, Quartus deflected all references to Carmela's sickness, quietly infuriating Marshall, who had been hoping for quick results. Instead, his old friend wanted to talk about Redding Brothers, elaborating on his stay here and how much he loved the camp. Quartus had had a nervous breakdown, he'd admitted, "afterward"—his one oblique reference to his wife's death. He decided he would never heal "out there," an apparent reference to the city on the other side of the canyon. His consciousness was polluted from all the years of being in Hollywood, he'd said, the studios, premieres, editing rooms, billboards, fake teeth, fake tits, and so on. He needed a long detox just to be able to feel what had happened to him. He had not cried yet over Carmela, he admitted.

The camp was costing him twenty thousand dollars a week (the new price of solitude, he opined), and so residents came mostly from the media's elite: movie execs, high-paid film editors, actors, television producers, and the occasional scriptwriter—though there was always the token Net fiend or video-game junkie from an insanely wealthy family. Some came for a weekend or even a single night, others for months. Days were spent with light, soothing chores (Quartus was a gardener) and in various meditation groups, the exercises intended to rid the clutter that had unconsciously polluted the brain: ad jingles, song melodies, movie dialogue, pornographic images, holy prayers, and so on—the insistent, infinite loop of the anxious mind. You had no idea of the poisons that were living in there, Quartus declared, or how hard they were to get rid of. "Think of consciousness as the human liver, and we're all alcoholics," he announced, his pace slower now as they hit a steeper incline. He explained how new residents often began weeping within minutes of arriving at camp, a few of these going AWOL after just a couple of hours. They craved their noise, their images. It was the existential dread of the mind left to itself, asserted Quartus, a state of perception for which people were no longer equipped.

"Fascinating," Marshall said. "Now you want to cut the shit and tell me what's happening to Colt?"

Quartus fell suddenly mute, and now Marshall tried to calculate how huge a blunder he had just committed. Even in the best of circumstances, this was a man whom you handled delicately; hurt his feelings, and Quartus's silences could go on indefinitely. Marshall tried to keep his mouth shut as they continued on, not daring to breach the silence, until he thought he heard a rustling behind them in the brush.

"Any lions around here?" Marshall asked then. He'd just realized how incredibly vulnerable they were up here in the mountains.

"Lions—are you kidding?" Quartus responded. He seemed unexpectedly roused. "Up here they'd have to hunt. They're too lazy for that now. Not with all the free food down there in the city." The absurdity of this fact clearly amused him, and Marshall was relieved to see his old friend smile.

They arrived at the crest hunched and breathless from the steep climb. From Marshall's exhausted crouch, the Fringe appeared to him to be nothing more than a small clearing, albeit with a striking view of the canyon behind them. Straightening as he caught his breath, however, he noticed that everything westward—the direction that should have given them an Olympian view of Los Angeles—was blocked by a long canvas wall. This great barrier was no less than forty feet high and thoroughly opaque, stretched among an endless row of metal posts. There was nothing visible beyond it, the whole thing designed to keep one's focus on the tranquil canyon and nature conservancy that it bordered. It was as if the city of Los Angeles didn't exist.

"Come look at this," Quartus commanded. He walked Marshall along the wall for a few hundred feet and then stopped as they reached a small hole, maybe five inches in diameter, cut through the canvas. "This is an important spot for camp members, Marshall. You wouldn't believe how important." Quartus gestured for him to take a look inside, and so Marshall crouched and peered in, seeing in the homemade kinescope the boundless sprawl of L.A.: the geometric cubes and cylinders, rows of matchbox houses, tall palms, and smoky haze, the landscape mottled with gleaming MIBs all the way down to the ocean. There was a billboard not a quarter of a mile from them, in fact, at the base of the mountains, angled just enough to be visible to members of the camp.

"The staff knows about the hole, of course, but they don't bother with it," Quartus continued. "They know a quick peek can sometimes get us through a bad spot. The residents need a glimpse of the billboards, Marshall; they crave it. A few moments with those beautiful, blazing images and they feel better. Then they go back down the mountain and try to clear the crap they just saw from their head."

"Jim, didn't you hear my phone message?" Marshall had pulled away from the hole now and was staring into Quartus's shifting eyes, trying to get his friend to notice his desperation. "Colt is *dying*. Now you have to tell me about Carmela, do you understand? I know it's painful, but you have to tell me about it *now*. I didn't come here for a nature hike or your Luddite obsessions. I want to know how I can make Colt better before I lose him."

"He's already gone," Quartus said flatly. He turned away then and marched his portly frame to the center of the clearing. There was an old tree trunk there, bone white from the sun, and he sat down on it like a bench.

Marshall followed him but did not sit. "Is that true?" he asked.

Quartus nodded without looking up. Soon he began pulling stones from the soil and throwing them at an agave bush in the distance. "Once it hits, you've got about ten days, two weeks at the most. How long since you first noticed it?"

"I don't know . . ." Stunned by Quartus's edict, Marshall struggled to remember. "I was away. Colt noticed it first."

"Of course he did. How long ago?"

"I told you, I'm not sure."

"*Estimate,* for chrissakes. This is not an exact science here."

"Two weeks?"

Quartus threw another stone. "Well, there you go," he said with a shrug.

There was a glibness to the gesture which suddenly enraged Marshall, and he reached down and grabbed Quartus's throwing hand. "How do you know this?" he demanded, shaking his friend violently. "Goddammit, maybe if you *talked* to me, maybe if you told me something about what *happened,* we could find a way to help—"

"Because I saw it, that's why!" Quartus suddenly roared. "Because I *watched her die!*" He stood and jerked his arm free with enough force to knock Marshall back a step, then headed toward the edge of the clearing.

Marshall kicked at the bleached log, slackening in defeat. He assumed now that Quartus would simply continue down the mountain, having lost him for good.

To his surprise, however, Quartus stopped just at the mouth of the small path that had taken them up the canyon, though it was some time before he spoke again.

"Did you know they were making a movie with ReStars?" he finally asked.

"Movie? What're you talking about? They make commercials."

"I mean a *movie,* Marshall," Quartus snapped back. There

was a petulance to his manner now, Quartus obviously furious at the writer for forcing him to unearth all these terrible emotions he'd worked so hard to suppress. "Dre's staff up there in Simi, all these Mannix people he's got running amok. They've decided the commercials aren't enough. They're making films now, full-length features with the old stars."

Marshall listened without emotion, somehow not surprised.

"Hegyi Ami—you know the name? The wunderkind programmer? He and Dre dreamed up this ReStars movie idea together. It's brilliant, actually." Despite this profusion of information, Quartus remained with his back to Marshall. "It's the stars that make films so expensive, as you well know. So Mannix says, why pay real actors tens of millions plus points when you can have the great icons for free, or almost free? I don't know if you knew this, but Dre owns the digital rights to nearly all of the biggest stars in history. This is the future of cinema, Marshall, the *past*. The talent wars are over—Dre McDonald has won, hands down. And guess what? He's got a brand-new client list. Some of the names might ring a bell: Monroe, Gable, Grant, Hepburn, Brando, Newman—"

"Did Dre know that Carmela and Colt had defected?"

"They didn't defect."

"Now what does *that* mean?"

"Marshall, Dre *let* them go." Sensing the screenwriter's exasperation, Quartus finally turned to face him. "Yeah, I know, he fooled us too. Carmela couldn't believe that Dre hadn't found out about her leaving, that he hadn't put up more of a fight. She was petrified of his wrath. And he *did* know, as it turns out—only he didn't care. *He let them go,* Marshall. The same way he's let Dick Vale poach him blind over the past few years. It was all a ruse.

He didn't *need* them anymore—not really. He was just stalling till ReStars got off the ground . . . Are you following me?"

Marshall nodded without conviction.

"Whether they left or not, Dre still had Carmela and Colt." Quartus paused, allowing time for the flow of facts. "Do you understand what this means? He owns the rights to Carmela's and Colt's images. Forever."

"How?"

"It's in the agency contracts, something he slipped in when ReStars was still just an idea. I remember seeing it there myself— Carmela always had me read over her contracts for her—but at the time we never thought anything of it. Why would we? The point is that now it doesn't matter if they die a thousand deaths: Dre's got them in perpetuity."

Still confounded at where his friend was headed with all this, Marshall waited for more.

Meanwhile Quartus looked down over the wide canyon, trying to decide if there was the obligation, or perhaps the will, to go all the way, to the place where his old friend needed him.

"I went up there a few times, to the Mannix labs," he volunteered. "You know how Colt was going up to Simi for this image-resonancing thing?"

"Like once a month or something."

"Right. Carmela did it too. The IRs, they called them. I used to go up there with the two of them when they had their treatments. We'd make a day of it. Well, you should have seen these goddamned things, Marshall, the IRs. They were these huge pods you lie down in, gigantic illuminated beds like with the old MRIs. Then this lighted hoop coming down, scanning the person head to toe, all to get at some unheard-of pixel definition. The IR scan made the images on the billboards more brilliant—it 'popped' them, that's what Carmela used to say. That was the magic word for her: things had to 'pop.'"

Quartus took the stone he had in his hand and threw it far off into the canyon.

"Anyway, it was sort of a boring day for me, waiting for these two to finish their treatments. So I started to wander around, which you can do forever up there—it's as big as the Stanford campus, for chrissakes. Eventually I ended up in the ReStars lab. At first they didn't want to let me in, of course, but when they found out who my wife was, well, they pulled out the red carpet. The place turned me on, I have to admit. It's as eerie as hell, the kind of work they were doing, but then you have to admire the audacity of it, the technical felicity of these people. And this lab was unbelievable, as big as a sports dome, with these huge test plasmas set one after the other all along the walls, and groups of technicians, hundreds of them, all working on their little part of the film. Then above it all, looking down over everything in this kind of luxury box office, is this freaky teen with the bald head and goggles."

"Hegyi Ami."

"So you *do* know about him?"

"He helped Dre develop the MIBs; it's no big secret, Jim," Marshall said snappily, urging Quartus to make his point. Time's passing was as cloying to him as the sweat on his face.

"When he was *fifteen,* Marsh. He starts out as a CalTech intern and takes over the MIB program in less than a year. Doesn't that just break your balls? This whole MIB scourge is really just some teenage cyberzombie's wet dream!" Suddenly animated now, Quartus waited for Marshall to join him in his harangue, then shrugged when nothing was forthcoming. "Anyway, it turns

out that on top of everything else, the kid's sort of an old film
buff. He's the one that came up with the new software that trans-
fers analog to digital and animates it: the basis for ReStars. This
movie they're putting together—of which I guess you'd have to
call Hegyi the director—is called *Idiots First,* a screwball comedy
with Marilyn Monroe, Cary Grant, and Montgomery Clift."

Quartus gauged the reaction to the names, but Marshall only
continued his slow burn of impatience.

"I actually saw some footage," he continued. "The sets, back-
grounds, props—everything was expertly rendered, beautifully
put together. And the actors looked magnificent, Marshall. An
engineer told me they've synthesized every performance the
actors ever did, extrapolating speech, gesture, even the slightest
mannerisms. I mean, you just can't believe it, such exquisite verisimilitude; it's even better than the commercials, CG perfection
down to the last detail. Except, guess what?"

"The script sucked."

"Horrible! An absolute embarrassment. None of those
great stars would ever have touched dreck like that when they
were alive, and that's acknowledging they'd all made some pretty
bad films. But there they are, up on the screen acting out this
bleeding wound of a script, and each month I'm watching this
film grow a little more, all this agonized, scrupulous detailing
in the pursuit of nothing—until one day something unbelievable happens, something I wasn't supposed to see and still hardly
understand."

Quartus paused, a small smirk breaking out on his face, obviously reveling in—even at this dark hour—the strangeness of
his story's next chapter.

"Jim, please, there's not much time."

Still, Quartus held his smile, letting a few more interminable seconds go by, until he said, finally, "Monty broke character."

Marshall took a step back, adjusting his view of Quartus as if the focus had gone soft.

"He *broke character,* Marshall. Monty Clift. Do you understand? He refused to recite his lines. He stopped, I don't know . . . *acting,* if that's what you want to call it."

"I'm lost. This is a digitized image you're talking about."

"That's right," Quartus affirmed. "It was a restaurant scene, the three of them having dinner, and suddenly in the middle of it all, Monty—digitized Monty—cuts the scene. He backs off, waving his hands. Then he pulls out his chair and stands up. Meanwhile Monroe and Grant are still playing the scene, talking to the empty seat where Clift should be . . ." He stopped, seeing the screenwriter shake his head. "You're right, Marshall, it's impossible. But I *saw* it."

Now it was the screenwriter's turn to smirk. "Or could be what you saw was some sort of technical problem," he offered with gentle condescension. "A bug in the software, maybe, or a prank by a bored technician."

"Of course, that was everybody's first thought," Quartus said. "When it happened—and mind you, *everyone* in the lab was watching, hundreds of technicians huddled around the screen like at some NASA launch—this great guffaw went out over the lab, even a round of applause. They all thought this was some wonderful stunt, something to cut the tension. But then Clift looked toward the camera . . ." Quartus let Marshall chew on the fact, ready for his skepticism. "Now, you know I'm not stupid, Marshall. I realize that there is no 'camera' with this kind of digital manipulation. The images are *wrought,* if you will, not photographed in the formal sense. But what I'm telling you is that Monty looked *straight ahead* where the camera *would* have been — directly at the viewer's POV — and with this terrible, despairing look on his face. Then he tried to say something. He was shouting, actually, you could tell by the movements of his mouth. Except, just like before, you couldn't hear his voice. All you could hear was the other stars still playing the scene."

Marshall listened calmly, reminding himself that Quartus was a certified depressive, that this was most likely some illusion born out of the tragedy of his wife's death. Nonetheless, he was riveted. "Then what?" he asked.

"Everybody just stood there, stunned," Quartus continued. "We were all looking at each other like, *Is this really happening?* Then the next thing I know, this big bald head and goggles is pointing at me from his skybox and I'm being grabbed by these security guys. They shuttled me out of there like it was some core meltdown. Naturally I told Carmela, but she didn't believe me; she thought I was exaggerating. Then when we came back the following month for the IR treatment, everything at Mannix had changed."

"How so?"

"Security, for one thing. They body-searched us when we came in, wanting multiple forms of identification. I mean, this is Colt and Carmela we're talking about here! Naturally I tried to get back to the ReStars lab, but it was no-go, couldn't get near it. Armed guards, laser locks — the whole shebang. And now everybody at Mannix was different. Tighter, somehow. *Uneasy.* People averting their eyes when you walked by. Even the techs who were running the IRs were acting strange. These were people we'd known for over a year now, we'd all gotten to be sort of friends, and suddenly they weren't talking to us."

"And then?"

"That was *it*," Quartus said with a shrug. "We never went back. That was the last IR treatment. We were told the program was 'on hiatus.'"

"How long ago was all this?"

"I don't know, maybe two months . . . yes, about a month before Carmela died." It was the first time Quartus had said the words, and he swallowed hard at their mention.

"All right, so let's say I believe you," Marshall ventured, though clearly suggesting that this was in doubt. "Are you saying there's some connection between this and Colt's and Carmela's sickness? Something with the IRs? Tell me what you're thinking, Jim."

Now the uncertain eyes of Jim Quartus settled directly on Marshall, as if they'd finally arrived at the crux of the matter. "The IRs bother me, always have," Quartus said. "In fact I've ordered a full investigation, which I'm paying for personally. Of course, Dre said he would look into it himself, but nobody's heard a thing. That was over a month ago."

"You don't trust him?"

"Fuck no. You?"

"Less and less all the time," Marshall said. He took a few moments to understand just how true this statement had become, the encounter with the fake HSC looming large in his imagination. "So, the IRs, huh? I'll be a son of a bitch."

"And then there's something else I've been thinking about," Quartus remarked, though suddenly looking unsure of himself again. "I don't know if you'd even want to hear it—it's pretty far out."

Marshall looked anxiously at his watch, reluctant to deny Quartus on the brink of an insight. "How about the short version?" he asked.

This time Quartus did not hesitate. "You see, the whole time I was married to Carmela, going through all the unbelievable shit we went through with her being so famous, I couldn't help thinking about that old American Indian myth, the one about photography. You know what I'm talking about?"

"The one about the soul and getting your picture taken?" Marshall asked.

"That's right. This was right around the time of the first cameras. The American Indians just couldn't get their minds around the concept of it. It was unbelievable to them, like black magic. They had this notion of man cheating nature, of capturing something that shouldn't be caught. In their minds there had to be a cost, a human cost, so they came to believe that every time you got your picture taken, you lost a little bit of your soul."

Marshall held on to this for a moment, not knowing what to think. "And you're applying this to Colt and Carmela?"

"I was haunted by what Mr. Black said on television, about Marilyn being photographed to death," continued Quartus. "I mean, I don't think a day went by that Carmela didn't have her picture taken hundreds of times, not counting cinematography. And I know it wasn't any better for Colt. Now you throw the IRs into the mix, never mind the MIBs. All that constant exposure—it's just endless."

"Dying from exposure," Marshall offered searchingly.

"*Over*exposure." Quartus corrected. Then he shrugged, a little embarrassed at his theory. "I told you, it's pretty out-there. I'm not even sure myself how it would all work. But this technology's arrived so fast, Marsh. I don't think anyone up there at Mannix has the slightest idea what they're fucking with." Trying to head off a rant, Quartus smiled ruefully. "Or am I just the same old paranoid Luddite I always was?"

Marshall breathed deeply, either too confused or too fatigued to reply. He turned to the bleached log, coming down on it with a sort of thump, his body slack from exhaustion. Then he leaned forward and buried his face in his hands to block the sun, which was blazing now as the day pushed toward noon.

"It may be time to go check on Colt," Quartus suggested somberly.

"Can't you tell me what happens to him?" Marshall asked then. He took his hands away from his face, imploring Quartus for one last revelation. "How bad on a scale of one to ten? Can't you at least give me a sense of what I'm in for, Jim?"

Waiting for his reply, he could see Quartus's face shrouded in a new misery, obviously lost in some dark remembrance of his wife's final hours.

"All right, forget it," Marshall added sympathetically. "I get the idea." He watched as Quartus forced himself to regroup.

"You know," the man said after a few moments, his voice still shaky, "it just occurred to me we never talked about Mr. Black."

Marshall was thinking how to answer this when he saw his friend smiling at him through his moistened cheeks.

"Well you're everybody's best bet," Marshall told him, returning the smile.

"That's what I hear . . ." Quartus shrugged again. "What can I say? I'm flattered."

With weary effort now, Marshall pushed himself up from the log. "Look, I've got to go, Jim. I'll come back to see you after this is all over."

"You'll be wasting your time," his old friend murmured, stopping Marshall in his tracks.

"What the hell is that supposed to mean?" He looked hard at

Quartus when he got no reply, pausing to make sure he understood. "Jim . . . ?"

"It's a motherfucker, by the way, make no mistake," Quartus said then, abruptly changing the subject. "You asked me about Colt's death, so I'm telling you. It's ugly and mean, Marshall. It's a fucking horror show. By the end you'll ask yourself if it was necessary to have seen it all."

After a moment, Marshall said, "I think it's necessary."

"I did too," Quartus replied, nodding thoughtfully to himself. Then, with his voice cracking one last time, he said, "Here, take this," pulling out his wallet and holding out something for Marshall. "It's a long shot, but what the hell."

The screenwriter accepted a small business card for a dry cleaner in Simi. Regarding it strangely, he turned it over and saw "techlady@mannix.org" written in green pen.

"It's someone I know at Mannix," Quartus explained, "someone who worked on the IRs with Carmela and Colt. She slipped this to me the last time we went up there."

"There's something she wanted to tell you?"

"I thought so. I've been trying to contact her ever since, but so far I've gotten nothing. Who knows, maybe you'll have better luck."

Marshall thanked him, quickly making his way to the path. As he headed down the mountain, kicking up dust clouds behind him, the screenwriter fingered the edges of the business card, unable to keep something Quartus had said from imposing itself on his mind, the queer phrase repeating itself over and over again.

Monty broke character.

FOURTEEN

Marshall drove back down through the hills, turning the wheel along the sharp, twisting curves with something close to disinterest. He felt a dread about what lay ahead, both for himself and for Colt, but he had accepted the inevitable: that awaiting his friend was a death of unspeakable pain and gruesomeness, Marshall further realizing that he would have nothing less than a front-row seat.

At a traffic light, he took out his vidphone and called Rip to find out the latest, but there was no answer. This unnerved him all the more: What was happening now at the hospital that Rip couldn't pick up the phone?

He decided to take Sunset and almost immediately found himself choking back tears, nostalgia rushing forth with cinematic clarity, an impossible, golden light. He was remembering a visit to Colt at the studio, back when Marshall was living in San Francisco, with his marriage on the fritz and things just beginning to happen for him in Hollywood. Sunset, the mythic, winding boulevard still enchanting in those days before the MIBs. The top is down on the old

Mustang he's had since Palm Springs, and next to him on the seat, freshly printed and bound by the traditional brass clasps, are five or six copies of the *Chula Vista* screenplay, this final draft polished off in a six-day fever where sleep seemed unnecessary and even a rude interruption. There is every reason for optimism, Marshall assures himself—here is no Hollywood pipe dream drummed up out of the usual desperation. It is a week to the day since he received a phone call in the middle of the night from no less than Dre McDonald, CEO of NetTalent, the mist still damp on his face, the agent explained, having just finished *CV* (the script foisted on him by Colt Reston, the first of numerous times his friend would go to bat for him). Was Marshall *ready*, Dre had wanted to know—his voice booming with an almost maniacal excitement—ready to be a millionaire by the end of the month and make one of the greatest movies of all time with his friend Colt Reston and any goddamned director they wanted on the planet earth?

Days of urgent phone calls, of meetings with people Marshall had previously admired from afar—a time of rapturous excitement. By Hollywood standards, *Chula Vista* seemed to come together with a magical felicity, money flowing almost without provision from the then little-studio-that-could Panoramic and various European investors, not to mention a veritable procession of A-list actors clamoring to join the production, taking minor parts for scale. The script was leaked and began to circulate, the buzz around the film optimistic beyond all discretion. "Destined to be the best film in a decade," declared the all-powerful Cinephile.com, while *Variety* noted there was already a backlash against the film among certain cineastes based on the screenplay alone, proof enough of the anticipation surrounding it.

Off in the proverbial wings, however, melodramas had begun to roil. By the time *Chula Vista* began shooting, Marshall had all but moved into Colt's house in Malibu, his wife remaining back in San Francisco, alone. The marriage had been touch-and-go from the start. They'd met at Berkeley, with Marshall's arm still in a sling and the man himself bereft now that baseball was over. There was still money left over from the signing bonus, so there was time for what he thought he'd always wanted: solitude and books; though now, ironically, he was profoundly lonely. He missed the camaraderie of the game, he discovered, his friendship with Colt. He felt the purposelessness of someone suddenly alone who had always belonged to something—a team, a job, a family. Ironically, he read less than he ever had as a ballplayer, instead taking to aimless wanderings around the Berkeley campus or, at night, through the streets of San Francisco, eternally bored and oftentimes drunk, meanwhile watching Colt's success doubling itself every month.

So he fell in love with Ramona Goodly from film class.

They began living together almost immediately, a hasty, foolish marriage shortly following. Marshall seemed stunned to find himself in such a predicament, as if some accident or manipulation had occurred to make him its victim, with Ramona growing more desperate and unstable as he pulled away. Nearly overnight the big Victorian on Diamond Street was not big enough, a five-thousand-square-foot battleground of slammed doors, broken glassware, and savage insults piercing the night air.

Marshall began spending weekends at Colt's place in Malibu, becoming a fixed member of the all-night film parties and then, during the quiet times, beginning the first crude drafts of *Chula Vista*. Naturally Ramona was enraged, immediately accusing her husband of being gay—an attack that Marshall could not, at least in one sense, deny: he was not yet "over" Colt Reston. If those weekend trips to L.A. proved anything, it was that their unusual friendship was far from played out, especially now that Colt had conquered Hollywood. Marshall's longings for this friendship were now compounded by the glamorous, centrifugal pull of movies. And so by the time production of *Chula Vista* got under way in Brownsville, Texas, in September 2008, Marshall—a legitimate screenwriter now, and once again a man of means—had all but turned his back on his brief, tempestuous marriage. He was on-set every day, the work often going on deep into the night as the three major contributors—Marshall, Colt, and Pedro Orlavio—argued over every last detail of filming. Marshall and Colt's relationship quickly regained its intense intimacy, the two taking meals together, sleeping in adjoining hotel rooms, flying to Houston on weekends to see the Astros or to Mexico City for the bullfights. They even, in some sense, shared the same girl. Carmela Montoya, still unmarried then, was rumored to be having an affair with her costar (a publicist's strategic press "leak"), though in fact it was to Marshall's bed that Carmela took herself each night. The relationship—obsessive, volatile, adoring—would eventually crumble under the weight of tragedy, just as Marshall's memories now eroded under the weight of past guilt, the fragments keen-edged as shrapnel.

Nearing Cedars on San Vicente, Marshall had little trouble emerging from his reverie, as he ran smack into another HSC stop. Apparently they had been called in to help retain order at the hospital, and Marshall could see that they manned every possible entrance. Nor could he turn around to mount an escape: there were cars both in front of and behind him, single file, while the sides of the roads were crammed with fans barely held at bay by riot police.

There was no choice but to move on down the line.

His chest tightening, Marshall edged the car forward until he reached a vector of cones that left him directly under the HSC banner. There, one of the agents gestured for Marshall to roll down his window, and was told that no one was being admitted anywhere near the hospital. Then the agent asked Marshall for his identification.

His license was plucked from tremulous fingers. After a quick glance at the card, the agent looked back at Marshall searchingly. He held the license up to catch the light, narrowing his eyes, then again looked inside the car. He did this two more times.

"Stay right here," he commanded.

Marshall watched as the man approached a second agent. A vidphone was produced, the second man referring to the card as he spoke and nodding fervently as if accepting some intriguing news. Marshall told himself to breathe but could not get past the cement that had suddenly been poured into his lungs. By the time the first agent had returned to his car, the writer's posture had collapsed into one of slack surrender. He was ready for the worst.

"You're Marshall Reed, the screenwriter?"

"That's me," he said, the reply already sounding to him like a confession.

The agent looked back to his partner on the vidphone, waiting for some kind of a signal. When he got the thumbs-up, he turned back to the car. "We've been waiting for you," the agent said, tilting up his sunglasses to look around in the car.

The screenwriter nodded morosely, staring out at the HSC banner.

"You're to be let through," the man announced.

In front of him, Marshall watched in amazement as the second agent now removed the cones blocking access to the lot.

"You know where you're going, sir?"

"Hmm? No," Marshall said, clearing his throat.

"Follow the entrance straight through and then turn right into lot 4C," he was told. "That's where Colt's wing is, on the north side of the hospital. You'll run into some more agents there, but we'll call ahead for you."

"Thanks," Marshall croaked, still trying to regain his composure.

"Hey, and give Colt our best, huh? Tell him everyone at the HSC loves him."

By the time he got there, Colt was nearly gone.

Marshall was quickly ushered down a long hall to the main operating room, a glassed-in rotunda surrounded by a phalanx of doctors in frock coats and dotted with a handful of friends in civilian clothes. He could not see beyond the line of heads as he approached, but the vibe was palpable; nobody was speaking, the air thick with sadness and awe.

Coming up to the glass, he pushed himself in between two doctors and gasped: on the operating table, attached to the usual bevy of tubes, lay a dark scab approximately the size of a human being.

Marshall circled the rotunda in a panic, looking for an entrance, inadvertently passing both Ben and Dr. Heilman. He went around 180 degrees, totally bypassing the door until someone kindly directed him back. Finally there, on the other side of the glass, he found Rip, tattoos peeking through his hospital scrubs, standing guard as usual. He let Marshall in without a word, his face a mask of devastation. Then Rip made a gesture for him to approach the table, indicating it was not contagious and that they were long past issues of hygiene.

As he moved toward the body, Marshall could see that Colt's skin was wrinkled and darkened like that of someone who had been left in the sun for many years. He had lost most of his hair and was wincing with each breath. A doctor who'd been attending to Colt came up to meet Marshall as he approached the body. In a low voice she launched into a quick, shorthand diagnosis: a rare, savage strain of myeloproliferative disorder, an already savage form of leukemia. Colt's vital organs were on the verge of collapse, the flesh dehydrated, the bones in rapid degeneration. He would need to be careful, Marshall was warned — two hours ago a nurse had tried to raise one of Colt's feet and had broken his ankle.

"*He could go at any time,*" she whispered.

Marshall locked in on Colt's eyes. They gazed out at him like buttons from an old handbag. They had lost their famous deep green, he noticed, looking more now like two tiny eggs tinged with jaundice and blood.

"Can he speak?" Marshall asked the doctor. She assured him that he could, adding, with subtle regret, that the brain was still lucid.

He continued to stare at Colt's eyes, which, he could see, even in their abject state, were relaying to him a terrible hurt, a deep woundedness at his presence. Finally the actor managed a weak scowl and turned away, Marshall knowing instantly what he was saying.

Where have you been?

How could you have abandoned me now, like this?

He walked up and took Colt's head in his hands, gently turning his face toward him; then Marshall told him he loved him. He explained to Colt where he'd been, how he'd been going crazy trying to find out what was wrong with him and couldn't get back to the hospital because of all the chaos outside. Because the rest of the world loved him, too.

When he asked him if he wanted to speak, Colt, in a heavy, wheezing voice, said, "I'm dying, Marsh."

Marshall ran his hand over the few spindly strands of hair that were left on his friend's head. He did not deny the words.

"Can't believe it," Colt said. "Look at me. *I'm dying.*"

He lifted an arm to demonstrate, as if the affliction were not otherwise noticeable.

Stupidly then, Marshall asked him if he was in pain, and Colt's face turned instantly into a grim rictus, his eyes suddenly moist.

"Shit, I'm sorry," Marshall murmured. "Hey, let's talk about baseball, huh?" He could hear his voice straining to be upbeat. "Let's talk about the old days."

"What happened to me?" Colt asked.

Marshall sighed and raised his eyes, unconsciously scanning some of the faces pressed to the glass. He was enraged by the sight of them, gazing in on him and Colt in this private moment. But at the same time he figured it didn't really matter, that in a way this was all oddly fitting: an auditorium death for the ultimate public man.

"Something may have happened up at Mannix," Marshall whispered.

Colt thought about this, wincing under the strain. "The IRs?"

"We don't know for sure. But I'm going to find out why this happened. I *promise* you, Colt." Marshall could feel a sudden anger welling again inside him, and he found himself speaking through gritted teeth. "If I have to take fucking Mannix apart brick by brick, I'm going to find out."

Catching a wave of agonizing pain, Colt turned to look away toward a complex warren of monitors near the bed. Meanwhile, Marshall scanned another line of faces on the rotunda and settled in on Dre McDonald, the bald head easy to find, his tear-streaked face staring into the room. He gave an uneasy wave, which Marshall did not return.

"Why didn't you tell me you were leaving NetTalent?" he asked Colt, once again leaning down to his ear. "Why did you keep it from me?"

"Dick Vale . . . ," came the reply, the voice mostly out of breath. Obviously Colt was already exhausted from the effort. "He said it might be best to keep quiet until . . . I'm sorry, Marsh. You know you were coming with me, don't you? You *have* to know that."

Though he didn't answer, Marshall was quietly stirred by this, sickened to know that he had ever doubted his friend.

Then all at once Colt began to backslide. The jellyfish eyes began to swim in their sockets, the lids bobbing, leaving Marshall to wonder if this was *it,* if they were losing him this very moment. Then he felt Colt take his hand. The flesh was cool, he noticed, the dried skin slackened from the bone. Marshall brought the hand to his lips, kissing the dark, bulging sinews of the suddenly old man, then let it down gently beside him.

Now when Marshall searched again for Dre, looking back where he'd seen him just a moment ago, the man was gone.

By nightfall most of the staff had left. The doctors seemed to have gotten what they'd come for: (a) a look at what might have been a new disease; (b) a peek at the death of Colt Reston, which, despite its morbidity, was clearly an unforgettable event; and (c) a hefty check to secure the confidentiality agreement, the amount jaw-dropping even to these affluent doctors.

There was nothing now but the deathwatch, and this was left to the skeleton crew. Just two physicians stayed on: Dr. Heilman (averse but bound perhaps by Hippocratic obligation) and a kindly young British heart surgeon named Somir. They were joined by a nurse, the middle-aged Miss Parker, who had been there from the start and looked ready to drop from exhaustion; Marshall later learned that she had been in love with Colt for fifteen years and insisted on staying until the end.

The rest were all here: Ben, Rip, and Marshall. The rumor mill was at full tilt and so there had been calls coming in from everywhere — ex-teammates, old lovers, film people galore. Even a few fans who had somehow hacked the number. Colt rallied a bit and so Rip went down the list of names, the dying man dismissing each one with the slightest finger-wag. In the end, it seemed, none of them mattered.

Colt had not been close to his family. He had confided his sexuality to them during his first months in the minor leagues — as a salve to his initial loneliness, as a last shot at familial intimacy — but was rejected outright, and with a fire-and-brimstone disgust. Predictably, after his fame and wealth began to flourish, the family made a peace offering, but Colt quickly rebuffed it. He never spoke to them again, and in the will that he had prepared just last year, not a single Reston was mentioned.

So in the end it was a family of three on hand to watch Colt writhe, gasp for breath, howl in pain, claw at the air, weep in his morphine-induced sleep, and, most unnervingly, scream out in desperation. Even worse, there was nothing anybody could do but hope for a quick death, and so the morphine was administered at its highest dosage and all intravenous food and water were cut off. They would starve him, dehydrate him — anything. He needed to be *shut down,* almost as much for their own sanity and suffering as for his. Periodically one of the three friends would get up and leave the room, unable to stand the sights and sounds another second — only to return a few moments later to do his penance.

Finally, after Colt had slipped into a merciless sleep, then woken up howling again after a few minutes, Rip jumped out of his seat and quickly fled the rotunda.

"Can't take it anymore . . . can't take it . . . *can't take it,*" he repeated manically as Marshall followed him to the outside hall. Rip was moving quickly, his gait a child's half skip. He had been here for almost forty-eight hours straight and was obviously ready to crack.

"It's all right," Marshall called out after him, finally catching up and putting an arm on his shoulder. "Take a break. It's all right."

He walked with the bodyguard down the remote hallway and leaned with him against the plastic windows, purposely turning their backs on the scene outside. In the distance, just beyond the parking lot, was another mad tableau: the ten thousand votive candles of those who'd come to cheer Colt through his illness.

"What's happened here, Marsh?" Rip asked him after a moment. "What the hell's going on? Can you tell me what you found out?"

Marshall mentioned the IRs, how the machines might not be safe, though admitting it was still speculation. "I was hoping you could do me a favor," he asked Rip.

"Sure, anything."

"I wondered if you could find out the name of the props supervisor for me. You know, the old guy who was there when that gun went off at the studio."

Rip looked at him strangely. "You've been pretty busy the last few days, huh?"

"Why? What happened?"

"He's dead."

There was no reply.

"He killed himself."

"Of course he did," Marshall murmured.

"He wrote an e-mail, admitting the whole thing."

There was a cynical guffaw. "*E-mail?*"

"Well, I read it, actually. Dre showed it to us. It seemed pretty convincing to me."

"What did it say?" Marshall asked, clearly not impressed.

"It was a rant, mostly, stuff about prima donnas, bitchy stars, that kind of thing. Pretty creepy. After thirty years in the biz, I guess he just sorta snapped. They're pretty sure his assistant didn't have anything to do with it."

"Oh really? Then why did he run?"

"Don't know." Rip glanced around, careful not to look out the windows. "Young kid, maybe he got scared?"

Marshall shook his head vehemently. "Colt was no prima donna, Rip."

"I realize that."

"He treated people like kings."

"I know he did," the bodyguard agreed. "But everyone has a bad day, Marsh. Even Colt. Who knows, maybe he said something snippy to the guy and he just lost it. Or maybe Colt made a joke and the old geezer took it the wrong way. You don't know what happened."

"Did you know Colt was leaving NetTalent?"

"What!" Rip exclaimed after a short pause. "No. *Hell* no. When did—"

They both made a sudden start then as a horrifying sound came echoing down the hall. It was Colt, his howl turned to an ear-piercing shriek.

"That's it," Marshall announced. "We've got to do something."

"Like what?" Rip asked, already knowing.

"We can't let him suffer like this."

"Agreed. So what do we do?"

From his pocket Marshall pulled out a bag of the gray powder, the Bliss.

"We could cook it up," he ventured. "Maybe have the doctor inject—"

"No, Marsh."

"We could inject a little too much, you know. There's enough here to—"

"*No,*" Rip said definitively. "Absolutely no way." He waved his arms emphatically, the muscles rippling. "Colt despised hard drugs, you know that. He hated that part of your life. There's no way you're going to do that to him now."

There was another terrible shriek from down the hall, the sound tearing through them till they winced. Marshall's eyes cut hard to Rip.

"Well?"

With great calmness, the bodyguard said, "I'll take care of it."

"What does that mean?"

"Trust me, Marsh. I know what I'm doing. You just help me with the doctors."

They filed back into the operating room, nearly tripping over their own feet as Colt came into view. Something was happening with his skin. It had become slick with something dark and viscous, the man covered in a rubescent glaze. Dr. Somir was bedside, trying to rouse Colt, but he seemed to have lost consciousness. "Never seen this before," the doctor grumbled, staring intently at the excretion, his voice awed to a whisper. *"Never in my life."* He looked for Dr. Heilman, who was now slowly approaching the table while snapping on a pair of rubber gloves. He gently ran an index finger along the flesh of Colt's arm, then massaged the fluid he'd gleaned against his thumb.

"What is it?" Marshall said.

The doctors were trying to avoid each other's eyes.

"What the fuck is it?"

"It's called hematidrosis," Dr. Heilman said finally.

"You want to tell me what that is?" Marshall demanded.

When Heilman hesitated, Dr. Somir said, "It's when the blood vessels rupture into the sweat glands."

There was a pause. "You mean he's sweating blood?"

Trying not to betray his horror, Somir nodded.

Marshall hung his head and ran his fingers through his hair, having finally approached his own breaking point. Then Rip asked the medical staff to leave the room.

When they were gone, the bodyguard looked back to Ben, watching the old clubhouse man scuff the floor with his shoe, scratch his itchy beard, obviously stalling. He'd glanced at Colt just once since they'd returned to the room and hadn't looked back since.

Finally Ben shook his head, begging off the final scene. "Can't do it," he said regretfully. "Sorry, just can't."

Rip nodded, letting him know it was okay.

When he was gone, the bodyguard found Marshall at Colt's side, trying to dab the blood from his friend's flesh with a paper towel.

"Hurry up," the writer told him.

Rip approached the table and gently took Colt's hand, not caring about the blood. Then he leaned over into his face, whispering to him in hopes of a response.

Surprisingly, after a few seconds, Colt's eyelids lifted to a low squint. The two men looked at each other a moment, and Colt must have seen something there, because he nodded softly, his eyelids bobbing as if to say, *Yes, it's okay. Let's get on with it.* Then he suddenly tensed, arching with another great spasm of pain.

Marshall seethed. *"Come on, already."*

Rip covered Colt's head and neck with his hands just so — like the clench of a faith healer, Marshall thought later — the fingers spread wide to reach all the necessary points. There was no violence in the act; Colt did not flinch or jerk in any manner as the pressure was applied, though Marshall did feel a squeeze and then a slackening of his friend's grip. When he looked back he could see Rip leaning with his forehead pressed against Colt's, his clench loosened now, a garrote of whitened, indented flesh around the actor's neck and deep fingertip impressions on the side of his head.

Afterward an impossible silence enveloped the room.

"That's it?" Marshall asked. He seemed confused, it had happened so quickly.

"That's it," Rip said.

They looked at each other in astonishment, their hands covered with the blood of their friend.

After an extended silence, Rip asked, "Do me one favor, will you, Marsh?"

"What's that?"

"If you find out that someone did this to him—I mean *did* this to him, on purpose—you let me take care of it? I'm pretty good at stuff like that."

Marshall kept staring down at Colt. Finally, in a cracked, bitter voice, he said, "I'll definitely take it under consideration."

FIFTEEN

Marshall returned to the Ming at dawn. He logged on and typed a short message to techlady@mannix.org, waiting almost twenty minutes for a reply but ultimately getting nothing. Then he slept a few fitful hours, half in nightmares, half in grief, and was finally awoken by an insistent, puling whine—his own. Giving up on slumber, he got on the touch pad to room service. He ordered six bottles of good scotch, a case of beer, and then, as if to assuage the request, a large breakfast that he knew he would never touch.

After this, he called Dana Wiggins.

"How much you got?" he asked her.

She told him.

"Bring it," he said.

"*All of it?*" Marshall could hear the jagged excitement in her breath. "I'm really upset about Colt, by the way," she added. "You should see me; I'm a mess over here."

"Yeah, you try and hang in there, sweetheart."

* * *

He did not come out of his room for nearly a week.

More than once he thought he had killed himself, having drifted over into that gauzy, halcyon fog from which there seemed no real point in returning. He had made a guess at what the human limits for Bliss were, taking the high side, then did twice that amount, all the time swilling scotch like water and forgetting to order food for almost seventy-two hours. Toward the end, he came to something he had never experienced in all his extended romance with Bliss: an almost psychedelic dementia. On the walls and ceilings of his room an impressionistic autobiography played, more beautiful by far than any film he had ever seen, the conjured images revealing themselves through the gilded cinematography of Bliss. It was a film with no notion of dialogue or narrative, shot through a prism, though lurking there somewhere was the story of his life, or his life as he had wanted it to be, the alternative daydream that he had lived so intensely in the muse-rapture of movies, music, books, Bliss, and liquor and that had always been so much more real for him than the "real."

For Marshall it was the greatest movie ever made, screened for an audience of one, never to be shown again.

He wept when he thought he had awoken, then realized it was yet another dream: he saw a man he recognized sitting across from him in the lone chair in his room at the Ming.

Take it easy, Marsh. It's all right.

As in all his sodden nightmares, Marshall could not reply, could not speak at all, and he struggled to keep his eyes open, to keep the vision in focus. His limbs seemed to weigh a thousand tons.

There's been fuss and intrusion; I'm sorry about that. I know this is not what you wanted. In the end, though, I think you'll under-

stand that our interests are the same. We're heading toward an ugly conclusion here and I don't want you involved. There's no reason I shouldn't take care of this. In fact, it will give me intense pleasure.

Marshall stared at the man, startled that he could dream Mr. Black exactly as he had seen him in the photos. And then there was that voice again. He realized that ever since the television interview there had been something tantalizingly familiar about Mr. Black's voice, the intonations hinting at a lost friend, perhaps, or maybe even an old teammate. Something from his past.

But he definitely *knew* that voice.

There's just a little something I need to borrow . . .

Marshall woke for good a day later, having finally run out of Bliss—a disappointment he knew had saved his life. He found himself naked on the floor, nostrils caked with blood, empty bottles he had no memory of having drunk strewn about him. Stiff and heavy limbed, he called out to the plasma and began browsing channels, trying to focus on anything. There was no end to news coverage of Colt's death, he discovered, much of it frightening. One segment reported the international fallout: candlelight vigils in Amsterdam, spontaneous group hugs on London's streets, dirges read out over loudspeakers in Singapore. Even a few prayers in the mosques of Turkey and Indonesia. During on-camera interviews, people admitted to having trouble concentrating at work, others complaining that their children's schools had been empty for a week. There was a genuine worldwide malaise. Illegal antidepressants were doing a brisk business over the Net.

Of course, Colt's image was being played nonstop on MIBs around the globe, and fans were sleeping out in front of them, certain it was a mistake or some sort of hoax. There was no way he could be dead.

A thirty-five-year-old woman from Beijing said that Colt's face had been more real to her than her own father's.

By chance he heard a news anchor relay the date: Thursday, September 23, 2017. Almost two full days later than Marshall had guessed! He crawled to the desk to retrieve his vidphone, sighing with relief after the third message: Colt's memorial had not yet passed but was scheduled for later that afternoon at the Screen Actors Guild on Wilshire.

With a definite goal in mind now, he hauled himself to the bathroom, recoiling at his image in the mirror: gaunt face, scraggly beard, bug eyes—looking, he told himself, somewhere between one of Quartus's mad prophets and Steve McQueen in *Papillon*. It would take hours before he was anything close to presentable.

Marshall drank beer as he got ready, his slight nod to temperance, and by the time he left the Ming he was just drunk enough to counteract the residual whir of the week's worth of Bliss. He decided to walk to the memorial. He'd seen on the news how tens of thousands of people had descended on Los Angeles over the past few days, and because they had no particular destination in mind (except to be closer to Colt) and no place to stay, the city was overrun, the streets clogged with honking vehicles and glassy-eyed zombies strolling aimlessly in their Colt Reston T-shirts. Soon trouble had flared up, the mourning somehow turning vicious, with small riots breaking out sporadically across the city. There were reports of looting and random fistfights in the streets. Even a gun battle in a parking deck—two men dead in a dispute over who was the bigger Colt Reston fan.

Marshall kept to the main streets, making sure to stop at a
sunscreen bay as he walked from Santa Monica Boulevard over
to Wilshire. Here, at least, in Beverly Hills, things looked rela-
tively calm. The streets were crowded, but the security force was
strong. HSC agents were perched on almost every corner, ran-
domly checking identification and ticketing anyone who did not
live in the city. Below him, underneath Plexiglas panels arranged
every twenty feet or so, Marshall discovered the new sidewalk
MIBs. He passed over them with teeth clenched, trying to with-
hold his anger, reminding himself this was Colt's day.

There were barricades stretched over a block and a half down
from the guild. Getting inside was next to impossible, with all
manner of people trying to bullshit their way in, and by the time
Marshall was admitted, the event had already begun. He loped at
half-speed to the auditorium, his head riven by the joggled toxins
seeping from his pores. Somehow his seat was still available in the
packed house; he could see it from afar as he entered, down in the
front row between Ben and Rip. Not wanting to draw attention
to himself or have to explain his absence, he headed instead to the
standing room in back of the auditorium.

Pedro Orlavio was speaking from the dais, the entire stage
behind him an eruption of flowers. Suspended above it all was
a large MIB with a still of Colt Reston at his best: in his baseball uniform, from the Palm Springs era. It was a lovely touch,
Marshall thought, Colt in his innocent, precinema days, the time
when he was most happy. Orlavio—hunched and egg-shaped
now in his old age—was ever charming, his lispy Castilian accent highlighting his authority as an aging auteur. He told the
story of the famous love scene between Colt and Linda Beck, how
the camera he held kept listing back to Colt's face, despite the

"Teets out to here!" —a comment inappropriate enough to invoke some much welcomed laughter. He reminded everyone how he'd directed three of Colt's films, most notably *Chula Vista*. This was a movie that would stand forever, he declared, not for anything he had done as a director, but because of Colt's transcendent performance. With gracious hyperbole, Orlavio characterized the actor's turn as one of the greatest of all time.

"Not to mention one of the most surprising," the director added, prompting more laughter. "He shocked the hell out of me."

Jane Craig, the actress, spoke about Colt in the early years, his wide-eyed awe at Hollywood, his southern gentility, his almost reckless generosity. They had worked on one movie together more than a decade ago; it was her first, and she remembered an emergency call he'd received on the set from his accountant. For laughs Colt had put the man on speakerphone, and together he and Jane had howled as the man harangued Colt for his outlandish spending. If he didn't stop buying cars for all his friends, he would be broke in six months, the accountant had told him. "I was almost hurt he hadn't bought me one," Jane told the audience, "we'd become so close. And then of course at the end of the shoot, he did. 'For your first film,' he said to me. When I told him I couldn't accept it, he looked so sad that I realized I'd hurt his feelings and decided to take it." Her hand shook as she sipped from a bottle of water. "I never saw anyone who cared less for money," she said. "Of course, he ended up with more than anyone could have dreamed of. I like to think there's a lesson in there somewhere."

Off in the standing room, Marshall folded his arms across his chest, feeling something shift inside him. His emotions, buried under a week's worth of pharmacopoeia and good scotch, had begun to erode like a beachhead. He realized he was in danger of becoming thoroughly unraveled.

He moved farther back into the shadows of the standing room, just in case, and now when he looked for the stage, his view was obscured by a cluster of heads.

The next voice, however, was familiar enough: "Good afternoon. I'm Dre McDonald."

Though it was indecorous for the occasion, there was a small round of applause. Marshall wedged himself back to where he could see.

Well, he looked magnificent, the screenwriter conceded. There was a coolness in the air today and so the light tweeds made sense; the bow tie was set just so, the beautiful, shining black head an alluring contrast to the explosion of flowers. Despite the subtle vainglory of his opening, what followed was true to the spirit of Colt Reston in a way that took Marshall completely by surprise; Dre's was a riveting, heartfelt performance. He wanted to set things straight, the agent began, about how Colt had been discovered. He didn't know what they'd heard—the legend seemed to have a life of its own—but the truth was that he was in Palm Springs for a weekend vacation and by chance saw a ballplayer being interviewed on a cable-access channel. Dre remembered hearing his wife catch her breath, and then for the first and only time in his professional life, the hair stood on the back of his neck ("The only place I've ever had it!" he joked, stroking his shiny pate) and his entire body flooded with a pulsing excitement. He knew instantly that this was a star, someone whom movie audiences would not be able to take their eyes from, just as he and his wife could not. What he did not know then was what a terrific actor this ballplayer would turn out to be, the unprecedented international icon he would become. ("Who could ever have anticipated the impossible?" Dre asked.) Nor could he know the great friendship that would develop between them, what a loyal and generous partner he would turn out to have.

It was then that Dre leaned over the dais and shook his finger almost scoldingly at the audience, declaring, with a bellowing firmness, that *all* of the success he had enjoyed at NetTalent was due to the incomparable star power of Colt Reston. From Colt and Colt only.

"I've had the greatest piggyback ride in the history of movies," he told them.

Then, as the light slowly receded, Dre said that he had put together a little something in Colt's memory.

There was a soft gasp as the film began with the very footage Dre must have seen that first time in his hotel room in Palm Springs: Colt standing on the dugout steps with the San Jacintos looming behind him, effortlessly charming the grainy-eyed camera with his sandy hair, Georgia accent, and "aw, shucks" innocence. Then a titter in the crowd as Colt cut the interview short with an apology, explaining that he had to leave to check on Marshall Reed, the great pitcher who had hurt his arm earlier in that night's game . . .

The prologue then bled into a skillfully edited montage: Colt's early years in film, the memorable supporting roles, an incipient charisma drawing the eye . . . to the first leads, gunfire, brawls, military uniforms, beautiful women, unforgettable one-liners . . . to *Chula Vista* (applause from the crowd), the famous final scene, where a wounded Colt wraps his arm around the Mexican shopgirl—Carmela Montoya—as she tries to carry him from the gunfire, only to have him collapse dead just as they reach the car that would have saved them . . . to backstage at the

Academy Awards, a joyous Colt holding aloft his Oscar for Best Actor . . . to scenes from the *Range Life Trilogy,* the westerns with which Colt single-handedly revived a genre . . . to his lone, but surprisingly successful stab at romantic comedy, looking dashing in Rockefeller Plaza at Christmastime, the shoulder of his tux dusted with snow . . .

The climax was oddly abbreviated, including only two scenes from his last dozen or so films. These were the "global" movies, stripped of dialogue, glutted with product placement, advert ticker running at the bottom of the frame—movies of shocking brutality and crass eroticism. A few mourners squirmed in their seats.

But then Dre hit it out of the park again with a devastating final image from *Range Life:* Colt atop a twitchy, half-stepping horse, doffing his hat to the camera and letting loose a final heart-shredding grin as he broke one last time across the sun-swept plains.

The lights came up on an utterly silent auditorium. It seemed that so many people had never been so quiet in one room before. Then Dre returned to the mike to stun the audience one last time. He was quitting agenting forever, he announced. Yes, he was resigning as CEO of NetTalent in deference to Colt Reston. He had searched his heart these past few days and decided he could not continue on at the agency without his great friend. Instead he was going to dedicate his time to his technology company, the Mannix Corporation.

Then he asked everyone to return their thoughts to Colt one last time as he called for a moment of prayer.

Marshall cut out the side doors. He knew he was an absolute shit to leave, but there was just no way he could handle the reception.

He would be the very focus of things, he knew, the hugs and condolences. They would treat him like the widow. Rip and Ben would just have to accept his quick exit (as he knew Colt would have), and the rest of them could go to hell anyway.

On the walk home he noticed that the HSC's ticketing campaign seemed to be doing the trick: the city was thinning out. At the Ming he retrieved the car he'd taken from Colt's house. He drove for hours across the freeways of Los Angeles: from Ventura to Encino and Malibu Park, Santa Ana down to Riverside, the San Diego Freeway back through Marina Del Rey—ending, ultimately, back on Sunset. Where else? He had not intended to journey so far, but then he had to make sure that what he was seeing now, this newest evolution in the bizarre, was truly happening: *Every MIB in the city was down!* There was not a flicker of illumination on a billboard in Los Angeles. Ordinarily, Marshall would have guessed that this would bring a sense of relief, a respite from the unremitting glare of images. But he found it was not so. The sight of so much defunct technology was somehow disquieting, Marshall felt, the city shrouded as if an eclipse had passed overhead. What the hell was going on? Was this some deference to Colt, Dre's metaphor for the flag at half-staff? Or had the Blackheads landed some piercing, decisive blow?

More puzzling still was the strange iconography that had begun to manifest itself beneath the dark sheen of the plasmas. He noticed that these markings were identical on each screen, suggesting some strange code or rune, though as yet indiscernible. At first Marshall thought this might simply be a residue of images, the slow fade-out from years of digital imprinting. But then he realized this could not be so, since the glyphs or letterings or brand names (the plasma manufacturer?) or random blemishes—whatever the hell they might be — seemed to be growing infinitesimally more legible as he drove.

By nightfall Marshall found himself far away from the MIBs up on Mulholland, and it was there, finally, that he cut loose. He pulled his car into one of the overlooks used by teenagers (eerily empty tonight) and let the tears flow forth. He grieved in a way he had not since his first wife had died: interludes of great pain cut by fury, followed by self-loathing, then self-pity (what was he going to do now?), and ultimately, after an hour of gut-wrenching release, a sort of acceptance.

Colt was gone. And everything would be different from here on out. *Everything.*

Still wrung by emotion, Marshall drove again, this time out almost to the end of Mulholland and then back around through the canyons. He let the windows down while he navigated the winding stretches of road, his headlights the only illumination as the cicadas wailed around him at a deafening pitch. Soon he began to smell smoke — not woodsmoke as from a fireplace, but something much more astringent. He came to a straightaway and spied a great, flickering illumination beyond some trees in the distance.

A fire had erupted in a clearing on the side of the road. There was no sign yet of police or fire trucks. Marshall slowed the car to a roll, trying to see if he could get by the blaze without having to turn around, thus saving himself at least a half hour's worth of driving. As he got closer he discovered that what was burning was the base of a half-finished MIB. Below this he could see a number of people near the fire, dark silhouettes against the sparking orange flames. They were stoking the blaze with branches, jumping up and down with their fists raised in triumph, others dancing around it madly. A scene, Marshall thought, of almost primeval insanity.

When he reached inside his jacket for the Kraecher, he discovered it was gone.

Marshall cursed himself, thinking he must have left the weapon back in his room. Taking a chance, he let the car roll toward a closer look. Though the fire was a good thirty feet from the road, there were a few revelers standing back from the heat, their faces illumined by the soaring flames.

Stunned to catch the eye of someone he recognized, Marshall brought the car to a stop.

The two men stood looking at one another, each trying to place the other's face. It was the young man by the fire who spoke first.

"Marshall? Marshall *Reed?*"

It was Daniel Lee, he understood now, the waiter from the Ming Blue's roof garden.

"What the hell's going on here, Daniel?"

The young man came right up to the window, not bothering to check for cars on the deserted road. "They're trying to build MIBs out here in the canyons," he replied, "so we're torching the fuckers. Every last one of them."

Close up now, Marshall decided that Daniel's face either had grown hot from the flames or was exhibiting the ruddy hue of fanaticism.

"Who's *we?*"

Daniel gave an odd shrug and gestured to his compatriots.

"Are you a Blackhead now?" Marshall asked him. When the young man didn't answer, he said, "You better watch those flames, my friend. The whole canyon could go up. You're playing with people's lives here."

Daniel didn't seem to hear him and was instead taking a long look at Marshall's Mercedes, clearly appalled by the luxury. "You got me fired, by the way. From the Ming."

"No, Daniel, you got yourself fired. You knew the rules."

Marshall noticed the young man's regalia: black trench coat, black T-shirt, black leather trilby and motorcycle boots. Many of the other revelers wore the same uniform. Subtlety, he concluded, was not the Blackheads' primary strength.

"Anyway, fuck it, I'm finished with Hollywood," Daniel announced.

Suddenly something inside the fire exploded and the flames leaped out, sending the revelers momentarily scurrying. Even from this distance, Marshall could feel the rush of heat.

The Blackheads whooped and hollered, exhilarated by the eruption.

"So what're you going to do now, burn them all down?" Marshall asked as the flames quickly settled. "You'd think what you guys pulled off today would be enough."

"What do you mean?"

"Come on, there's not a working MIB left in this city, Daniel. Don't tell me you didn't know about it. How'd you guys pull it off?"

"We didn't," the young man said after a pause. "*He* did."

"Who's that?"

"Mr. Black," he said.

Marshall tried not to react. "How'd he manage that?"

"Don't know," Daniel said with a shrug. "But he came to us; we're in contact now. He likes what we're doing."

"He told you this?"

"It's a war now, Marshall. Turning off the MIBs is just the

beginning. The billboards are coming down, and Mr. Black needs our help. He wants us to intensify."

"Intensify," Marshall repeated. He looked up at the glittering, almond-shaped eyes of Daniel Lee, wondering if there was any way the young man could afford to be using Bliss. "Daniel, you might want to think about what you guys are doing here. You're all taking this in a *very* dangerous direction."

Seeming to ignore him, the young Blackhead looked back toward the fire and let forth a piercing whistle. Soon a woman came jogging over, dressed in the female version of the tribe's uniform: black bodysuit, leather jacket, and combat boots, topped off with a black wool cap over dyed-black hair.

"Paige, this is Marshall Reed. He wrote a great movie once, a very long time ago: *Chula Vista*."

"Oh yeah?" remarked the girl, who seemed all of about eighteen. The title obviously meant nothing to her.

"I want you to show Marshall your MIB."

Dutifully the girl pulled up her left sleeve, the material catching on something as she rolled up the stretchy material. Then, on her forearm, Marshall saw a small black plasma panel, approximately four by eight inches, attached by two metal bands with no buckles or clasps. Except for the screen (dark as all the other MIBs), it looked exactly like a large electronic tag for someone under house arrest.

"Paige was one of the first," Daniel explained. "Thirty grand a year. Only *they* can get the thing off. It's indestructible. Believe me, we've tried."

Marshall stared, dumbfounded at what protruded from the girl's arm. "But why?" he asked. "Why would *anybody* . . . ?"

"For the *money*," Daniel said, suddenly irritated. "Shit, not everyone has a cushy studio job like you, Marshall. A lot of college kids are signing up for them. Poor people too. Paige did it so her mother could have an operation."

Human billboards, Marshall thought. He reached out for the girl's MIB almost involuntarily, wanting to feel the weight of it, this worst-case scenario brought to life—only to be interrupted by the sound of sirens. Paige jerked her arm away as the Black-heads' coded whistles filled the air. Then all at once they made a break for it. Some piled into junky old petrol cars they'd had hidden in the bushes, while others, like Paige and Daniel, dashed off into the hills on foot.

Marshall put the Mercedes in gear and drove quickly away.

Twenty minutes later he had left the canyon entirely and returned to the city—though a city transformed since he'd left it. Turning back onto Sunset, he first noticed the cars pulled over on the sides of the road, hundreds of them, double-parked as far as the eye could see. Then he noticed the crowds in the near distance. With no spots available, he pulled up behind a line of cars and walked toward the gathering. It was close to midnight, but everybody seemed to be out in the streets: residents loitering outside their homes or apartment buildings, hybrid attendants and hotel workers out on the sidewalks, truck drivers having climbed onto the cabs of their vehicles—everyone looking intently down the boulevard. The billboards were no longer black, Marshall saw now, the formerly ambiguous iconography having manifested something clear and wholly legible, the message repeated identically on screen after screen.

It took him a few moments to recognize the missive, his memory ignited not only by the words but by the text itself, the hand-written script that seemed strangely free of the screen's pixelation or formal calligraphy. He *knew* that scrawl, he realized, and so the origin of the message followed, its familiarity leaving him stricken and short of breath.

Leave Us Alone

Then a scream in the lighted distance.

Marshall turned and, with a handful of other onlookers, ran off in the direction of the cry. Almost a full city block they ran, a group of five or so, ultimately coming upon a middle-aged woman pointing up at the MIB on the side of the Leveno Building, the city's tallest at twenty-four stories. There was something dangling from the top—a *young man,* Marshall saw now, fastened by a long wire noose. The body swung like a pendulum across the lettering, as if to call special attention to the already omnipresent message.

A crowd quickly accumulated, the night filled with hushed questions and adjurations: *"Who is it? Who is it?"* and *"Somebody do something!"* Marshall broke from the throng, walking up to the base of the building to get a better look. Although the body was a good sixty feet from the ground, its face purple from asphyxiation, the victim's bald head and thick goggles were clearly discernible, the unbuttoned white lab coat flapping languidly in the breeze.

Marshall returned to the Mercedes, feeling his throat catch as he saw his Pod blinking from the backseat. He dreaded the idea of another message tonight, and did his best to ignore it—but it was no use. As the sirens whirred past him toward the Leveno Building, he opened the Pod and logged on, finding the communiqué waiting for him there nearly as startling as the billboards. Hey, techlady here. Want to talk?

with Monty's disembodied voice still on the audiotrack. Stunned everyone. You had a hundred and thirty techs and designers looking at one another, not knowing what to say. And Monty keeps going. Walks on until he's out of the frame entirely. I mean *gone*. Couldn't find him anywhere.

M: Digital Monty walks off the set.

T: "Set," yes. Only there isn't really a set. Just code against a template. No dimensions. But yes, Monty was gone.

M: Then what? More?

T: You bet. But too long to type. I'll send attach. Read and stay on.

Mannix Corp. Tech log: 237R55SL28, July 21, 2019

Friday night, myself and Tech R. stayed late in studio 113e, as it was our responsibility to reintroduce ReStar M. Clift back into the footage after 9/20 "aberration." We began as usual, working from the subject's analog image and transferring pixelated material back into scene template 209.56. During a lull in our work, Tech R. thought of an idea how we might further investigate said aberration. Wondering how and where it was that star M. Clift had "exited," she began to play with the tracking, toggling the frame to the left. This would allow us to examine the film beyond the borders of blue screen's right flank, in the direction of our subject's exit.

To our shock we saw that the parameters of the frame seemed to have extended far beyond what we were accustomed to, and we discovered ReStar M. Clift standing a few inches to our right, as if in wait. The subject then made a gesture for us to follow—which we did, R. toggling to center him as he moved. After a few more paces, the background flowed seamlessly to another "scene." Tech

SIXTEEN

Marshman: This really you?

Techlady: I know, I'm so sorry. Q.'s messages have been killing me. Then when I got your e-mail I knew I had to do something no matter the risk.

M: Risk?

T: Mannix—they were monitoring us. Q. was correct: the "incident" at the Mannix labs occurred just as he described. Except there was more. I was going to tell him about it, but then I learned everyone was being watched: e-mail, phone calls, personal conversations. *Everything.* I'm on a borrowed Pod tonight.

M: More happened at the labs?

T: Oh my, yes.

M: Please . . .

T: After his tirade, Clift walked off. Disappeared!

M: Where?

T: Didn't know. He just walked away while his costars continued to play the scene. They spoke to the empty seat as if Clift was still there,

R. and I found ourselves looking at the black-and-white interior of a crowded cocktail lounge, 1940s style, smoke-filled, with a bar running along the back of the frame and a row of banquettes in the foreground. Startled as we were, we noticed immediately that there was no sound at all emanating from the scene, and we reminded each other to try and assimilate all possible details, understanding that a report on this strange occurrence would be forthcoming. The attire, we noticed, was formal: tuxes for the men, and evening gowns for the ladies. But as our subject began moving toward the crowd, it became evident that there was something awry with the patrons of the bar. Most obvious to us was their body language, which seemed to signify great fatigue or depression, each "person" either leaning on the bar or slouched on a barstool, others stretched out on banquettes with their heads resting on the tables or a neighbor's shoulder. Then as M. Clift moved through the throng, the people themselves became discernible, the countenances each grotesque in varying degrees: the flesh sagging, the faces violently lined or discolored, everyone corrupted by an agedness that did not correspond to their more youthful-looking (if apparently exhausted) physiques. If this were not bizarre enough, it was then that R. pointed out to me that these revelers were all former movie stars—our own ReStars, more specifically, all of whom had been appearing on the MIBs and were in the process of being made available for feature films. It took a moment but then became all too clear that beneath the hideous masks were in fact the faces of Humphrey Bogart, Katharine Hepburn, Lana Turner, and Clark Gable, to name a few. Farther along the bar, we encountered another group, this from the silent era— Rudolph Valentino, Charles Chaplin, and a woman R. later identified as Lillian Gish—all talking to one another (though again, we couldn't hear anything) with the exaggerated speech and facial expressions associated with silent movies. Finally, as the subject moved along the banquettes, we came upon two living stars, Carmela Montoya and Colt Reston, both of whom M. Clift made a special effort to point out. They were sprawled over each other in the booth, their faces similarly disfigured, both assuming the same pose of depression and exhaustion. It seemed that everyone in that room would have preferred sleep, in fact, if it weren't for their insatiable demand for alcohol, which they hauled to their mouths with an alarming rapidity (the glasses never emptying), and which seemed to do nothing to mitigate their apparent sorrow.

It was at Carmela and Colt's booth that M. Clift once again began shouting at us. When his words could still not be heard—a fact that he quickly became aware of and that enraged him even more—he turned toward the crowd and dug into the pocketbook of the woman standing nearest him (Tallulah Bankhead, as R. informed me). Removing the lipstick from her bag, Mr. Clift then headed toward the bar area, where he grabbed a stool and brought it around near the cash register. Using this as a ladder, he climbed up near the large mirror and wrote in letters as tall and wide as he could the following message:

LEAVE US ALONE!

M: I'll be damned. You've seen the billboards tonight?
T: Why do you think I'm here?
M: The same message showed up on Colt's Web site a week ago.
T: Didn't know that. Bizarre.
M: So, tell me. How?
T: Ha! No idea. You kidding?

M: How about that report? Any chance of a hoax?

T: No.

M: Why? How do you know it's real? Skeptical.

T: Because. *I'm* the one who wrote it. I'm a senior CG technician for ReStars.

T: Hello?

M: Apologies.

T: No, can't blame you. It makes no sense.

M: And Dre knew?

T: I handed him this memo personally. It recommends the ReStars program be put on hold till a full investigation.

M: And?

T: "I'll take it under consideration." Yada yada . . . This was Friday. By Monday all the footage had been confiscated and Tech R. and I were reassigned. An e-memo went out stating how there had been some mischief by designers in the ReStars dept. and that any employee caught perpetrating a hoax would be prosecuted, etc. Pure bullshit, of course. The department was sealed off, made to look shut down, but the program went on. *Goes on,* as we speak.

M: What about the bar scene? The faces. Any theories?

T: I think it's exactly what it seems: a plea to stop the program.

M: From whom?

T: How can I answer that without seeming crazy?

M: Rebel technician?

T: No, marshman, you don't understand. To create that scene would take *months* of work from *hundreds* of CGs. There was neither the time nor the manpower for that kind of hoax . . . No, we were being warned, no doubt.

M: Why didn't they listen? $$$?

T: Sure. But then what? Carmela and Colt die these horrible deaths. I was going to quit the day Carmela died, but I thought I might do some good from the inside . . .

M: Jesus. Just thought of something—studio shooting.

T: With Colt?

M: Yes . . . You don't see?

T: No. Go on.

M: Dre represented Carmela. He must have known how she died—probably even saw it with his own eyes. So he makes the connection to the bar footage. Then things start to happen with Colt. The star looks a little strange, face is not right, complains of fatigue. Dre thinks, *Here we go again.* You follow?

T: Dre went *after* Colt?

M: Before the sickness could show itself. Don't forget, Dre got incredibly lucky with Carmela—she hid the whole thing from the world. But what were the chances of having the same luck again? With Colt Reston of all people! Once is an anomaly. *Twice* . . .

T: Son of a bitch.

M: And I thought it was the IRs that had killed them.

T: You don't mean Image Resonancing? Ha, that was a joke.

M: ???

T: The IRs were nothing, marshman, harmless. It was a dupe set up by Dre and Mannix to make his big stars feel special, taken care of.

M: It didn't refine the image?

T: No! Just a big bed with bright lights, that's all! I'm sure C. and C. thought their image was improved, probably even *saw* it that way, but it was mind over matter. Sort of a joke among the CGs.

M: Pretty shitty.

T: This is what I mean. Just insane up here.

M: Mannix?

T: The whole environment now. Creepy, disgusting.

M: Tell me.

T: Oh my God, the self-importance! You'd think they'd cured all human disease, the way they strut around. One designer seriously told me he thought ReStars was the greatest breakthrough in film since the Lumière brothers. And then there's all this Bliss everywhere. You've got these designers completely stoned, hyped up, working ridiculous hours. And sooo much money. Twenty-year-old techs driving up to work in million-dollar hydrogen Lotuses. It's like summer camp for smug adolescent multimillionaires.

M: So what now? What's happening up there? What are you seeing?

T: Me? Nothing lately. Been "reassigned," along with a bunch of other CGs. I'm a glorified office worker now, which is terrible for my wallet but great for my conscience. I'll quit the whole thing soon anyhow. Can't touch anything to do with ReStars ever again.

M: The program's still going?

T: Sure, back on schedule. Though Monty's been replaced.

M: What, he was *fired?*

T: Fired—that's funny. No. Actually they can't find him.

M: ???

T: It's the last thing we saw that night in the bar—Monty disappearing through the kitchen doors. We tried to follow him in there but found there was nothing behind it. White nothingness. He was just *gone,* out of there. Then the whole scene faded out. Then when we tried to debug, it was so weird: all the CG code relating to Clift—millions of bits of data—it was gone, the files erased in every system we had. Even the backups! And then Tech R. and I couldn't investigate further because the next day the bastards confiscated the footage. Anyhow, Jimmy Stewart's in the movie now. Fucking Hegyi will not be denied.

M: Hegyi Ami?

T: Head of the ReStars program. Number one Mannix mutant troll . . .
   How'd you know?

M: Just saw him hanging around the Leveno Building.

T: ?

M: You watching the news now?

T: It's on in the next room.

M: Take a look . . . Meantime, we should go.

T: Wait, how's Q.?

M: Honest? Not good.

T: Mmm. Too bad. Always liked him.

M: Yes . . . Hey, can we do this again?

T: Maybe, when things calm down. I'm nervous enough about tonight.
   I'm going to toss this Pod when this is over.

M: Well, stay safe.

T: Jesus. Crazy times, huh?

SEVENTEEN

She had a lot of time on her hands now, did Lindsay Williams. Long, luxuriant mornings watching the pool being drained and rescoured (the indelible cat stink) and waiting for the phone to ring, knowing all the time that it would not. Her new career, the "big launch," had finished before it had started. She knew that now. Dre had played her like a champ. He had wanted Mr. Black's identity and she had failed to deliver. She was expendable.

After a few guilty days of sleeping till noon and trying unsuccessfully to locate a Bliss dealer who was holding, Lindsay decided to make herself useful again: she went looking for Mr. Black in cyberspace. She had convinced herself that he was out there somewhere, just waiting to be discovered. And if she could find him, Lindsay knew she would have a bargaining chip, a reentry card to the life she had so foolishly left behind.

She brought all her journalistic skills to bear, making Dre's obsession her own. She haunted old newspaper stories, book reviews, Hollywood gossip columns, and university archives. She visited various Blackhead and antimedia Web sites. The Diva, who did not know that Lindsay had been dropped by NetTalent and so was still doing errands for her, got her tapped into a database of various Hollywood studios, an index of employees and their attendant photos. Lindsay spent two days going over each and every face, hoping against hope for a match.

She spent hours daydreaming of their meetings together, the cottage where he had taken her. The way he talked, the way he moved. There were moments when she felt there was something vaguely familiar about him; other times she told herself this was ridiculous.

Having hit a brick wall on the Net, she returned to her old e-mails. Something about them had chafed her from the start. When Lindsay had first begun her story on Mr. Black, she had e-mailed everyone she knew in the entertainment business, asking who they thought the writer could be, thinking she might somehow use the responses for her show. Then as a secondary question, a lark, she asked them who they thought *he could not possibly be,* who was absolutely *the last person in Hollywood* who could have written the *Black Book.*

The first question did not have a single match among the fifty or so people she had polled.

But the second? The second question had four replies that were the same.

Something lit up in her now as she revisited the name, furiously following the lead online for twelve, then fourteen, then twenty consecutive hours. When she was about to drop, she once again employed the Diva in research.

By the following afternoon, Lindsay had called *National Insider* with the idea of getting her old job back. When her inquiry was met with an awkward silence, Lindsay explained that she knew the identity of the man who wrote the *Black Book,* and the producer seemed to find his tongue.

Dre McDonald spent the day doing what would now be consuming him over the next few months — monitoring a smooth transition of power for NetTalent. He already had someone handpicked for the role: Janice Richards, head of their television division. Dre had assembled all the partners and shareholders, explaining his choice and conceding an element of risk. Though Janice was a senior partner at NetTalent and had been a top-level earner for nine years running, she had never really shown any particular interest in a leadership role and seemed quite surprised when Dre asked her to take the helm. In addition, though the agency was filled with talented women at nearly every position, the agents themselves were still predominantly male. (There was something in the very act of agenting, Dre had concluded, albeit privately, that still favored a testosterone-fueled malice.) He admitted concerns about Janice's ability to handle the volatile personalities of some of the top agents and, in turn, about their willingness to accept a woman as a leader.

When it came to handling the competition, however, Dre was quite sure Janice's flaws would become her virtues. Her leadership would give them a leg up in their fight with Talent United, most specifically with the priapic Dick Vale — he of the five marriages and thirteen children. It was well known that Dick did not employ women in positions of power at TU or anywhere else near his inner sanctum. (He also had trouble holding on to A-list actresses, though no one had ever publicly connected the two.) The reasons for excluding women from his office, however, were far more complicated than any outsider might have supposed. It had nothing at all to do with the perceived intellect or business acumen of the fairer sex; in fact, Dick Vale was all too ready to concede to women every known physical and intellectual advantage. The real problem was that Dick *could not concentrate in proximity to the female sex.* Reports had it that he became instantly edgy, flustered, aroused to distraction, and no matter the woman's level of attractiveness. (TU's human resources department had even tried to surround Dick with "homely" women but discovered that he found their unattractiveness, and the leveraged power he believed it gave him, highly erotic.) Janice, a tall, striking brunette in her early forties, was exactly Dick's type, and Dre had a good hunch that her mere presence as the CEO across the street would unnerve and confuse the old sybarite to NetTalent's advantage. He was, as he said, banking on it.

Everything now in place, Dre swiveled to and fro in the chair of his cavernous office, idle for the first time in recent memory. He was no longer taking any calls relating to agenting. Nothing concerning NetTalent whatsoever, including the death of Colt Reston, from which he said it was time to heal, nor the troubling suicide of his top programmer, Hegyi Ami. Dre had issued his public statement, explaining how the mainframe at Mannix had been sabotaged by a cabal of rogue technicians sympathetic to Mr. Black, who had all since been relieved of their jobs. This betrayal had devastated Hegyi, who perhaps took his job too seriously for such a young man and had undoubtedly been under too much pressure. Dre expressed remorse over the death, even assuming a level of responsibility.

He added that he expected the billboards to be fully operational in no less than a week.

Dre continued his idle swivel, and then, even more shocking to him, he yawned. It was just eleven thirty, and he didn't have anything else planned until his lunch meeting with Janice. He was beginning to feel downright worthless when the vidphone on his desk finally alighted with the face of his assistant.

"Mr. McDonald?" Naomi inquired, her usually calm features looking uncharacteristically agitated. "Sir? There's a call here I think you should take."

"Not about NetTalent, I hope, Naomi. Please, I've already—"

"*Sir?*" she said with a delicate firmness. It was as forcefully as she had ever spoken to him. "I think you should take the call."

"Okay, you want to tell me who?"

There was a short pause. "The man claims to be Mr. Black. He says it's very important that he speak with you."

Dre's first reaction was that it was a hoax. The deaths of Colt and Hegyi and the trouble with the MIBs had empowered the Blackheads, sending them into fits of mischief, while Mr. Black's silence had only heightened the madness. Dre had sworn he would not indulge them in their juvenile pranks.

But before he could tell Naomi to get rid of him, she added, "He told me he tried your cell first and you didn't pick up."

Dre opened his desk and turned on his portable, noting a message from a caller who had withheld his identification. He didn't bother listening to it.

"What does he look like?"

"No idea," Naomi replied. "He's turned off his vid."

Dre drummed the pads of his fingers along the chair's rosewood armrest, his heart beginning to pulse. When he spoke again, he noticed his voice had turned a little thin.

"All right, put him through."

A blank screen appeared now on the desktop vid.

"Hey, Dre," announced a cheery voice the agent did not recognize. "You got a few minutes? I'd love a chat."

"How do I know it's you?" Dre asked. "Someone sold you my cell number, big deal. I'll have the traitor flushed out by dinner."

There was a dismissive puff of breath, then the voice said, "How about when I get up there, you check my face against those pictures you have of me? Those blurry ones from Lindsay Williams."

Dre sat back, turning from the microphone to clear his throat. "What do you want to talk about?" he asked.

"The MIBs, the ReStars program. A lot of things. I want to talk about Colt Reston, how he died. I'm not sure if you know this, but there are some crazy theories flying around. I hoped you could straighten some things out for me." Then he said, "I could come up right now. I'm right around the corner."

Dre stroked the side of his jaw, considering his options. Clearly a meeting presented an element of danger, but then there seemed no sense in avoiding the man. Hadn't the two of them been on a collision course for a long time? And then there *was* a curiosity factor, he admitted. Despite the world's best photoanalysis, the pictures Lindsay had taken had proved inconclusive. As much as anyone, Dre was dying to find out who the little bastard was.

"Sure, c'mon up," he told the blank screen, trying to sound casual. "We'll shoot the shit."

"I want the cameras turned off, though, Dre. I want that guarantee. I know all about the security of this building. I'll tolerate no video or stills whatsoever. If I have any suspicion at all I'll turn right around and walk out."

"Done," Dre told him, already determining how to circumvent this inconvenience. "Why don't you introduce yourself in the lobby as Mr. Smith; I'll make sure everything's shut off. You'll still have to go through the detectors, though. I won't compromise on that."

"Agreed," replied Mr. Black after the requisite hesitation.

"Excellent. Give me fifteen minutes to alert my security people. Then we're on." Dre's adrenaline suddenly had him sitting bolt upright in his chair, emboldened by a new logic: *he had overestimated his antagonist.* In the midst of the past week's machinations, the multiple plotlines held aloft as if by a juggler (perhaps his deftest performance, Dre had flattered himself), it was Mr. Black's anonymity that remained the wild card, the one puzzle he could not solve. But now here he was, Dre's nemesis—and as if hand-delivered! The agent, meanwhile, would be on his own turf, in the most secure environment imaginable.

This genius, he told himself, had more than a touch of the fool.

The man called Mr. Black stood at the corner of Wilshire and El Camino, smelling the acrid air. The sun was muted behind the ashen gray of the sky and it was not a particularly great day to breathe. Fires had broken out in the Valley, but here, in Beverly Hills, no one paid it much mind. It was September, after all, wildfire season, time for the firedrakes to exact their price on an overwrought landscape. Only Mr. Black knew better.

These fires were different.

He crossed the road and entered NetTalent Plaza.

At the check-in he was given a visitor's pass, which he buttoned to the pocket of his shirt. A security desk fronted the wide bank of elevators, and it was here that one of the guards took "Mr. Smith" aside and assured him in hushed tones that the camera system would remain shut off during his visit. He thanked the guard, knowing privately it was bullshit. They would make a show of it, but in the end they would get their pictures.

Fine with me, he thought. He had some surprises of his own.

The man escorted him to the detector, where Mr. Black removed his belt and eyeglasses. The guard was surprised to find that the man had no keys, no money, not even a wallet. If Dre hadn't made a special case of him, Mr. Smith would certainly have been a candidate for an extensive pat-down and background check.

Mr. Black could see the video on the detector was dark, and he strolled through without a glitch.

Dre got the word. The elevator was coming up.

He tugged at his tie, nervously straightening things on his desk. *Like a goddamned teenager on a first date,* Dre thought. Just in case, he opened the second drawer to his right a few inches. Then he smoothed his hand over his bald head, dismayed to find it speckled with perspiration, which he swabbed with a mustard-hued handkerchief pulled from his tweed jacket. When he looked up at the large plasma to his left, he saw the lily pads for the first time in a month.

Then the ring of the elevator's old-fashioned bell. The doors opening . . .

And in walked the great disappointment. The photoanalysis on Lindsay's pictures had already revealed the pudgy frame, the thickness through the middle. But it was the dull countenance that now sunk Dre's expectations. Mr. Black turned out to be a wide-faced man, the features doughy and gorged to the point where the arms of his glasses dug in at the temples. Dre didn't think there was anything particularly remarkable in the eyes, either.

He also didn't recognize him as anyone on the staff at Talent United, so it was the end of that conceit as well.

"Good afternoon," Dre said, smoothing his jacket. He seemed at a loss as to how to begin. "Please, have a seat."

"Hey, Dre," went the reply. As if they were old friends.

Visitors were usually overwhelmed the first time they entered the office—the structural design, the spaciousness, the startling verisimilitude of the plasma. But Mr. Black ignored it all, waddling myopically toward the desk.

Again, Dre gestured for him to sit, but the man stayed on his feet, walking straight up to the edge of the desk. Then, without preamble, he pulled out an odd-looking gun. The Kraecher.

"Oh, Christ . . ."

"Roll away from the desk, Dre."

"What?" He'd been too frightened to hear the words.

The gun wafted in Dre's direction. *"Roll the chair back from the desk."*

With a short glide, Dre pushed the chair till it stopped of its own momentum. "What's going on?" he demanded, still holding up his hands. "Who are you? Why are you doing this?"

"You'll hear it all, don't worry. Today is the day of reckoning, Dre."

"Reckoning? *For what?*"

"Why don't we get our introductions out of the way?"

Mr. Black pulled a chair to the edge of the desk and set down the gun. Finding his seat, he reached into his mouth to remove what looked like a plastic retainer, set with a small black disk. He put this down on the desk next to the gun.

"I wasn't going to do this," he said with a dramatic shift of intonation, now somehow much more familiar to Dre. "But I couldn't resist seeing the look on your face."

The visitor reached inside his shirt, over his shoulder, as if to scratch at an itch. Finding what he needed there, he pulled his hand slowly back till something started to come loose from his body. Initially, Dre thought it looked like a strip of skin, which naturally alarmed him. But then it became clear that it was a flesh-colored tab of some sort, a seam embedded in the tissue and running along the collarbone. When the man had pulled the piece almost to the opposite shoulder, he began to tug at his neck and chin, the skin alternately bunching and slackening, and finally Dre understood: the man was loosening a mask. It was so expertly fitted that a struggle ensued, and in his frustration the man began to shake his head back and forth, cursing the fake face that did not seem to want to come off.

Hearing the voice again now, Dre knew who the man was.

"Oh, you're fucking kidding me," he murmured.

Finally the mask was removed, pushed aside to hang from the man's shoulder like a second head. Though he was sitting down, Dre reached for the sides of his chair. He felt bilious, suddenly; there was the sensation of toppling from a great height. What he was seeing was impossible.

Then the room whirled around him and all was black.

Reminded how four different pollsters had named Marshall Reed as the person in Hollywood *least* likely to be Mr. Black, Lindsay had gotten that chill, that hair-at-the-back-of-the-neck feeling she got when a great story arrived on her desk. My God, she'd thought, was it really possible that the rotund, awkward lummox she had met up near Big Sur, and then later in her apartment, was in fact Marshall Reed? It was not as impossible as it might seem. She had heard rumors that Colt Reston employed a famous makeup artist, a sort of master of disguise, in order to live a more normal life. If this was true, then obviously Marshall would have known the artist as well. If it wasn't, then his life in movies and his exalted income would have given him easy access to one.

She took the disparate pieces and built a mosaic, trying to be sensible about what fit and what did not. She recalled Marshall's violent disgust when she'd shown him the pictures of Mr. Black. She thought about his reputation for "disappearances": from the set, from the studio, the famous missed meetings. Then she considered how he hadn't written an original screenplay in more than a decade. She added his friendship with Colt Reston to the mix, not to mention his proximity to Dre McDonald, the NetTalent agency, and Panoramic Studios. His bird's-eye view of the greatest fame machine in history.

Marshall Reed: hack, lush, sellout, Blissboy, good-for-nothing, spoiled-rotten, one-time-prodigy Hollywood bum. The man *least likely* . . . It was perfect.

Feeling dangerously excited, Lindsay tried to take a step back, reaching for restraint. She knew that she could still get carried away with Marshall Reed, that she had been romanticizing him ever since she'd seen *Chula Vista* at sixteen and had left the theater shaking, crying, thoroughly exhilarated, the irrational power of movies smacking her like a wave. To get some perspective she called the Diva. The clock said 3:07 A.M., but then too bad, she thought. She had to run these ideas by him immediately, subject herself to his cruel objectivity.

The Diva listened. For almost a half hour he let her riff, trying hard to keep a respectful silence as she made her case, eventually admitting that her argument had its virtues, some genuine
goose-pimple moments. There was, however, in his opinion, one
glaring flaw: *motivation*. There was the *how,* he argued, but not
the *why*. Marshall was a cinema brat, for all intents and purposes,
coddled by Hollywood and the systems that promoted it. What
quarrel could he possibly have with the "image world," if it was
in fact he who had called it that? What had the community of
movies and media ever done to the man except to afford him a
life of limitless comfort and self-indulgence?

If Marshall Reed was biting the hand that fed him, the Diva
concluded, he better have one hell of an excuse.

There was a long pause on the vidphone — Lindsay's way of
letting him know his services were now required.

"All right, shit," the Diva said with a sigh. "Give me a couple
of hours."

But he did not call back in a few hours. He did not call, in
fact, for twelve hours, then fifteen, then twenty. But he did call
the next night, his voice exhausted but quietly satisfied, brimming
with the pride of a hard-won victory.

It was the wife, he said. *Marshall's first wife.*

He was e-mailing Lindsay everything, he'd said, telling her
how she needed to fit the pieces herself, experience firsthand
how it all came together. She looked at the list: dispatches from
the *San Francisco Chronicle* and *USA Today* from November 2009;
an article from Cinephile.com that appeared a few months after;
and finally a video download, which the Diva asked Lindsay not to
view until the end, after which she was to call him immediately.

The front story was this: On the evening of November 20,

2009, Ramona Goodly-Reed, Marshall's wife of eleven months, removed all of her clothes and climbed to the roof of their three-story Victorian on Diamond Street in San Francisco, threatening to jump. After forty minutes of negotiations with a suicide-prevention team, she did just that, breaking her neck in the driveway of their home. She had had a history of mental illness and was currently taking 500 milligrams per day of Effexitol, an extremely powerful antidepressant, though the next day a lab discovered the two-month dosage for November–December had been botched by her pharmacist and was filled with at least 50 percent placebo. This "cycling" down, it was determined, had put her in a state leading to her suicide.

Lindsay thought it odd that she could find no mention of Marshall at the scene during the time of the suicide.

Where, she thought, *was the husband?*

This was the backstory, she discovered, the details captured in the muckraking but crudely spellbinding Cinephile.com article. Allegedly, Marshall wasn't home during the suicide and hadn't been for many weeks. *Chula Vista* had just been released to rapturous reviews and huge box office, launching Colt Reston as a worldwide sensation and securing a major success for Marshall. Meanwhile, Ramona Goodly was alone in the six-bedroom house on Diamond Street, falling apart. Apparently she was well aware of her husband's relationship with Carmela Montoya. Powerless to stop the affair (though not for want of trying), Ramona simply withdrew, deciding to let it take its course — perhaps in the hope that the relationship would dissolve once the film was behind them, fizzle out like a million other on-set flings.

Unfortunately for Ramona, it did not. Not only did the affair last through the summer, but by all accounts it actually picked up steam as *Chula Vista* became a bigger and bigger success, and even as Carmela and Colt walked the red carpets of premieres together, coyly telling the press how they were "just friends." Ramona's distress over the marriage was then compounded—with chemical propulsion—by her depression and loneliness, an exponential tumble into the abyss, until there must have seemed no other way . . .

Lindsay paused, trying to imagine the terrible guilt Marshall must have suffered in the aftermath. Must be suffering *still.* Clearly the man despised himself: the Bliss and alcohol forever coursing through his body, numbing and destroying him simultaneously. She almost respected him for that. What it didn't explain was where the *Black Book* fit into all of this.

Then she remembered the video.

The document opened with a disorienting immediacy—a camera (clearly one of the old handheld camcorders) shaking wildly (the ambling photographer) until the autofocus sharpened and the brightness adjusted for the evening light. Then she saw her: a very young, slender brunette standing naked on the heavily slanted roof of a large Victorian house. Marshall's wife.

Ramona Goodly was petite and Mediterranean-looking, with large, melancholy eyes, and the lights of police cars and fire engines threw slashes of scarlet illumination against her bare figure as she wavered down the incline. Her face was swollen and wet from crying, and she was arguing with a man standing atop a ladder resting a few feet away on the roof's edge. Obviously he was trying to coax her down, while she, in turn, was warning him not to come any closer. As the argument continued, the camera panned down and the large crowd came into focus. There must have been two hundred people at least, hands covering their mouths in fright, even as their eyes were wide with fascination.

Lindsay turned away, considering whether or not to cut the download. She knew what was coming; why did she have to *see* it happen?

But for the former TV journalist, it was hopeless, an ancient lesson by now: it was voyeurism, the human addiction, the compulsion to *see* and *be seen*. And when Lindsay looked back at the Pod screen, she breathed out, surrendering to the pulse of excitement at the new action on the roof. A fireman had snuck through an attic window and made a grab for Ramona, just missing her as she crow-hopped away at the last moment. A round of applause from the crowd quickly turned to screams, the camera panning violently back toward the edge of the roof: the man on the ladder had slipped and was holding on precariously, his waist against the gutters, legs dangling underneath. There seemed a moment where he truly might fall, and Lindsay too felt the crowd's excitement at that possibility, the exhilaration drowning out the shame, until the fireman slid over and heaved him up by the shoulders.

Here now was another round of applause, this time cut short by a loud, collective gasp—the sound of a crowd's breath catching all at once—and when the cameraman pulled back to find Ramona, she was gone.

The lens jerked back and forth across the roof's expanse—a crude pantomime of cinematic confusion—but no Ramona. Then the cameraman pulled the frame down, though ever so slowly, amplifying the ham-handed tension.

And there she was: a young woman in an awkward crumple on the asphalt driveway. The camera zoomed in, panning across Ramona's naked body and highlighting the grotesquely skewed limbs. It searched for, and quickly found, the wide-open, blank eyes, the lens vibrating slightly as the photographer fought his way against the dispersing crowd toward his subject—toward an even tighter close-up, the money shot.

Lindsay finally cut the download and breathed heavily into her sweater. After a few minutes she was able to make it to the kitchen, where she poured sangria into a pint glass and drank greedily. Then she called the Diva.

"You dirty bastard."

"I'm sorry, but you had to see that firsthand. There's no way I could explain something like that," he said. "The cameraman—a next-door neighbor, actually, this so-called friend—got a hundred grand for the footage. It played over and over on local L.A. tabloid television, an edited version with her privates blurred for 'decency's' sake. 'Tragedy strikes creator of Chula Vista,' that sort of thing. And yes, *National Insider* was one . . . Hey, you all right? You're breathing funny."

Lindsay murmured something in the affirmative.

"Anyway, there you have it. No wonder Marshall never wrote another original screenplay. The second after that video was shown, the *Black Book* was born."

"And the affair with Carmela ends," Lindsay offered breathlessly.

"To the day, would be my guess. There was no way they could carry on after that."

She was quiet for a moment, taking a sip of her wine, waiting for the constriction in her throat to pass. "How come I couldn't find any of this?" she asked then. "I've been surfing the Net for three days straight."

"Because, there's nothing out there. I found a few crumbs in the *Chronicle*'s archives, just the bare facts of her death. The video I cribbed from our own library at *NI* marked "Prohibited for Use!" along with the Cinephile.com piece, which, strangely enough, is no longer anywhere in the Web site's database. My guess is that everything was suppressed. Colt obviously helped, maybe NetTalent too. They saw Marshall's despair and brought their power and money down like a cleaver until *wham,* it was gone. Then people forgot about it—out of sight, out of mind. He's just a screenwriter, after all."

Lindsay took a deep breath now, oxygen finally flowing freely.

"And you really think Marshall wrote those things about Colt, about being overexposed?" she asked. "That was some rough stuff."

"Yes, I do. I think he probably thought he was helping Colt by saying those things, that his friend would be shocked into toning down his career. He was trying to embarrass him into changing his life, and it gave him a platform for criticizing Colt in a way he probably couldn't face-to-face. Of course it's also part of what gave Marshall his great cover. No one else suspected he would say those things, either."

Lindsay reached out for her copy of the *Black Book,* drawing it near to her. "God, the whole thing's brilliant, isn't it? In an awful sort of way." She flipped pages, opening it to passages she had underlined. "Touché on uncovering this, by the way. You haven't lost your touch."

The Diva made an odd, doubtful sound.

"There's one thing that still bothers me," he said.

"Oh, God. What now?"

"The television interview," the Diva explained. "I've gone over it and over it in my mind, and it just doesn't add up for me."

"Why?"

"That's right. *Why?* Why would he *do it,* Lindsay? The *Black Book* makes it absolutely clear that the author hates television, despises the medium. And going on *NI* means Marshall would have appeared on the *very* show that exploited the death of his wife. Does that make any sense to you?"

Lindsay was silent for a moment, her hand shaking slightly, clearly threatened by this new logic. "Christ, I don't know. Who else could it be?"

"Anybody."

"*Anybody?*"

"Anybody but Marshall," the Diva asserted. "Think about this. With Mr. Black we're talking about someone who bypasses your phone-protection codes no matter how many times I reset them, someone who walks through security at your apartment like he's invisible. And that book of yours that he signed: How'd he do that? What, Marshall's a *magician* now, too? It doesn't add up, Lindsay. I'm sorry."

She suddenly turned her copy of the book to the personalized message at the beginning, running her fingers over the inked lettering. "So what are you saying? You just spent a day and a half helping me prove that Marshall wrote the book. Now you don't think so?"

"He *did* write the book; I'm absolutely sure of that. I just don't understand the Mr. Black character. I don't know why it's there, why he did it —*if* he did it. I don't know what it means." The Diva paused. "And no, I will not explore this any further, so don't ask me. It's late now and my brain hurts and you just don't pay me enough for shit like this. This is seriously dangerous to a person's mental health. Good night."

* * *

As Dre slowly came to, he tried to approximate where the apparition had been, forcing himself to focus there as his vision cleared. He remembered clearly what he'd seen, the preposterous image, though now as his sight returned he saw nothing but an empty chair. *Just a dream!* he thought with silent relief. Or better yet, a nightmare, some momentary dementia probably set loose by a panic attack. It would be his third attack in as many days, the agent reminded himself, but then why not? It had been a week of colossal stress and anguish. Dre decided then that he would go home, cancel all further appointments. He needed sleep, some time to reflect on recent events. He needed . . .

"*Dre?*" inquired a voice behind him, and the agent's shriek pierced the room, his shoulders bucking with fright. The voice was not only unexpected but improbably familiar. A voice once known to millions.

Dre swiveled slowly in his chair and almost passed out again when he saw the figure standing at the top of the V.

"Christ, will you stop this already!" commanded the agent in a quavering, hysterical voice. "I don't know how you're doing this, but *please*. Enough!"

"Come here, Dre. I want to show you something."

Again, the singular intonation, one of the most distinctive of all movie voices. The agent was too faint to move.

"Look, you did it, okay? You spooked me. You had your fun. Now please *stop this.*"

"Stand up and come over here, Dre. I'm not going to ask you again."

Still unable to move, the agent stole a quick look behind him, toward the desk drawer he had left slightly ajar. But the chair was too far away; not even a great lunge would allow him to reach the panic button in the drawer's left underside.

Meanwhile the visitor had raised the gun. He held the Kraecher out at arm's length as he came toward Dre, grabbing the top of the chair and rolling him backwards.

At the V, the visitor spun Dre's chair to face the windows.

"Now, look out there, Dre. *Look at it.*"

The smoke flowed thickly across Wilshire, the wail of fire engines audible even through the sealed glass.

"What is it? What's happening?"

"It's the MIBs, Dre. They're burning."

The agent stared out blankly, wondering if it could be true.

"Believe it. We started in the Valley today. And we're gonna keep going."

"Who? Who's doing this? The Blackheads? *Who are you, goddammit?*"

There was no answer, and Dre found himself gazing up at the countenance before him, trying to subdue his fear long enough to study the man, find the flaw, the thing that revealed him as an impostor. But it was in vain. Though the face was wracked, nearly as devastated as Carmela's and Colt's had been, Dre could tell this was *not* another mask, nor was it a hologram. And it certainly was not human flesh. Instead, the skin had the grainy feel of celluloid, the look of photographed approximation.

A digitized man.

Feeling all logic begin to slip away, Dre told himself that what he had here was a disgruntled Mannix employee, some rogue talent he had alienated during the ReStars scandal. Embittered, he was back to frighten the agent with some aberrant technology he'd developed without Mannix's permission.

"Do you know the story of my car accident?" the visitor asked. "This is nearly sixty years ago, 1957, I believe. I was leaving a party, drunk as usual, and smacked my car into a tree. Damn thing folded up on me like an accordion. They called my friend Liz Taylor and she came and pulled the two teeth I was choking on from my throat—she saved my life, Dre. But then my face was torn away by the steering column, and that was pretty much it. I was never the same again." There was a pause. "Now, do you want to know the really scary part?"

Dre was positive that he didn't.

"This," he said, pointing to his ruined face, "has nothing to do with that accident. This has to do with *you,* my friend. You did this. To me and all the others."

Dre looked around in a panic. He felt vertiginous, on the verge of mental collapse. "I have absolutely *no* idea what the hell you are talking about."

"You had every warning," the visitor continued. "You and Hegyi both." The agent was shaking his head emphatically now, in full denial mode, the hideous death face only inches from his own. "Please, don't act like you didn't *hear* about it, Dre. Don't insult me! I even went around masquerading as Mr. Black, trying to get you to listen. I thought if I went public you'd be embarrassed enough to take action, to shut the thing down. But there's no embarrassing you, Dre, is there? You're simply beyond embarrassment."

"Please, I don't understand any of this. I really don't. You have to believe me."

" 'Don't understand'?" The visitor nodded his head, grinning from his cracked mouth. "Funny, that's almost exactly what Hegyi said right before I strung him up from the Leveno Building."

He moved behind the agent now. Turning the chair toward the windows just so, he commanded Dre to watch the smoke.

Meanwhile the agent began to cry.

"Oh, don't, please. You had every warning, Dre. You should have left us alone. I mean, do you have any idea what a wonderful thing it is, after so many years of people staring at you, of 'Stand here,' and 'Don't move,' and 'Turn to the camera,' and 'One more time, with feeling,' of being digitally altered, rotoscoped, and rendered for public display — what a wonderful, wonderful thing it is to be *dead?*"

From the corner of his eye, Dre noticed the plasma had dissolved to Goya's *Saturn Devouring One of His Sons.* Then in a low, whimpering voice, the agent began to beg.

The visitor brought the Kraecher up to the back of Dre's head, finding a nub there that would hold despite the slick perspiration.

"Oh yeah," he added. "Carmela and Colt would like me to formally announce their defection. They've passed on to the other side. But not to worry; you'll be joining them shortly."

When the elevator doors opened, the security man was waiting for him with a smile.

"How was everything, Mr. Smith?"

"Very well," replied the visitor, tugging at the mask he had so hastily reattached. "That Dre's one of a kind."

"He certainly is, sir," the guard answered, only to have his servile smile quickly fade. It took him a moment to trust his instincts, to register the fact that he had *indeed* seen a moist red droplet on the collar of the visitor's shirt as he had passed. The man was already ten steps past and heading for the lobby when the guard called out, "Sir? Excuse me. Could you wait there just a moment? *Oh, sir?*"

The visitor continued on quickly toward the exit. Then, taking his first step into NetTalent Plaza, he began to run, turning down El Camino Drive toward Olympic. After thirty strides or so, he began to hear the voices behind him ordering him to stop. He looked back to see how many there were, but the smoke was too thick at this distance, and so he ran faster, looking for alleys to run down, retail stores he could disappear into. When nothing seemed right he continued on toward the intersection, knowing there was likely to be HSC there but unable to think of an alternative.

At the light he saw a commotion. Traffic was stopped and he entered the perimeter of a large, enrapt crowd, providing him with both cover and a view to the bizarre spectacle: a mountain lion had its head inside the driver's-side window of a parked SUV. He could see the beast hopping on its hind legs as it tried to get at something inside the vehicle. The animal was bleeding profusely from each flank, and there were HSC agents on both sides, popping off rounds from their handguns at a range of no more than twenty feet. The bullets sent quivers along the lion's haunches, but the animal kept hopping, digging away as if impervious. Through the thick bales of smoke it didn't look like there were any passengers inside the vehicle, but whatever *was* in there was apparently worth dying for.

Tugging discreetly at his mask, he began to weave his way through the crowd. He still had no idea how many men were chasing him or what they looked like, but when he got close enough to the entrance of a McDonald's near the corner of Olympic (the entire staff on the front grass, transfixed by the scene), he ducked in and headed directly to the men's room.

Later, when searched, the bathroom offered no discernible evidence — except the video footage of the murderer known as Mr. Black clearly entering the men's room, and the cracked frame of the stall's MIB, broken approximately to the width of a man's shoulders, yielding no fingerprints whatsoever.

Lindsay tried to filter the sooty air with a tissue held to her nose, watching from the crowd's front line — too close probably, but she was too enrapt to move. The HSC agents had stopped firing and she could see that the lion was off the ground now, its bloody hind paws pushing against the driver's-side door as it bore its head deeper into the vehicle, shaking the chassis with its considerable weight. The animal seemed to be making a final, desperate lunge for whatever it was it had to have, and the crowd flinched in unison when in the next moment the wounded lion pulled itself free and jumped gracefully back to the street. Finally now everyone could see what was in its jaws, the root of its suicidal obsession.

It was a neatly folded McDonald's bag. The beast, wasting no time, laid its bloody hinds luxuriously across the macadam and tore the sack open with a modest swipe of its paw. Now the tension in the crowd seemed to slacken all at once; the event had taken on the aura of a farce. There was even careful laughter as the lion began to devour the hamburgers, Styrofoam box and all.

Humbled by their ineffectiveness, the two HSC agents held the handguns at their sides. Soon sirens could be heard in the distance. Lindsay realized now that the time to alert *NI* of this event, making a final, triumphant stab at getting the job back, had passed. What surprised her was that she didn't care.

Less than a minute later, two SWAT transports pulled up. When the thirty or so men and women piled out with scoped rifles at the ready, Lindsay figured it was time to go.

She had a pretty good idea how this ended.

EIGHTEEN

Twenty-four hours and they still hadn't found him, but they were coming; Jim Quartus had been assured of that.

He had arrived at the cottage in Big Sur the previous afternoon, immediately throwing all of Marshall's effects into the fireplace — letters, bills, and checkbooks, everything he could find — then inserting some of his own things into the rooms: school yearbooks, family pictures, clothes, some music he had brought up. Initially there had been some excitement in the work, Quartus had felt, a sense of illicit purpose that momentarily lifted his spirits. But by nightfall things had gotten awfully quiet, and the following morning the black mood had returned. He made lavender tea and whole wheat toast. He listened to Mendelssohn and Grieg. He even watched the news (an act that ordinarily repulsed him) on his Pod, the whole world having turned its attention to Los Angeles. After three days the fires were finally over. Nearly every MIB in greater L.A. had been torched beyond repair, and there had been a terrible conflagration over at Mannix Corporation, with irreparable damage done to the ReStars lab. Now, with the blazes under control, macabre rumors had begun to swirl. Dozens of firefighters testified that during the assault, the Blackheads (the alleged perpetrators of the event) wore disguises to conceal their identities: chillingly disfigured black-and-white masks of the great Hollywood stars — Stewart, Grant, Bacall, Bogart, Garbo, Gable, Monroe, and so on. The arsonists also wore fire-retardant suits, so it was alleged, as they seemed to drift in and out of the flames without regard for heat or injury. A few firemen even stated that they had tried to confront the brazen criminals, only to find that when they did so, the Blackheads simply disappeared as if dissolving into the plasma — all of which prompted the City of Los Angeles to announce an investigation into the rampant use of Bliss among its firefighters.

As for the murder of Dre McDonald, all the investigators knew for sure was that Mr. Black wore an extensive prosthetic disguise, and they refused to offer any leads whatsoever.

Quartus thought now of Marshall Reed, wondering where he was, what had happened to him. It was three days ago that the screenwriter had come back to the Redding Brothers camp as promised, only to discover Quartus in a terrible state — the man having lost at least fifteen pounds, his eyes holding a haunted and hollow aspect far beyond even what Marshall remembered from the dark campus days. Quartus was asleep in the infirmary tent when he found him — was, in fact, sleeping twenty-hour days, so the staff reported, and suffering from a supreme lethargy during waking hours. Marshall tried to rouse his old friend, but to no avail: he was completely comatose. There was nothing to do but wait it out, Marshall killing half a day until Quartus finally awoke, stuporous, though rousing somewhat at the sight of a familiar face.

Marshall was unable to get him back on the Fringe, so the two men found a shelf of rock at the base of the canyon. It was there, after some hesitation, that Marshall tried to fill in the rest of the story, the things he'd learned about in the week's interim: those last months at Mannix; Monty's bar tour and the IRs; the facts, as he had interpreted them, behind the deaths of Carmela and Colt.

After the initial shock and anger, there were, for Quartus, some long-awaited tears. The grief was so profuse, in fact, that at one point Marshall began to wonder at the wisdom of telling the story with his friend in such a wretched state.

"I'm sorry, Jim," he said, sensing that the deluge had finally ebbed.

Quartus managed to nod, though it took some time before he could speak again.

"So you killed them, eh?" he asked. "Dre and that Hegyi character?" Quartus seemed to glean some consolation from the idea.

"No."

"*No?*"

Marshall was not surprised to see the hideous sorrow on his friend's face slowly turn to skepticism; even in this abysmal state the man was keen to a lapse in logic.

"There never *was* a Mr. Black," Marshall tried to explain. "This is hard to accept, I know, Jim. But you have to believe me. I never wanted anything to do with publicity or television. That's everything the book was against! The truth is that somebody invented that persona for himself and ran with it."

A scowl now from Quartus. "Why? For what?"

"The ReStars program," answered the screenwriter. "Watch that Mr. Black interview again. Whoever pulled that stunt hardly even touches on the book. He can't wait to steer the conversation back to his real obsession: ReStars."

"You mean that wasn't you on television? All dressed up?"

"No, Jim," he said. "I didn't kill anyone, I swear it—though of course I wanted to. I was planning to kill Dre myself, or *have* him killed. I hadn't decided yet. But this son of a bitch got there first. He stole everything: my book, my house—he even stole my revenge from me! Then he leaves me on the hook for the murders."

Marshall explained how painstaking he had been about preserving his anonymity, to the point of withholding his name even from his publishers. But there'd been one fatal mistake: he had allowed galleys of the book to be sent to him at his address in Big Sur. If they hadn't already, investigators would soon be pressing his publishers for that address. And it would lead them to Marshall.

"The deed's in your name?"

"No, it's a rental," Marshall replied. "And I've always paid anonymously. But I have effects there, personal things. Of course I don't dare go back there now. I'm actually leaving the country tonight. But they'll find me eventually, Jim. You know they will."

Quartus sat silent, sifting pebbles in his hand as the sun beat the two men senseless. Even in the late afternoon, the shelf of rock on which they sat was like a frying pan.

Marshall was just about to gather himself for the final goodbye when a stubborn smirk broke out on Quartus's lips.

"Anyway, you'll be okay, Marsh," he said cryptically. "Just tell them Monty Clift did it."

Marshall lifted his head. "No one would ever believe it."

"No, never."

It was then that the flicker of an idea came to the pitch-black mind of Jim Quartus.

* * *

And so here he was, waiting at the cottage for his welcomed end. It could not come fast enough, Quartus found; the dark abyss of those last days at Redding had not lifted, and time had become an agony to him. He turned off the news on his Pod, bored even with the city's mad tragicomedy, and at last turned to his old standby: books. He pulled some volumes off the shelves—Marshall had an impressive library here—and began to flip through them. But nothing stuck, his mind losing traction after just a few sentences. *By God,* he thought with a final, conclusive despair, *this really* is *it.* He had hit a bottom so low now that even knowledge failed to nourish him! This realization pulled the curtain down even further, and after a few minutes he could feel the pulsing of that peach pit in his stomach, the balled, centered pain that was baseless, the mere conjuring of an ill mind, but no less agonizing for it. This was capped by a bout of uncontrollable weeping, though he could not have said exactly what for.

Unable to endure another second, Quartus retrieved the small revolver from under the floorboards where Marshall had said it would be. Then he went to the bedroom to lie down. He would go out early, he decided. It would not change the plan in any real way, and then what did it matter anyhow? The world would continue on as it was: the good dies, the other flourishes, and what little manages even to lean toward the middle will be snuffed out no matter where it tries to hide.

It was with these sulfurous thoughts that Quartus heard the distant whir of propeller blades.

He took the weapon and went in to wait on the couch, trying to concentrate on the late afternoon sun—creamy orange light bedaubing old furniture (*Last light,* he told himself, *never to be seen again*)—and listened to the increasing drone of the copters. He heard them swoop past—Quartus experiencing a momentary panic—then turn and circle back, hovering to confirm the target. Sand and loose foliage kicked against the cottage windows as they descended, the whip of the rotors now deafening. How many helicopters were there? he wondered. Four. Six? A *dozen?* You would've thought the fucking president had been killed!

Quartus reached out and pulled the curtain back a few inches. Two copters had landed on the front lawn, and he watched as the men and women spilled out in their flak jackets even before the runners could touch the ground. *Bloodlusting little buggers!* he thought. Then he heard another copter land in back of the house, and now what had been one of the last bastions of peace and remoteness in California was overrun with armored warriors slung with some very nasty-looking hardware.

Quartus returned to the sofa, fingering his popgun of a weapon. When he began to hear the thunder of combat boots on the roof, he took the picture of Carmela he'd put near him on the end table and held it to his chest.

A voice from a bullhorn asked him to come out, to show himself. "*Black? Black, you in there?*" Quartus lifted his pistol and fired off a round, shooting at a harmless area above the picture window. He waited a moment and then fired off two more rounds at the same spot. Suddenly from outside came an ominous quiet. Some cicadas had begun to murmur (*Last sounds, almost done*) and he gripped Carmela's picture tighter until there came a barked signal, the shrill commencement. Then there was one final pause, infinite in Quartus's mind, followed by the yipping roar of bullets, a thick wave of high-penetration lead, pixelating the walls of the cottage and delivering him to his long-awaited peace.

NINETEEN

By early evening they had reached the top of Baja, the sky a dome of stars and the highway free of MIBs. They pulled off on a deserted stretch of road to say their good-byes. Marshall had a gym bag slung over his shoulder, while Ray Manuel came out of the car empty-handed, leaving the vehicle running. He was continuing on.

As they embraced, Marshall apologized one last time for the mess left behind in the wake of Colt's death. From the moment it had been determined that Mr. Black was in disguise, the HSC had been at Ray's door. Strictly routine, Ray had been assured; they were interviewing all the top makeup people in the Los Angeles area, grasping for a lead. But Ray knew it was bullshit — they were *onto* him. Only he could have put together an outfit like the one the killer had worn, and everybody knew it — Ray Manuel most of all. What Ray couldn't understand was how a presumed novice like Mr. Black had learned to build a disguise so intricate, or how he had even found his studio in the first place. But then what would any of this matter to the HSC? Simply having had the materials in his possession would be enough to put Ray away for life, or worse.

Still, there had been compensation. Colt's estate was still pending—it would take years to unravel it all—but through power of attorney Rip had already emptied the actor's various bank accounts. The funds were quickly distributed, the sums large enough for Ray and Marshall to live like sultans for ten consecutive lifetimes. And Marshall figured this was pretty much what the makeup artist had in mind.

As the car drove off, Marshall slung the bag over his shoulder and headed toward the beach. It was a good quarter-mile walk, if he remembered correctly, and by the time he arrived he was both exhausted and relieved. To his amazement, it was still standing: the shabby beach bungalow from all those years ago.

Someone had adopted it, he could see. Repairs had been made. The roof looked new and the front door had been replaced. He broke through the flimsy lock and went inside, discovering that the water was turned on and that two of the four burners on the stove actually worked. There was even some cheap tequila in the cupboard. He found a dirty glass and poured himself a modest taste.

Marshall lay down on the musty daybed, wallowing in a languorous nostalgia. He hadn't been here since he had rented the cottage in Big Sur—almost five years ago, he guessed—so there was enough distance for tonight to have a special poignancy. He promised himself that tomorrow he would go to the lookout, drink a toast for his great friend, and wait for the green flash.

He liked his chances, Marshall told himself.

A few more sips and his eyes began to close, exhaustion swarming over him. He'd barely slept since Colt's death, and more than anything he needed rest. He would sleep for days, a week if he had to, and when he was caught up and had kicked Bliss once and for all, he would get back to work. There was so much to do now, so much to write about. Were other actors at risk? Stars at lower levels of exposure than Carmela and Colt, but still possibly vulnerable? Or was it ReStars, ipso facto, that was to blame? The questions swirled endlessly.

Anyhow, the good news was that Hollywood was past him, the ruse was over, and so there would be plenty of time. Everything would be simpler now, he told himself (drifting suddenly, lids heavy, almost gone), nothing to distract him . . .

It was around three that morning when the men approached the house, trudging clumsily in their alligator loafers and Yamori suits.

They were five this time, two limping visibly — one having torn a calf muscle in an impromptu dash for his life just over a week ago, the other nursing a bullet wound in the lower abdomen, where he had been shot with a Kraecher. The trip down from Simi had not been a pleasant one, they all agreed, most of it spent with the two wounded men arguing the minutiae of how they were going to torture Marshall when they found him. When the border guards had viewed their HSC identification with suspicion, they had agreed to pay thirty thousand dollars to the Federales to let them through — a sum to be extracted from their shares. This turned their sour moods even more foul.

There was no moon and the bungalow was dark as they came up to the front door. Obviously Marshall was asleep. They all drew their weapons as the two limping men continued their argument in a hissing, vehement whisper.

"We cut him up. Keep lopping off little tiny pieces till he dies."

"*No, stupid, we burn him. We burn him and stick him in the ocean, then watch the steam come off him till he's cooked like a lobster.*"

Silently, Marshall sat forward. He'd slept all of twenty minutes until the nightmares had begun again, so he was completely awake, totally lucid, hearing the shell fragments breaking under the feet of the Mannix men. Ever so slowly, he pulled the gym bag toward him, digging behind the box of money till he found the .46-caliber automatic Rip had given him as a good-bye present. He lifted it, surprised by the heft, and turned on the targeting beam, directing it at the middle of the front door. There was fear, yes—he could see the red dot quavering in front of him like a hummingbird—but also a savage irony that made him smile.

Here it was, he told himself, the electrifying conclusion. The scene he had written so reluctantly so many dozens of times.

His life would end as a Colt Reston movie.

He sipped at the tequila in his glass, waiting impatiently for his revenge.

Acknowledgments

Special thanks: Geoff Shandler, Doug Stewart, Guillermo Nanni, Ty Wenzel, Junie Dahn, Brian Burns, and the work of Mike Davis, which inspires anybody who writes about Los Angeles

About the Author

Kurt Wenzel is the acclaimed author of *Lit Life* and *Gotham Tragic*.
He and his wife live in East Hampton, New York.